NEAR NEIGHB

Gordon Legge was brought up in Grangemouth. He has published two novels and one previous collection of stories. His work was represented in the recent *Children of Albion Rovers* anthology.

Gordon Legge

NEAR NEIGHBOURS

V

VINTAGE

Published by Vintage 1999

2 4 6 8 10 9 7 5 3 1

First published in Great Britain by Jonathan Cape in 1998

Vintage
Random House, 20 Vauxhall Bridge Road, London SW1V 2SA

Random House Australia (Pty) Limited
20 Alfred Street, Milsons Point, Sydney
New South Wales 2061, Australia

Random House New Zealand Limited
18 Poland Road, Glenfield, Auckland 10, New Zealand

Random House South Africa (Pty) Limited
Endulini, 5A Jubilee Road, Parktown 2193, South Africa

Random House UK Limited Reg. No. 954009

Acknowledgements are due to the following publications: *The
Big Spoon*, *Children of Albion Rovers* (Canongate), *Cutting
Teeth*, *Dog*, *Edinburgh Review*, *Intoxication* (Serpent's Tail),
Rebel Inc., *Rebel Inc.* website, *Scottish Short Stories* (Flamingo),
Soho Square VII (Bloomsbury)

The author would like to thank the Scottish Arts Council for a
bursary which enabled him to devote more time to completing
this volume

A CIP catalogue record for this book
is available from the British Library

ISBN 0 09 927267 9

Papers used by Random House UK Ltd are natural,
recyclable products made from wood grown in sustain-
able forests. The manufacturing processes conform to the
environmental regulations of the country of origin

Printed and bound in Norway by
AIT Trondheim AS, 1999

CONTENTS

FOR MARION SINCLAIR AND WALTER CAIRNS

MANNERS

You can just never get rid of him, this new bloke. Never budges, just stands there. Hanging round waiting for God knows what. Never utters a word to it either, not a word, not a blooming word. Just concentrates on whatever it is you're saying, whatever it is you're on about. Could be anything, no difference to him, just absorbs every last wee detail while all the while you're trying your best to shift, right – ready to go, raring to go, a million things to do, right – well, he's just there, just there, right on at you with this attentive thing of his – giving it all this wee gesturing carry-on, taking it all in – nodding away, keeking away – taking everything in. And I mean everything, oh, absolutely everything. Oh aye, you've got to be careful, got to watch, got to watch what it is that you say 'cause, well – heh heh – you never know, do you? Not that you ever get a peep out him, of course, but, here, listen, maybe that's just the type as to head off rabbiting and land you right royally in it, right there in the thick of it. Could well be, who's to say? Granted, he's good at his job. I'll give him that. No complaints on that score. He's good at his job alright. But, well, you don't really know, though, do you, mean you don't really know him? But *listen* I lose the rag. I do, I really do. I get wild. I get raging. You should see him. Sometimes you just feel like stopping and shouting and getting really, really angry – getting really, really, really, really, really, really angry – and just starting on him, just having a go, you know, just going, 'Hey you, pal, just hold on a minute there' and enquiring exactly why it is that he's like that, what exactly it is that's wrong with him, what it is that's the matter. But, of course, you don't, do you? No, you don't, you never do. I mean it's the knowing what's the

I

right way to go about it, though, isn't it? I mean you don't want to appear rude, do you? God forbid. 'Course you don't. Got to be civil in this day and age. So, so it never gets mentioned, the matter is never raised, not a word is ever even spoken on the subject. And you, you're just left to go on and on and on and on and on and on and keep raving away, trying desperately, and I mean desperately, absolutely desperately, to avoid, to avoid at all costs, to avoid having anything remotely at all to do with those reactions of his. Oh, my God, those reactions, those reactions. No, 'cause, telling you, see when he comes away with those reactions of his you've got to be blooming well ready with your responses to those reactions. You have. You've got to. You've got to. You have. You've got to respond or you're going to be standing there looking like a right sad thicko, aren't you? You are, 'course you are. And damned if I'm going to look thick. Damned if I am. Damned if I am. In front of him? Huh. No way. The cheek of it. With those eyes of his bearing down on you? Oh aye, those eyes, those eyes, those eyes of his. Oh, he's got those eyes alright, that type always have, those beady wee types with their beady wee eyes; them that are never off you, know what I mean. Not for one second. Never even blooming well blinks just waits for you to sodding well slip up and fall flat on your flaming, flipping face. That's right. That's what I say. That's all it is. One big joke. That's what it is. Just one big joke, one big joke to him. Ha bloody ha. Ohhhh, and hey, hey listen, listen to this, now that I remember, now that I'm thinking about it, there's another foible of his he's got – shakes his arms. That no queer? Like that, goes like that. Shakes his arms, shakes his arms. What a carry-on. Thinks I never see him but I blooming well see him alright. 'Course I do. But is that no just a wee bit funny? Aye, a wee bit too strange that one, eh? 'Cause see, see if that's no the case then well can someone please tell me why in the world does he need to want to have to go and do that for 'cause I haven't a clue, a blooming clue, and hey, if that's no bloody queer then I don't know what there is that is. I don't. I truly don't. I just don't. Hanging round like that waiting for God knows what. No, but it's a shame for the laddie, right enough, young laddie like that. No, I mean it. I do. Basically, he's a nice enough laddie, very presentable, good at his job — very good at his job, in fact. No complaints on that score. He's good at his job, alright. But see all this carry-on of his, it does your head in, it does, it really does. I'm telling you. I'm telling you. I'm telling you. For goodness sake, listen, it does.

PAST MASTERS

This was a good wall. None of your cheapo muck. Nah, this was built to last. One good headbutt and ...

'It's that lassie again, isn't it?'

Adam flung his spanner in the toolbox. 'Aye,' he said. 'Suppose so.'

Mrs Hanson rested her hind-end against the table. 'You mustn't blame yourself, son. If it wasn't to be, it wasn't to be.'

'I know, I know. It's just . . . ach.' Almost apologetically, Adam looked up at Mrs Hanson. In her own words, she was as brittle as a biscuit with skin like a wet paper hankie. The first time Adam had ever went round, he'd stayed on and watched *Countdown* with this frail old biddy. She thrashed him out of sight.

Mrs Hanson put her weight back on her zimmer. 'Do you think she was the one, Adam?'

'Don't know.' Adam put the doings back on. 'To be honest with you, just now, the way I'm feeling, I don't think anybody'll be the one.'

'Away, away and don't be daft. I'm sure many a lass would jump at the chance of you. You should hear what they all say about you down the centre. Oh, that Adam, with his fine wavy hair. All the time in the world for you he has. An awfy nice laddie.'

Adam stopped what he was doing. It was headbutt time again. Slowly back. Then release. And, just at the maximum speed, impact.

'Sorry, I said it, didn't I?'

'Aye, you did, you did that.'

Mrs Hanson leaned right forward, like her zimmer was a pulpit. 'Well, you know something? I'm glad I said it, because you are, you are nice.'

'Aye, but anybody can be nice, eh?'

'Och, Adam, lassies play games. Half the time they never know what they're on about. Half the time all they want is a response.'

'Maybe. Anyway, change of subject, I think we're ready. You want to give Telstar a go again?'

Mrs Hanson edged her way to the banister. Adam took her weight as she fitted herself into the seat.

'Fingers crossed, Adam.'

'Fingers crossed.'

Mrs Hanson pressed the button. The chairlift – Telstar – was working okay.

'Well,' said Adam, 'that'll have to do for now I'm afraid. Any worries, give us a buzz. Day or night. No problem.'

Mrs Hanson came back down again. 'Listen, Adam,' she said, 'I was thinking: there was this mannie on the telly the other day there, a doctor mannie, and what he was saying was how folk can always go on for ages about all the times they've ever been miserable; but seeing being happy, you're lucky if you get ten minutes. Adam, son, remember the good times, fight to remember them. Believe me, if you don't remember them now, that's them gone, gone for ever.'

Adam laughed. 'Tell me,' he said, 'and tell me truthfully, do you think that what she said was right?'

Mrs Hanson got up onto her zimmer. 'Aye. Maybe it's true, son, maybe it is. But, mind, it's only true when you're playing a game. Only when you're playing a game.'

Out in the van, Adam dialled Geordie McIntyre's number, let it ring twice, then hung up.

Geordie lived in a terrace of old miners' houses, five minutes' drive out of Muirside, which itself was a quarter of an hour's drive from anywhere.

In other words, the back of beyond. Where the roads were empty, where it was pitch black. Just think: foot down, seatbelt

off, one wrong turn – that could be that. Smack into a tree.
Down the side of the hill.

Nah, just didn't appeal, though. Wasn't quick enough. Too
much chance of failure.

Adam thudded the door with the heel of his hand. The door flew
open.

Geordie called his machine The Catapult. Adam called it The
Catastrophe. On average, it broke down twice a month. Most
days, Geordie only used it for going up and down to his bed.
Only when visitors were in would he use it for the toilet.
Otherwise, the kitchen sink and Geordie's all-purpose bread-bags
sufficed.

The Catapult was one of the originals. Next to nobody got
new models. Like the walls that encased them, these machines
outlasted their owners. About the only thing they had in
common.

On his hands, knees and belly, Geordie crawled through. 'It's
yourself. Tea's on.'

'Cheers. And what is it this time then?'

'Well, I'll tell you this much, it's no a sexually transmitted
disease, anyway.'

Adam gave Geordie a mournful look. The jokes were chronic.
'Just the usual then, aye?'

'Aye, thing's about as much use as a fiver made of meat.'

Adam took the doings off. It wasn't beyond the bounds of
possibility that Geordie had tried to fix it himself. In fact, going
by the evidence, and past history, it was more than likely.

'Eh,' said Geordie, 'have I still no to say that word, no?'
'No!'

Geordie rolled over so's his back was against the front door.
Geordie liked sitting on the floor. He liked crawling about the
floor. Said it minded him of being down the pit. 'Now, take a bit
of advice from an old bid that's been round the course a few
times. Lassies? Ken what they're after?'

'Aye, guys that are as thick as shit, guys that've got shoulders the width of your staircase and guys that horse their money like you horse your faeces.'

Adam mimed a gentle throwing motion. Notoriously, Geordie shat into his bread-bags, then hurled the bread-bags out into the fields out back.

'Now,' continued Geordie, ignoring the last remark, 'correct me if I'm wrong, but this lassie gave you the heave-ho, and you said, "But I thought you were nice?" and she said, "Anybody can be nice." That about right, aye?'

Adam picked up his spanner: thoughts now veering from termination of self to termination of Geordie.

'Well,' said Geordie, 'have you never stopped to think and ask yourself exactly what she meant by that?'

'No,' said Adam, shaking his spanner, 'funnily enough, now you come to mention it, I never have. D'you think maybe I should like?'

'Hey you, less of the cheek. No wonder you can never keep a bit of skirt. Ken what I think? I think she was talking about you. Anybody can be nice.'

That done it. Adam switched on the motor – without its covers it was as loud as a road-drill – and set to work.

That was what she'd said alright. 'Anybody can be nice.' The last words she'd ever said to him. It was like saying anybody can say please and thank you, you just don't have to mean it.

And God, did it hurt.

And every time it hurt Adam wanted to headbutt the wall. He lay awake at night, feeling sorry for himself, crying. The only thing that kept him going was this daft idea: to design the perfect wall. Just bash your head and that would be that. No need for notes or posthumous explanations. Medical records would just record another 'death by headbutt'.

Adam had it all worked out. He'd build this place, like a big sports hall, with this long, low wall as its centrepiece: like one of these old folks' houses, great walls, purpose-built. There'd be guys queueing up round the block. You'd come in, kneel before the wall, and then, when the moment struck, the moment when it hurt, you'd *Adam* yourself.

Adam switched off the motor.

'Oh,' said Geordie, 'you're back again.'

'Back to listen to you and your blethers, aye.'

'By God, see if I was a younger man – I'd take my hand off your face before you could say Gazza. I've battered bigger than you, mind. Plenty bigger.'

'Aye, I think I mind you telling me – *hundreds of times*.'

Geordie was the type as would probably be quite happy if Adam were to headbutt. He'd live off it for years. 'Aye,' he'd tell folk, 'just right in front of my face. What a mess it was and all. Blood and brains all over the shop. Never get that cleaned. That's what the polis said. Said to me, "Geordie," they said, "long as you live, and hard as you try, you'll never get that cleaned." '

Adam replaced the seat. 'Well, want to give it a go, auld yin?'

Geordie made to get up. He adjusted his legs. He adjusted his legs like they were artificial. To all intents and purposes, they were.

No way was he going to make it.

'Well, are you no going to give us a hand then or what?'

In one back-breaking movement, Adam lifted Geordie up off the deck and on to the seat.

Geordie pressed the button, and said what he always said. 'If only it was taking me up to a brothel, eh?'

The chairlift went up, the chairlift came down. For the time being, it was working okay.

'Get my stick, son. You'll stay for your cup of tea, aye?'

'Aye, suppose so.'

They went through the living-room. Adam shifted some papers and sat down. The house was always covered in papers. Old folk seemed to have this thing about information. They read all the time, watched every news bulletin, had the radio on day and night.

Adam started playing about with teletext.

'What did you say the lassie's name was again?'

'Juliette,' said Adam. 'Juliette Binoche. Ken, her off the pictures?'

'Eh, I thought it was Eleanor.'

Adam cringed. It felt like his skin was trying to strangle him. Maybe he wouldn't need to bother with headbutts. Just visit Geordie enough – break your back and get asphyxiated by your own skin.

'Can I tell you what I think?'

'No! Look, you're no allowed to. I'm no letting you. It's against the rules, okay?'

'Here's what I think: best just to forget about her. Forget everything about her. Just like it never happened. Just get back out there, find some wee lassie, and go for it.'

Adam shook his head. As if it was that easy. Then again, who knows, maybe it was. Treat every experience as a learning experience. Sadie Callender said that. She also had views regarding 'Anybody can be nice'. The way she seen it, Adam couldn't have been treating Eleanor special enough. That was Sadie's answer to everything. Sadie didn't like men. To be fair to her, she'd had more than her share of bad experiences. She said Adam was alright, but then again she qualified that by saying she didn't really know him.

Sadie died a couple of weeks previous. The machine was awaiting its next owner. Sadie called it The Stick.

'Well,' said Adam, 'best be making tracks I suppose. Any worries, give us a buzz. Day or night. No problem. And, mind, no crawling up and down them stairs. I'm no wanting to open that door and find you all crumpled in a heap again.'

'Aye,' said Geordie, 'I've learnt my lesson. And you mind and learn yours. Forget about her, just you go out and find some young bit of stuff; and, hey, give her one for me, eh?'

Out in the van, Adam dialled Phil Hendry's number. Before it rang twice, Phil answered. Adam said it was okay, he was only phoning to say he'd be about twenty minutes.

To date, Phil was the only person who'd ever queried as to why Adam made his calls late in the day. Adam didn't really know. Maybe it was something to do with taking your time. Maybe it was something to do with ensuring they had a peaceful night. Adam wasn't really sure.

The Hendrys lived on the outskirts of town. Painted the purest white, theirs was the sort of house a tourist would stop and photograph. Truly, it was that beautiful.

As ever, Phil was waiting at the door when Adam pulled up in front.

'I hear you're nursing a broken heart.'

'Aye. So they say.'

'Nothing worse,' said Phil.

'Oh, I don't know. Toothache's pretty bad. Car breaking down. Getting burgled. Nah, when you come to think about it, there's plenty worse.'

'Glad to hear you're bearing up so well.'

Adam shrugged. 'Water off a duck's back.'

Up until fairly recently, Phil had still been carrying Marjory up the stairs. The doctor had advised against a chairlift, saying that with Marjory's life expectancy a nursing home would be cheaper. Typical of the man, Phil went out, changed his doctor and got the most expensive chairlift he could find.

'So there's no truth in all this headbutt nonsense then.'

'Ah.'

Adam tossed his spanner into the air. He let it do a couple of somersaults before catching it again, squeezing it like it was a certain *Countdown* expert's throat.

Phil laughed. 'Mrs Hanson likes to keep us all informed.'

'Bad news and all that, eh?'

'But not as bad as the car breaking down?'

'Christ, no. Now that would've been serious.'

Adam set to work. The good thing with new machines was that problems usually had to do with moving parts stretching: all you had to do was shorten them.

Phil sat down on the staircase. 'You know, Adam, I'm sure when that lassie said that to you, you were probably the last thing she was thinking of. She'd've made her mind up ages ago. Maybe just an unfortunate choice of phrase. Then again, maybe she just wanted you to hate her. A clean break.'

'Yeah, maybe.' Adam sat himself in the chairlift. He pressed the button. As if by magic, up he went.

'You're a miracle worker, Adam.'

'Something like that, aye.'

Phil laughed. 'If you don't mind, I'll just get Marjory.'

A couple of seconds later Phil returned. He was carrying Marjory.

Adam hadn't seen Marjory for a couple of months. It was hard not to be shocked.

'That's her under five stone now,' said Phil.

Adam helped Phil with the straps. There was nothing to say. Marjory never spoke. She never really did anything.

But then again . . .

Adam took Marjory by the hand. 'I wonder what you would tell me, Marjory, eh? Should I remember the good times? Should I forget it all? What do you think? Do you think anybody can be nice?'

Marjory gave one of her wee starts, like a shiver was running through her.

'It's okay, love,' said Phil, 'not be long till you're in your bed. Nice and warm up there.'

Phil called his chairlift Gabriel. There was always something religious about seeing Marjory going up. Something reassuring.

'Be seeing you then,' said Adam. 'Mind, any worries, just give us a bell. Day or night. No problem.'

The chairlift reached the top of the stairs. 'Right,' said Phil. 'And sorry but she probably did make her mind up ages ago. I wouldn't put any weight into what she said. Just something to say, that's all.'

That was Adam finished for the day. Tomorrow was just a few services. As yet, nobody had phoned with a breakdown.

On his way home, Adam drove passed Eleanor's house. He had this compulsion to tear the exhaust off her car, to get really drunk and shout abuse at her.

Anybody can be nice.

Anybody can be nasty.

Oh, maybe it all just was a game. Maybe she was having a go at him. Maybe she just wanted rid of him. Maybe he didn't treat her special enough. Who knows.

When Adam got in he phoned a mate and had a good rant about football. Mates never wanted to talk about Eleanor.

Adam was just about to settle down for the night with his telly and remote when the phone rang.

It was Phil Hendry.

'Sorry if I was short with you earlier there.'

'It's okay.' Adam hadn't noticed.

'It was just with you wondering what Marjory would've said regarding this "Anybody can be nice".'

'Yeah.'

'Well, it was just something Marjory said once. It's maybe not important.'

'No problem. Fire away.'

'Well, you know how she used to be a teacher? How we both were?'

'Yeah.'

'Well, when we used to fill out our report cards, I was always wary of my comments. See I taught maths, I was used to being exact. Marjory, though, taught English. She revelled in what she called the poetry of ambiguity. This, believe it or not, upset me. I thought, dealing with young minds, you had to be careful. Marjory never bothered. All she ever said was, "It's up to them to decide." I'm afraid she'd have been far more impressed with what your friend said than what it actually meant. It would be up to you to decide.'

There was silence at Adam's end of the line.

Phil laughed. 'That doesn't help you at all, does it?'

'No, to be perfectly honest, no.'

'Sorry,' said Phil. 'Anyway, I just thought I'd mention it. If it's any help, I'm sure Marjory would've liked you.' Phil's voice started to crack as he added, 'She was an amazing woman, you know. I wish you'd known her.'

'I'm sure she was.'

With that, they said their goodnights and hung up.

Adam couldn't be bothered with the telly. He just went to his bed.

As usual, he couldn't sleep. But this time, after a while, something of Phil's kept replaying itself in Adam's head. Something Adam would take from all this. Something from the past that made him feel good, yet somehow managed to make the future seem positive.

He wouldn't think of headbutts or whether anybody could be nice.

No, it was up to him to decide.

He'd think of Mrs Hanson and her *Countdown*, and Geordie and his flying faeces. He'd think of Phil and Marjory with their report cards, and Sadie with her sadness. He'd think of Telstar, The Catapult, Gabriel and The Stick.

And, of course, all the others.

He'd think of Eleanor.

He'd think of all these things, all these great things, and say to himself: yeah, I wish you'd known them, I wish you'd known her.

LIFE ON A SCOTTISH COUNCIL
ESTATE VOL. 3 CHAP. 1

I've got a new girlfriend. She's great. She's fantastic. She looks
like Maggie out of *Northern Exposure*. She wears stripey T-shirts.
She's got me wearing stripey T-shirts! She's into Stereolab and
P.G. Wodehouse. She's got me into Stereolab and P.G.
Wodehouse! Oh, she's fab. She's the best. She's the one. She *is*
the one . . . Anyway, we're dancing about to *Refried Ectoplasm
(Switched on Volume 2)* when the door goes. It's The Tank. He's
wearing the clothes his mam got him for Christmas. This is
weird. The Tank *never* wears the clothes his mam gets him for
Christmas. He only ever wears them on Gala Days and when his
terminally ill rich auntie visits. It's like he's had a makeover or
something: there's stuff in his hair; he's clean-shaven; Christ, I
can smell Hai Karate. The Tank goes over to my new girlfriend.
He shakes her by the hand and introduces himself. He's all nice to
her. Oh, come on. The Tank's never nice to anybody. Much as I
love him, the headbanging sonofabitch's got all the charisma of a
bag of cold chips. Like usually just comes in, sticks the kettle on,
sticks *If You Want Blood* on the stereo, and sticks round till it's
time to head off for his next meal. The day though, he's being all
polite and asking my new girlfriend all about herself. Not only
that, but he's going on about himself. He's talking about himself
as if he's halfway interesting. What is going on here? The door
goes again. It's Stuart this time. Stuart smiles and says, 'Hello
there, how you doing?' Stuart smells of Daz. You can see the
white bits on his jeans and denim jacket. He keeps smiling all the
time, like he's auditioning to be a weather forecaster or
something. He's asking my new girlfriend all these questions.
He's agreeing with things that she's saying. Come off it, Stuart

never agrees with a word anybody says. He comes round, argues all the time, pisses folk off and eventually I always have to sling him out. I goes through to make more coffee. The Tank follows us going, 'D'you think she likes me? D'you think she likes me?' The Tank's catatonic. This is getting well out of order. I tells him, I says, 'I spotted her; I approached her; I asked her out. She's mine. MY FUCKING GIRLFRIEND!' Stuart comes through. 'Alright,' he says, 'listen, I've got to go but any chance you could maybe spare a minute and put in a word for us? Just mention us or something. See what kind of reaction you get. Mean I'm fairly confident but . . .' I points to the door. I points to my sharpest knife. Stuart assesses the options. 'Eh, that's right. I'm supposed to be going, eh.' Now, in between Stuart going and me returning with the coffees, Wee Harry has somehow managed to steal in. Wee Harry is holding/massaging my new girlfriend's hands. Wee Harry acknowledges me. 'Just be a minute,' he says, and motions me, The Tank and our coffees back through the kitchen. Me, The Tank and our coffees duly oblige. I looks at The Tank. The Tank looks at me. 'Bastard!' says The Tank. The door goes. It's Carmel this time, with Edwin and English Edgar. Carmel says, 'I'm here to check out the new bit of stuff.' Carmel goes through the living-room. 'How's the wife?' she says to Wee Harry. Wee Harry starts greeting. He leans into my new girlfriend. My new girlfriend starts greeting and all. 'Nah,' says Carmel, 'she's not your type.' The E Boys are quick to agree. 'Nah,' they say, 'she's not your type.' Carmel disappears. Edwin and English Edgar request some coffee and start skinning up. The door goes. It's my ex-psychotic big brother. He gives me a big eccie hug. 'Alright, doll,' he says to my new girlfriend. He gives her a big eccie hug and all, sits down beside her and starts skinning up. 'Hey,' he says, 'you heard the one about Farmer Smith and Farmer Jones?' My new girlfriend shakes her head. 'Well,' says my ex-psychotic big brother, 'I'll tell you all about it. See Farmer Smith has this prize bull, right, and Farmer Jones has this brand new prize donkey. Now, thing is, this prize bull, it's been shagging everything in sight. *Everything*. Now, Farmer Jones says to Farmer Smith, "See that bull of yours, see if it so much as sniffs round my donkey, I'll toast its tadger for breakfast." Farmer Smith goes, "Nah, no problems, nothing to worry about. Look, all you have to do is, see at night, put a blanket over the donkey. That way, the bull'll no see the donkey, so the bull'll no shag the donkey. Okay?" Anyway, so that's what he does, that's what Farmer Jones does. That night, blanket over the brand new prize donkey. Following morning, Farmer Jones gets up out his bed. Looks out his window. No fucking donkey. All he sees is the bull, totally shagged out its brain. Oh, he's raging, Farmer Jones is raging, like. Heads off down the road, in search of the donkey. Sees the postman. Says to postie, "Excuse me," he says, "Excuse me, you've no by any chance seen such a thing as a donkey with a blanket over it, have you?" Postie says, "Noh, noh. No seen any donkeys with blankets over them." Farmer Jones goes to the village. Asks round the village. No, but nobody's seen a donkey with a blanket over it. Goes on to the next village. Still nobody's seen it, nobody's seen a donkey with a blanket over it. But then he comes to the next village, the third village, and there's this big, huge crowd in the middle of the square. Farmer Jones says to one of the boys, "What's been going on here then?" Boy turns round and goes, "You're no going to believe this but we just seen the most amazing thing, like." "Don't tell me," says Farmer Jones, "bet you seen a donkey racing down the street with a blanket over it." "Noh," says the boy, "it was a donkey, funnily enough, but it was a donkey with a wee hankie sticking out its arse." '

Old as the fucking hills, man. Mind you, my new girlfriend thinks this is great. 'Oh,' she says, 'tell me another, tell me another.' The Tank's looking daggers at me. Wee Harry's looking daggers at me. My ex-psychotic big brother is tickling the chin of my new girlfriend. I'm drinking cold, cheapo coffee while she's rubbing his inner thigh.

Last I seen, my ex-psychotic big brother and my ex-girlfriend were heading off down the town, the pair of them clad in matching stripey T-shirts, the pair of them harmonising along to John Cage Bubblegum.

MOVING TARGET

Rancey's old dear phoned him at his work one day, telling him as how he was to go round to his Auntie Teen's, over in Clouston Street, and pick up a wardrobe for his sister that had just moved into her own place over the old town.

Rancey said, 'Aye, no problem,' and once everybody was off home for the night, he popped out his hidey-hole – the domestic's station – pocketed Matt's spare keys, and helped himself to a wee shot of the work's van.

Now wardrobes were normally two-man jobs. Rancey, however, was never one to be bothered with such trifling diversions as hunting round for obliging volunteers. Nah, it would be a challenge for Rancey tackling this on his own: and Rancey fair liked his challenges, especially those that called for a combination of brain and brawn – mind and muscle jobs, as Rancey liked to call them.

It had been years since Rancey was last in at his Auntie Teen's, and as he cracked open a can and headed round – with the windows wide open and the stereo blaring out *Queen's Greatest Hits Vol. II* – Rancey tried to see what he could mind of the old place.

And the first thing that came to mind was his old dear's warning – 'Now don't you dare touch a thing, you hear me.' Reason being that Auntie Teen's was forever decked out with all these fragile-looking wee ornaments the two boys, Auntie Teen's sons, had brought back from all their travels with the navy.

Rancey had a wee laugh to himself.

For all that he'd never once got round to actually meeting up with the two boys, Rancey was never so shy when it came to mentioning them – as in, 'See you: mess with me and you mess with my cousins – and they're in the navy!'

Trouble was, the navy didn't sound hard enough; nah, the navy wasn't hard enough for Rancey, so Rancey changed it to first the army, then the marines, and eventually it became that his two cousins he'd never once met were nothing less than undercover agents on special assignment with the SAS. That did the trick. Whenever anybody was hassling him, Rancey would just grab a hold of them, usually by the throat, shake them about good-style and go, 'See you: mess with me and you mess with my cousins – and they're in the SAS!'

The funny thing, of course, about all this, was that the two boys out the navy weren't really Rancey's cousins at all, and Auntie Teen wasn't really Rancey's auntie. Rancey was just to call them that when he was wee. Not that Rancey was one to complain, mind you. See, where he came from, big families meant hard families, and Rancey adopted any rellies he could get. He even invented them: his Uncle Alec that was in the jail; his Uncle Grant that had the gun; his Uncle Davie that had beat up Sean Connery. His Uncle Duncan that . . .

Rancey's brain stopped in its tracks. It was like he'd forgotten something.

But no, it wasn't that he'd forgotten something – no, what it was was that he'd remembered something. Something that should've dawned on him ages before now.

Clouston Street! Flaming Clouston Street! He was heading round to Clouston Street.

Now his Auntie Teen was staying upstairs in a four-in-a-block in Clouston Street, 47 Clouston Street; and the veritable scum that was Whitey and Bammo and their brood stayed upstairs in a four-in-a-block in Clouston Street and all – 43 Clouston Street, if Rancey remembered rightly.

Nah, it couldn't be, could it?

But as Rancey finally pulled into Clouston Street, the two sad facts became just the one sad fact – his poor old Auntie Teen, all on her lonesome and coming to the end of her days, was having to live through the wall from the bog-washed, festering vermin that passed for Whitey and Bammo and their brood.

Rancey parked his van. He'd hold on a minute before heading up. This was something that was seriously needing to be thought about.

Whitey and Bammo were the lowest known scum that walked the face of planet earth – druggies. Day-in day-out, year-in year-out, all the pathetic, sorry scum could ever think to do with itself was just to sit in its poxy wee house with its poxy wee pals, listening to its poxy wee music, watching its poxy wee videos, while all the while spending its entire poxy wee life smashed out its pin-sized poxy wee skull.

But for all that – all that poxy stuff – the worst of it was, the thing that really bugged Rancey about druggies, the thing that totally done his head in, was just that arrogance, that arrogant look druggies always had about them, that *I know something you don't know*, like they were supposed to be really smart or something; going on like wee lassies in the playground. That's all they ever were and all, wee lassies, daft wee lassies. 'I know something you don't know/and I'm not gonni tell you/Nah-nah nah-nah nah-nah.'

In as many years, Rancey had only ever been dragged round to Whitey's and Bammo's the five times. Always, it would be the same. One of his mates would be wanting a wee bit blow, and what with every other source in the town run dry, they'd've ended up at Whitey's and Bammo's. Rancey gritted his teeth. Whitey's and Bammo's; where you got teased by the kids, you got attacked by the cats, and you had to listen to Frank fucking Zappa. 'Za-ppaaaahhhh!' as Whitey called him. 'Za-ppaaaahhhh!'

The last time he'd been round, Rancey'd looked through the pile of records, dug out the first Motorhead LP – *the* party classic – bunged it on and pogoed away to his heart's content. You want to've seen their poxy wee faces. Rancey thought it was a scream.

And so did all his mates when Rancey told them. See Rancey was always telling stories about Whitey and Bammo. The classic was the one when Bammo's old boy had went round to have it out with them. According to Rancey, like, Bammo's old boy was none too happy with Bammo for having teamed up with the slothful Whitey, and, to show his disgust, had went through their room, pulled the covers off their bed and dropped a runny, big brown one all over their mattress. Fucking classic.

But, despite the fact that Rancey told this as gospel, and with everybody duly passing it on as such, the origin of the story lay that bit closer to home – for in truth it was Rancey's ex who'd shat on Rancey's mattress.

Even so, Rancey saw no reason to waste a good story, so he gave it the most deserving home he could think of. Anyway, the likes of Whitey and Bammo just set themselves up to be laughed at. And Rancey hated folk like that. Rods, he called them, nothing but total rods.

Apparently, Whitey'd been in Rancey's year at the school; but Rancey could hardly mind of him. Just one of those ten-a-penny wimps Rancey and his mates used to waste when Rancey and his mates – inspired by Starsky and Hutch – were into spending their playtimes going round and wasting ten-a-penny wimps.

Bammo, on the other hand, was one Rancey did mind. Rancey had quite fancied Bammo at the school. Mean she was nothing special, like, but she was alright, she was worth a poke. But when Rancey had grabbed a hold of her one day and told her that, told her how she was worth a poke, Bammo'd went all funny. Not that Rancey was too bothered, mind you. He'd stole a decent feel of her tits before she'd got away.

These days, Rancey wouldn't've went near Bammo even if she'd been gagging for it. Bammo had went right ugly. Lost it completely. The last time Rancey'd seen her, she'd had her head shaved up the sides and what tit there was sagged worse than a wet Monday's washing line.

No, Rancey couldn't get angry with the likes of Whitey and Bammo, and as he made his way round the back of his van for his rope, his four cushions, his broom-handle and his slippy bit wood, Rancey couldn't help but notice just how run down and decrepit the old street was looking.

And there was no doubting in Rancey's mind as to who was

responsible – the bog-washed, festering, druggie vermin that passed for Whitey and Bammo.

Rancey went up the path. He chapped his Auntie Teen's door. He tried the handle but the door was locked.

The old bint was probably getting a bit deaf in her old age so Rancey knelt down and shouted through the letter-box.

'AUNTIETEEN! . . . IT'S . . . ME . . . RAN . . . CEY . . . COME FOR WAR—'

'Henry?'

'Ih?' The voice came from behind. Rancey turned round. It was this wee wifie in T-shirt and jeans with Bammo.

'Auntie Teen?'

'Goodness, it's a fair old while since I last clapped eyes on you, Henry. Well, stand up and let me have a good look at you then.'

Rancey stood up.

'By jings,' said Auntie Teen, 'what a fine figure of a man you've turned out to be, Henry. Bet you don't remember the last time you seen me, do you?'

Rancey shrugged.

'Portobello. Summer of '76. You came through with me and your Uncle Tom. Mind, that was the day you shat yourself and wouldn't admit to it.'

'Did I fu—'

'Now, Henry, don't you go denying it – you did so. What a state you were in, laddie, the slitters all running down your bare wee legs.'

Bammo was laughing. Rancey scowled at her. Bammo still had her head shaved up the sides. What hair there was was yellow and all done up like string. In addition, she sported a bolt through her tongue, a stud through her left nostril and a ring through her right eyebrow. A fucking mess, in other words.

'I'll see you later then, Romy,' said Bammo. 'Thanks for all your help.'

Bammo went away.

Rancey said, '*Romy?*'

'My new name,' said Auntie Teen. 'You not like it, Henry?'

Rancey shook his head. 'No, I don't. If you don't mind, I think I'll just stick with Auntie Teen, Auntie Teen.'

Auntie Teen shrugged. 'Fair enough,' she said. 'No skin off my nose. Anyway, let's go up and see about getting this brute shifted, shall we?'

Rancey gathered up his rope, his four cushions, his broom-handle and his slippy bit wood, and followed his Auntie Teen up the stair.

'What was spaghetti-heid wanting then?'

'Sorry?'

'The pin-cushion, whatsherface?' Rancey tried to mind Bammo's Sunday name.

'What, Bammo?'

'Aye, her.'

'Oh, nothing in particular. Just having a rake through the old greenhouse, seeing if there was anything she wanted to make use of.'

Aye right, thought Rancey, anything she could sell more like. Right, that settled it. Auntie Teen was needing straightened out about a few things.

'Any chance of a cuppa 'fore we get started?'

'Oh,' said Auntie Teen, 'I'm sure we can manage to stretch to that, Henry.'

There was this right funny smell bugging Rancey as they went up the stair. The only thing he could think to compare it with would be sticking his nose into an old, empty crisp packet. That bad.

When they reached the kitchen the smell grew worse, and Rancey's jaw just about dropped like an anchor. The place was nothing so much as a bombsite. Every cupboard was open and the worktops and tables were covered with all these spice jars and stuff. Rancey picked one up. He had a sniff.

'Hey, Auntie Teen,' he said, 'this's off. No be best just horsing it in the bucket?'

Auntie Teen laughed.

'No, it's alright, Henry. It's supposed to be like that. Now, let's see, what sort of tea can we do you for. There's some . . .'

Auntie Teen listed half a dozen types of tea.

'Eh,' said Rancey, 'all the same to me. I'll just have whatever you're having, Auntie Teen.'

While Auntie Teen stuck the kettle on, Rancey started putting away all the spice jars and stuff.

'No, Henry, don't bother, just leave them. I won't be able to find anything if you put them all away.'

'But, Auntie Teen, they make the place untidy.'

Not for the first time, Auntie Teen shrugged.

This was starting to do Rancey's head in. The old bint couldn't've cared less. Yet, thing was, in Rancey's day, he'd always been brought up to believe that if there existed one wee bit of dirt or one wee bit of untidiness then there was always somebody somewhere that seen it – and for that reason, and for that reason alone, you should always keep everything clean and tidy. 'Cause if you didn't keep everything clean and tidy – then you got whacked on the back of the legs with the poker, got sent to your room and got told not to come down till it snowed blue snow.

'Now,' queried Rancey, still holding a couple of the spice jars, 'are you sure, Auntie Teen? Mean, really, it's no bother. I can just put them all away. Five minutes tops, no problem.'

'Oh, I'm sure alright,' said Auntie Teen. 'My generation's wasted too much time as it is with all this blasted clean and tidy carry-on. See when you think of it, when you really come to think of it, it's neither wonder we made such a right bloody mess of things.'

The kettle clicked off. Auntie Teen filled the mugs. Rancey meanwhile put down his spice jars and picked up his rope, his four cushions, his broom-handle and his slippy bit wood.

They went through the living-room.

Wherein . . .

'Eh, Auntie Teen,' said Rancey, 'why've you got a rug nailed to your wall?'

'You not like it, Henry?'

Rancey shook his head. He didn't like the tree sitting in the corner either. Or the fact that there wasn't a carpet. Or a telly. Or anywhere to sit.

All the chairs were upright chairs, and, as everybody knew, you only ever sat on upright chairs when you were sitting down to your Christmas dinner.

'Hey, Auntie Teen, where's your suite?'

Auntie Teen pointed through the wall.

Rancey was beeling. 'They did *what*? You wanting me to go get it back?'

'Och no, Henry. Don't be silly. They wanted a suite, I gave them one. No harm done. That thing was far too big for in here, anyhow.' Auntie Teen sat down. 'Anyway, these chairs are better for you. Good for the posture. Picked them up for a fiver at a silent auction. Not bad, eh?'

Rancey shook his head. He put down his rope, his broomhandle, and his slippy bit wood, then made a seat out of his four cushions and sank into it. 'If you don't mind me asking, Auntie Teen, much did your suite cost you again?'

'Oh, twelve hundred I think it was.' Rancey gulped. Auntie Teen continued. 'I never liked it, mind you. No, it was your bloody Uncle Tom that was into all that keeping up with the Joneses nonsense. You know, that daft clown was always out buying up rubbish that was neither use to man nor beast.'

Bloody Uncle Tom! That daft clown! You didn't speak of your dearly departed as being 'Bloody Uncle Tom', 'That daft clown'.

'Surely,' said Rancey, putting on his concerned voice, 'you must miss Uncle Tom?'

Auntie Teen shook her head. 'Nah, best thing that ever happened to me. See if I'd've murdered the bugger I'd only've got half the sentence I did when I married him.'

'Auntie Teen!'

'What, Henry?'

'But Uncle Tom was a nice man.'

'Oh, he was *nice* alright, there was nothing *wrong* with him; but he was a boring bastard, Henry, and, take my word for it, that's no way to go through life. Always the house: the house first; the house second; the house bloody everything.'

Rancey was just about to say something when his ears started twitching. There was music coming from somewhere. Rancey went over and leaned right up against the wall.

'Right,' Rancey flexed his muscles, 'you wanting me to go through and have a wee word with them, Auntie Teen? Mean it's no problem, like.'

'Away with yourself, Henry. Don't be daft. A wee bit music never hurt anybody. After all, it's only Za-ppaaaahhhh!'

Auntie Teen giggled.

Rancey freaked.

'That's crap, Auntie Teen, that is seriously crap. There's nobody alive should have to put up with that kind of nonsense. You know what that is? That's what you call noise pollution. You can get folk put away for the likes of that. Oh, aye. Tell you what, I'll just go and have a wee word with them. Promise, they'll never bother you again.'

'Away,' said Auntie Teen, 'away and behave yourself. Now, sit down, drink your tea and stop making such a fuss, will you?'

As always when confronted with one of his elders, Rancey did as he was told.

He sat down on his cushions and sipped his tea. Tea that tasted like nothing so much as the wrapping you got a boiled sweet in i.e. bogging.

'Tell you the truth,' said Auntie Teen, 'I actually think Zappa's shite and all. I'll put a wee bit of this on and we'll see what you make of it.'

Auntie Teen switched on this ghettoblaster that was down beside her chair. A few seconds later, this really freaky, spacey music started coming out from over beside the tree and from over beside the door leading out to the stair.

Ambient shite, as Rancey believed it was called.

In the meantime, Auntie Teen had leaned right back, stretching herself out as though she'd been poleaxed. Then she started speaking really slowly, like one of them hypnotists, really slow-l-y. 'Now, just you try and relax yourself, Henry,' she said, 'just take a good sip of your tea and just try and relax . . . Just concentrate on the tips of your toes; and just allow yourself to relax . . . Just concentrate on the tips of your fingers . . . Just relax . . . Just listen to the music . . . Just relax . . . Then all the way up, through all your veins, all your muscles, just slowly relax.'

As instructed, Rancey took a sip of his tea, concentrated on his fingertips, listened to the music and tried to relax.

But, after a few seconds, he was starting to feel really weird; so he decided instead to think about battering fuck out of Whitey.

There you go, that was better.

Rancey was due to give somebody a skelping, anyway, and Whitey was perfect: what with being a druggie; what with being a wimp and what with taking a loan off his Auntie Teen, Whitey was seriously singing for it.

'How you doing, Henry?'

'Oh, feeling good, Auntie Teen, feeling shit hot.'

All Rancey had to do was find something that pissed off his Auntie Teen when it came to Whitey and Bammo, something that would legitimise his impending outrage.

'So,' he said, 'that pair next door, been getting any bother off them of late?'

Rancey was watching her. She was thinking.

'No, not that I can think of, no.'

'What about the noise and that? I've heard that the likes of them with their music can give off some racket when they've a mind to.'

She was thinking again.

'Well, there was one time . . .'

'Aye,' said Rancey. That would do. One time would do.

'Yes, now that I think about it, there was the one time; but seemingly that wasn't them, just some clown that was round visiting, put on this really loud music – Motorhead, I think they said it was – and started jumping about all over the place. Bammo said that the poor fellow wasn't all there, mind you, so I suppose we should excuse him.'

Rancey was taking a reddie.

Wasn't all there? Wasn't all fucking there?

That was that then.

Whitey was getting wasted. No questions asked. Whitey was getting himself seriously fucking wasted. The hifi, it was getting wasted and all, the hifi was getting seriously fucking mega-wasted.

'Just out of interest,' said Rancey, 'where's your telly, Auntie Teen?'

'Oh, I bunged that hideous thing next door and all.'

Rancey shook his head. She was away. She was away with the God-damn fucking fairies.

'Henry, don't laugh, dear. But doesn't it bother you that in this day and age you know more people that appear on telly than you know in real life?'

Rancey thought about it. 'So?' he said.

'Well, I don't know about you, Henry, but I find that truly alarming. Mean how are folk supposed to know how to get on with each other when all they ever see of each other, when all they ever learn about each other, is from that stupid bloody box?'

'Hey, hold on,' said Rancey, 'just hold on for a minute, will you? Auntie Teen, are you feeling alright? I mean, in yourself, are you alright?'

Auntie Teen got up out her chair. She grabbed a hold of her right ankle with her left hand then wrapped the ankle round her neck. 'Feeling fine, Henry,' she said, 'feeling fine.'

Rancey shook his head. This was getting too much.

Now Rancey's brain always worked best once he'd worked up a bit sweat, so he drank up the last of his tea and said, 'Right, come on then, auld yin, let's go and have a look at this wardrobe.'

They went through the room. And there was the wardrobe. It was a fucker. The sort of wardrobe you'd expect the Queen to store her going-out gear in.

Auntie Teen said, 'You wanting me to go and give Whitey a shout?'

Rancey scowled. Aye, right. He gave the wardrobe a budge. It was about the weight of a small car. Rancey shifted one side eighteen inches. Then he went round and shifted the other side eighteen inches.

That would do.

The plan was to edge it to the top of the stairs – and once it was at the top the stairs? Well, it was easy enough to get to the bottom of the stairs.

Rancey gave it another eighteen inches. Good. The sweat was starting to flow. The brain was starting to work. 'Auntie Teen,' he said, 'I don't want to alarm you or anything, but what you've got staying through the wall there, right, is nothing but a couple of good for nothing druggies.'

Auntie Teen laughed. 'Come on, Henry,' she said, 'lighten up, will you, it's only hash.'

'What?'

'I said, "It's only hash." '

Rancey shifted the wardrobe eighteen inches. 'Auntie Teen, listen, listen to me, right; I know a bit about these things – it's a chemical, right, it gets in their brains, right, it messes them up, it makes them paranoid, it makes them scruffy.'

'Rubbish,' said Auntie Teen. 'It's all to do with how you use it, Henry. It's just like anything else: you mustn't be a slave. Like I always tell them, there's no such thing as freedom unless you exercise your freedom.'

Aye, aye, thought Rancey, as he shifted the wardrobe another eighteen inches; he could be on to something here. 'So you have the odd wee go at them then, do you?'

'Well, I wouldn't put it quite like that, but I certainly speak my mind. See, Henry, I've had all this before with your Uncle Tom: but see his drug was buying things, buying up useless rubbish. You know, over the years, he held me back. He never thought to exercise his freedom, so I never got any.'

Rancey was half-concentrating on this, half-concentrating on his eighteen inches.

'So,' he said, 'let me get this straight, you think, *at times*, that that pair through the wall are as bad as Uncle Tom was?'

Rancey was minding as how she'd said she'd wished she'd murdered Uncle Tom.

'In a way, yes; *at times*, they are.'

Hey, hey. Problem solved then. Rancey would just go round and say, 'See you, Auntie Teen says you're as bad as Uncle Tom was!' Then he'd start wasting. You know, it really was amazing, things did become that much clearer once you'd worked up a wee bit sweat.

'Aye,' said Rancey, getting back to the wardrobe, 'druggies: no consideration; wrapped up in their own wee worlds; smashed out their skulls morning, noon and night. Best just to keep out their road.'

Auntie Teen nodded. 'Like I say, *at times*, I think they go a bit far. Personally speaking, myself, I only ever tan a spliff if I'm wanting to get myself zonked out.'

And at that precise moment, in lieu of this wee bit of unexpected information, the wardrobe didn't so much appear to land on Rancey's foot as appear to wilfully fling itself on Rancey's foot.

'Goodness, Henry, are you alright?'

Rancey was staring at her. He wasn't going to scream. Much as he wanted to, no way was he going to scream. No way was he going to scream in front of nothing so low as a geriatric druggie.

'Henry, now think carefully; do you want me to go and get an ambulance?'

Rancey shook his head. With all his might, the might of ten men, he somehow managed to get a hold of the wardrobe and get it shifted.

Rancey looked down at his poor foot. It was throbbing in and out like something out a cartoon.

Rancey bent down. He counted his toes.

There were still five, but one seemed to be moving about awfy independent of the others – it was like trying to catch a goldfish, whenever Rancey touched it, it went away, it was like it wasn't . . .

Oh, shit.

'Henry! Henry, are you alright? Henry, you've gone a funny colour.'

He'd severed a toe. He'd severed a fucking toe.

Of all things, Rancey started smiling. He stood up, bold upright. He looked like a statue of Rancey. Here he was; he'd severed a toe, he was in absolute fucking agony, and he hadn't even screamed or shed a tear.

This was how hard he was. Fucking hard.

Rancey could feel the toe moving about. He didn't want to damage it or anything so he took off his trainer and eased the toe round so it came to rest under the arch of his foot. That way, if he walked with a banana foot, he'd be alright.

Rancey put his trainer on again. He got back to the wardrobe.

Eighteen inches.

Whitey was getting it good-style. For being a druggie, for being a wimp and for turning Auntie Teen into a twenty-four carat flake-head, Whitey was going to get the most seriously severe kicking any human being had ever yet got.

Eighteen inches.

Rancey was hoping and praying there would be others there, other druggies. Rancey was settling for nothing less than a mass-wasting, a mass-mega-wasting.

Eighteen inches.

The wardrobe was now at the top of the stairs. Rancey was sweating like he'd just stepped out the chip-pan.

'Now, Henry,' said Auntie Teen, 'have you worked out how you're going to get it down the stair?'

Rancey looked smug. 'Got a plan,' he said, 'got a ten-step plan.'

Rancey went through the living-room. He collected his rope, his four cushions, his broom-handle and his slippy bit wood.

On his way back, however, something truly disgusting happened, causing Rancey to let loose the most piercing scream this side of rush-hour at the abattoir.

Auntie Teen hurried through. 'My God, Henry,' she said, 'are you alright?'

Rancey nodded.

All it was was he'd forgotten to walk with a banana foot.

Hence, he was standing on his toe.

He was standing on his now truly squashed and squelched toe.

Rancey said, 'Just needing to get a drink of water.' He went through the kitchen, slamming the door behind him.

Rancey took off his trainer and his sock. Inside the sock, the severed toe looked like nothing so much as an uncooked oven chip covered in cheap tomato sauce.

Rancey opened up the freezer. He scraped the walls of the freezer with a fish-slice and scooped the ice into the sock that contained the severed toe. Once he had enough, he tied a knot and stuffed the toe-containing sock down his other sock. Then he scraped more ice off, and lined his trainer. It was agony to walk on, but Rancey suspected that in these kind of circumstances, following this kind of accident, then this was the sort of thing you were supposed to do.

Rancey hobbled out the kitchen.

Auntie Teen was waiting for him. 'Do you not think maybe we should just call it a day, Henry?'

Rancey shook his head. He picked up his rope, his four cushions, his broom-handle and his slippy bit wood. 'Got a plan,' he said. 'Got a ten-step plan.'

Rancey put his plan into action, his ten-step plan.

Step 1)   The wardrobe was tilted. The slippy bit wood slid underneath.

Step 2)   The rope was secured loosely around the wardrobe.

Step 3)   The cushions were placed between the rope and the wardrobe. The rope was tightened.

Step 4)   The remaining rope was harnessed round Rancey's legs, arms and shoulders.

Step 5)   The wardrobe was edged forward so's it was balancing on the top step.

Step 6)   Rancey, tug-of-war style, wedged his left heel against the frame of the kitchen door, and his right heel against the frame of the bathroom door.

Step 7)   Rancey picked up the broom-handle. He put it in his mouth. Gently, he leaned forward till the broom-handle made contact with the wardrobe.

Step 8)   A gentle prod. The wardrobe went flying down the stair.

Step 9)   Rancey took the strain.

Step 10)   As if by magic, the wardrobe came to rest at the foot of the stairs.

Rancey looked over to his Auntie Teen. Auntie Teen looked over at Rancey.

'It fucking worked,' said Rancey.

Auntie Teen nodded. 'Henry,' she said, 'forgive me for asking, but is that how they normally do it?'

Rancey shrugged. Who cared? He'd dislocated a shoulder, he'd scorched his hands to the very bone and the rope had cut dangerously close to his family allowance. He was in no mood to debate the finer points of accepted practice.

Rancey got his broom-handle and hobbled painfully down the stairs.

It was perfect. There was no damage to the wardrobe, no damage to the wallpaper and he'd left just enough room so's to get the door open. Fucking brilliant. There was no denying it, even though he was saying so himself, the man was a genius.

Rancey got his rope, his four cushions, his broom-handle and his slippy bit wood and hobbled the distance out to the van.

From a fixed point, in line with the edge of the lawn, it was exactly seventeen hobbles from the door to the hedge, with a further five hobbles from the hedge to the van.

Rancey lay two of the cushions on the floor of the van. He placed the other two upright behind the driver's seat and the passenger's seat.

As he was heading back, Rancey espied Whitey and Bammo up at their kitchen window. Even from this far away, and through the net curtain, Rancey could still make out that look, that arrogant look, that druggies look – that look that Rancey was going to wipe off their faces for once and for all. Rancey gave them the finger, mouthing the words, '*I know something you don't know – I'm gonni kill you.*'

Rancey got back to his work. He got the wardrobe out on to

the path no problem then gave it a quarter turn so's it was broadside on. Subtlety bit the dust – Rancey was tackling this turtle style.

It would have to go up to get over the hedge, then down to get into the van. Rancey repeated this to himself a couple of times so's he wouldn't get mixed up.

Rancey tilted the wardrobe. It weighed a ton. It wasn't even off the deck.

Rancey got underneath it.

He took deep breaths. When he reached ten he'd go.

One . . . two . . . three . . . four . . .

But Rancey couldn't be bothered with hanging about. He went on the five.

Seventeen hobbles to the gate . . . sixteen . . . fifteen . . . fourteen . . .

When Rancey reached hobble number two he shouted, 'Geronimo!' and straightened his arms.

The pain was beyond pain. Every part of Rancey that could snap, snapped. Every part that could burst, burst. Every part that could tear, tore.

Rancey managed four more hobbles then flung himself forward.

The wardrobe landed in the back of the van.

Rancey smacked his head off the bumper.

He gave himself a statutory count of eight before getting to his feet.

Rancey held up three fingers. He counted three. According to his brain, it was Tuesday. According to his watch, it was Tuesday.

Rancey was alright.

More importantly, so was the wardrobe. Perfect landing. Not so much as a scratch.

Auntie Teen came down the path.

'I did it,' said Rancey. 'See me, I did it.'

'That you did, Henry. That you certainly did.'

That was the worst of it, anyway. Rancey would just dump the wardrobe over at his sister's and let them get on with it. Then he'd head straight up casualty, get his toe stitched back on, get his shoulder reset, get his head, back and hands looked at then return and batter fuck out of Whitey.

'Well, it's been nice seeing you again, Henry,' said Auntie Teen. 'Hope you don't leave it so long before your next visit.'

Rancey nodded. Aye, right. He wasn't bothering whether he ever seen the old flake again or not. Without so much as a word, he got into his van, opened a can, downed it in a oner, turned the stereo on – 'I Want To Break Free' – cranked it up, sneered at his Auntie Teen in the sideview mirror and headed off.

Halfway down Clouston Street, however, things came to a head when a small ginger cat happened to come bombing out into the middle of the road.

Rancey swerved to avoid it.

Then he thought to himself – why the fuck was he trying to avoid running over a stupid bloody cat?

It was too late.

Rancey'd missed the cat alright.

But he didn't miss the lamppost.

Rancey went clean through the windscreen. His good shoulder shoulder-charged the lamppost.

The last thing Rancey was thinking before his head head-butted the pavement was how he hoped there wasn't a scratch on the wardrobe, because, if there was a scratch on the wardrobe, then his mum and his sister would surely kill him.

Back outside the four-in-a-block, Auntie Teen had been joined by Whitey, Bammo and a small ginger cat.

'And you're sure,' said Bammo, 'he doesn't have a licence?'

Auntie Teen shook her head. 'No, dear: no insurance; no licence; he's on probation; the van's been reported stolen; and going by his breath he's over the limit. This time, poor Henry's going from here to hospital to jail.'

Whitey took Bammo's hand. At last, the bastard was getting some kind of comeuppance.

'Well,' said Auntie Teen, 'I better go and tell the neighbours it's safe for them to come out now. See you later, fellow instigators.'

Auntie Teen headed down the path.

'Romy,' said Bammo, 'hold on a second, will you? Listen, there's still one thing I don't understand.'

'Yes, dear, and what's that?'

'Well, we've good enough reason to hate him, but – why you? Why do you hate him?'

Auntie Teen laughed. 'Do you know, Bammo,' she said, 'I'm really not that sure, but it's a funny thing, these days I really do get a kick out of knowing things that other folk don't.'

And with that Auntie Teen winked at Whitey and Bammo and headed off – whistling to herself as she did so a daft wee tune, a daft wee tune she hadn't whistled since schooldays.

SING AND SAY NOTHING

About twenty minutes of the film remained. Aileen got up out her chair, gathered the evening's dishes and went through the kitchen.

There, she filled a kettle and clicked it on. What with doing a washing and everything, chances were there wouldn't be any hot water left in the tank.

While the kettle took Aileen scribbled an entry in the wine diary — typical Australian, good not great, reliable — then proceeded to scrape her plate into the pedal bucket.

It was then the beeps started.

Aileen counted to herself.

One thousand and one, one thousand and two . . . Beep! One thousand and one, one thousand and two . . . Beep! One thousand . . . Beep! . . . Beep!

Aileen poured what remained of her bottle of wine down the sink. Then she took the two empty bottles through the back cupboard.

'Mind me to take the bin-bags out in the morning, will you?'

She'd meant to see to them earlier, had actually been in the process of tying them up, when something — the phone? The door? Aileen couldn't remember what exactly — had distracted her and caused her to forget.

In between beeps, a surprised-sounding 'A-ha' came from the living-room.

Aileen got back to her dishes.

Clem got back to his beeps.

She'd spied on him once. She'd made the noises of going upstairs, but had in fact hidden herself just outside the living-room door. Eavesdropping wasn't so easy, mind you: furtive as ever, Clem lowered the volume when Aileen was out the room. Anyway, after a bit, a minute or two, Aileen eventually discovered what he was up to — he was flicking between channels. He was trying to watch two programmes at the same time. This was what he did when Aileen was out the room.

He even planned it that way. Clem had this habit of ticking his night's viewing in the paper, but if you studied the timings closely you saw that some of the programmes not only overlapped, some of them actually coincided. You wouldn't have been able to watch one without missing all of the other.

It was all just so typical, typical of Clem. 'Cause when Clem was doing something he had to be doing something else, he had to be doing two things at once. Like when they were sitting down to supposedly watch their film: Clem would start off by devouring his meal; then they'd polish off their wine; then they'd talk for a bit (always Clem starting the conversations, always Clem talking about two things at once); then Clem would finish up by reading his paper.

It was crazy. He was like this about everything. This was the man who couldn't go for a message without bringing back something else, usually something that wasn't needed at all. This was the man who couldn't do an ironing without at the same time feeding his face with tea and toast. And the man who, when doing his morning stretching, had developed a routine whereby, say, he'd be adopting some sort of en garde position whilst at the same time grabbing his left ear with his right hand and leaning over. It looked daft: more akin to an exercise in pointless balancing than anything else.

Aileen stacked the dishes in the drying rack then steeped her hands.

The beeps continued.

God knows what it was going to be like when they got the dish installed. He'd talked her into it. Apparently, according to Clem, it would work out so's they'd be spending less on a dish than they were presently spending on videos. Aileen wasn't so sure. Not about the cost, that wasn't the issue, but about the notion of satellite dishes. The idea that another twenty-odd channels was supposed to be so exciting, was supposed to be something to aspire to, something to achieve.

The water in the basin turned tepid. Aileen filled the pots and pans with tap water and left them to soak overnight. She'd see to them in the morning.

Ten minutes to go. Time to head upstairs. As she passed the living-room door, Aileen stopped for a fly keek.

'I'm away up then. Okay?'

'Right,' said Clem, 'I'll join you in a minute.'

The remote was resting on the coffee table. Four feet away, four feet from the remote, Clem's arms were folded. A pen, though, was sticking out of the corner of his mouth. Aileen shook her head. To think, he couldn't even sit at peace without having to chew on a flaming pen.

Aileen left him to it. Halfway up the stairs the beeps started again.

One thousand and one . . . Beep! One thousand . . . Beep! One thousand . . . Beep!

Aileen looked in on Malcolm.

In a way it was all Malcolm's fault, all this business with remotes, videos and satellite dishes. You couldn't take a baby anywhere these days. Sitters cost the earth. Neither Aileen nor Clem had family local enough or reliable enough to call upon.

Sure, they managed the odd night out, when one of them had a work's do or whatever, and the other sat in, but as a couple they seen about as much nightlife as the average blue moon. And then there was the money, the cost of going out as a couple, when everything had to be doubled. Videos were cheaper.

Also, when they did go out, it was never enough for Clem to just go somewhere, to just do something, and come straight back home; to go to the pictures and come straight back home, to go for a meal and come straight back home. No, Clem had to have it so's they'd be meeting up with folk, or calling in on folk. Usually, colleagues from Clem's work. Colleagues Aileen didn't know, didn't particularly want to know, and didn't particularly feel disposed to once she did know.

Malcolm was needing changed. Aileen removed the nappy, gave a cursory wash, applied some talc then put on a fresh nappy.

Aileen supposed it had always been like this, that Clem had always been like this. But back then, back in the old days, before they were married, when they were going out all the time, going out just for the sake of going out, the unexpected was always an adventure. Nowadays, the unexpected was just always an irritant.

Aileen got herself ready. She set out an outfit for the morning then climbed into bed. She opened up her book and started reading.

The beeps were still going.

His twenty minutes were up. The film should be finished. Twenty minutes. He should be up here. He should be beside her. Beside Aileen. Beside his wife.

The beeps stopped.

Clem put the telly off. He picked up the apple from the mantelpiece. There were, at most, two bites out of it. He took the apple through the kitchen.

There, he deposited the apple in the pedal bucket then checked the entry in the wine diary, adding price and place of purchase to the comments column.

Clem rinsed out the pots and pans. He wiped them with the cloth, dried them and put them away. He dried the plates and cutlery and put them away as well.

Clem went through the back cupboard. He got hold of the bin-bags and took them out front for the morning's collection. On his way back, he stopped off to take in the washing.

How could she have forgot to take in the washing?

Clem went up the stairs.

He checked on Malcolm. Opening Malcolm's nappy, Clem discovered the wee man's wee man to be trapped pointing up the way. Had Malcolm peed, the bed would've been flooded.

Something caught Clem's eye as he finished up seeing to Malcolm. A shimmer of silver paper down by the foot of the dresser. Clem went over to investigate. It was a bar of chocolate. Or, to be precise, most of a bar of chocolate. All bar two bites of a bar of chocolate. Clem shook his head. He folded the paper over to cover up the exposed section then left it on top of the dresser.

Clem went through the bedroom. Aileen was asleep. Her book was resting on the bedcovers.

Aileen always got these books, these seven-hundred-page potboilers, that she never got anywhere near finishing. It was like everything she did. Her meal. Her wine. These daft apples she left everywhere. The bars of chocolate. The dishes. Taking out the rubbish. Taking in the washing. Seeing to Malcolm. She never finished things.

Every night when they sat down to watch their film, Aileen would get up with still twenty minutes to go. Every night. She'd sit there and watch the whole thing then with twenty minutes to go she'd up and head through the kitchen.

It was the same when they went out. Aileen never wanted to make a night of it. Almost as soon as they were out the door she'd be itching to get back home again.

She never seen anything through. There was a time, Clem reminded himself, when this had been enticing, when this had been one of the qualities that attracted Clem to Aileen in the first place. Defiantly individual, she would forget to do this, not finish doing that. Always thinking ahead was our Aileen. Always thinking about something else. To get her attention, to get her time, was one hell of an achievement.

Clem checked the alarm clocks.

In a way, Clem supposed, it was probably best to be like this. It was a reminder, a test. After all, these things were just quirks. You could get attracted by quirks. Equally, you could get irritated by quirks. But only ever irritated. Only ever an itch. What they had, what Clem and Aileen had, amounted to a whole lot more. A lifetime's worth of attention. A lifetime's worth of time. The ultimate achievement.

Clem climbed into bed. Totally at peace with himself, totally at peace with the world, he put on his Walkman, turned the volume way down low, pressed play and started reading his book.

THE PAPER

Yet again, the hoity-toitys had beaten him to it.

Sandy went over to the rack and got himself a copy of *The Sunday Times Magazine* instead.

He sat near them this week. Just two tables away. Close enough maybe to get on their nerves.

'In the name of God!'

The two women looked over.

The Sunday Times Magazine was doing a famine special. Page after page of starving weans. Sandy hadn't realised.

He liked the reaction, though. He kept an eye on the two women as he turned the page. 'Tch,' he said, 'that no terrible. Break your flaming heart, so it would.'

But no, the women never reacted. Sandy gave up and looked at the page he'd turned over to.

'Christ almighty!'

This time the two women did look over.

The photo was of three weans. Sandy'd never seen the like. 'No real,' he mumbled to himself, 'just no real.'

The young thing over at the desk was watching him. Her that went in for them big, thick woolly tights with the wee flimsy skirts you'd've struggled to get a decent sneeze out of.

She was giving him a look.

Sandy gave her a look back.

You could get away with looking when you were old, giving them the once-over. To them, you were just a crabbit old git, capable of nothing other than crabbit old thoughts.

The young thing got up. She walked over to the store-room. She'd boots on. Cherry reds. A bonny lass alright. Sexy. She entered the store-room and Sandy turned his attention back to his magazine.

'Jesus God!'

And there had been him thinking all manner of thoughts when next thing, staring him right in the face, was a poor lass laid out as naked as the day she was born. Just skin and bone.

'Excuse me. Are you alright?'

It was her with the boots.

Sandy shook his head. 'Just these pictures,' he said, 'mean, hen, what can you say?'

Sandy'd got out of jail with that one, answering a question with a question.

Her with the boots looked at the picture. She was leaning over Sandy. She'd on enough jewellery to sink the *Titanic* but her wee black vest might as well've been Marmite.

And then there was that poor lass in the photo.

Her with the boots said, 'O-kay,' as if she'd been thinking about it. 'As long as you're sure you're alright.'

Sandy pointed to the lass in the picture.

Her with the boots put her hand on his shoulder. 'I know,' she said. 'But could you just keep it quiet, please.'

Sandy just acted the dafty. 'Mean, God love them, but can you no see, they're only weans? Couldn't harm a soul even if they tried.'

Her with the boots put her hand on his shoulder again – they were awfy into touching, all these young folk – then she put her finger to her lips and winked at him.

As she headed back to her desk a great big woman with a right torn face came storming in. Bold as you like, she marched right up to the hoity-toitys.

'Excuse me,' she said, 'but do you think I could possibly bother you to have a wee look? Just that I want to check and see if my niece's photo's in. Mean you don't want to go out and buy it if it's not in, do you?'

The woman skimmed through the paper.

Sandy was raging. This was his job. This had always been his job. He was the one that got the paper on the Thursday afternoon. He was first on. He'd always been first on.

'No,' said the woman, 'can't say as I see it. She did say, right enough, mind you, that it would most likely be next week's. Still, you don't want to miss it, do you? I mean . . .'

Would you listen to it? Talk about hoity-toity. And talk about tight-fisted, if Lady Muck here wasn't willing to part with a few bob for the paper then what hope was there for these poor buggers that had to feed themselves off scraps.

Lady Muck got the jacket off and sat herself down beside the two hoity-toitys, yapping away.

That was that then. They'd made a boo-boo on that one. This was a strict no-yapping zone. There were signs up. No flaming yapping.

Being a life-long card-carrying user of the premises, Sandy felt duty-bound to draw to their attention the error of their ways.

Sandy went ahead and cleared his throat.

'Ach-hemm . . . Oh shit.'

The contents of Sandy's throat, a dollop of phlegm the size of a two-bob bit, had flown across the room and found a home for itself on the spine of Cassell's English–French French–English dictionary.

Her with the boots was attending to somebody but Sandy could tell she was watching him all the same.

Lady Muck and the hoity-toitys were giving him the if looks could kill treatment.

Sandy reset his teeth.

He wasn't going to clean it. No way was it his fault. Damned if it was his fault. It was the flaming hoity-toitys. It was their fault. It was them as was to blame. If it hadn't been for them none of this would've happened in the first place.

Her with the boots was on the phone.

Oh no – that would mean Mavis on the warpath.

Sandy laughed to himself. Mavis on the warpath, that was a joke. Mavis was one of them nice folk – and Sandy hated nice folk. You never knew where you stood with nice folk. You were that busy being nice to them and they were that busy being nice to you that you always forgot what the hell it was you were all supposed to be so worked up about in the first place.

The squelch of sticky slippers announced the arrival of Mavis.

Mavis stopped at the desk. Mavis was talking to her with the boots. Her with the boots was pointing at Sandy.

Sandy was praying she wouldn't come over.

This was a new one of his, this praying lark. Not that he was turning all Holy-holy or anything, just that these days he spent half his time wondering what atheists did when they were told their plane was about to kiss the mountain.

Her with the boots and Mavis were still at it. Mavis was doing the talking. Her with the boots was doing the listening. Mavis was wagging her finger. Her with the boots kept nodding.

Mavis went back through and Sandy allowed himself a sigh of relief.

They hadn't seen it. Sandy was convinced they hadn't seen it.

It was then that Sandy noticed something – the blob on the spine of Cassell's English–French French–English dictionary hadn't moved.

Sandy looked at it.

Then something really weird happened – the blob looked back.

Sandy took off his reading specs and put on his seeing specs.

It did, too, the thing was staring at him. It had the exact shape and consistency of an eye.

Sandy got himself up and started heading across for a better look. When he reached halfway, though, he decided it would be best to kill the two birds with the one stone and returned for *The Sunday Times Magazine*.

In close-up, the blob on the spine of Cassell's English–French French–English dictionary not only managed to retain its optical illusion but actually looked even more realistic.

Sandy took off his seeing specs and put on his reading specs.

It had a kind of milky consistency, while suspended at its centre there was a dark brown dollop that gave the impression of being a dilated pupil. Sandy had half a notion to take it round and show it to the doctor.

Sandy removed the book from the shelf. He held it close to him, then he held it at arm's length. He held it out to his left, then he held it out to his right. Whichever way he held the book the eye continued to stare at him.

Sandy was fair tickled. He raised the book above his head so's the eye was looking down on him.

At this point, however, the forces of gravity intervened, bringing to an end the short-lived bond between the blob and the spine.

The new bond, between the blob and the right lens of Sandy's reading specs, got off to a stormy start when a full-scale flinch caused Sandy first to recoil, then to bang into a chair and finally to mutter something about Jesus.

Her with the boots was watching him.

Lady Muck and the hoity-toitys were watching him.

Sandy thought about what he was doing. In one hand he was holding a copy of Cassell's English–French French–English dictionary above his head. In his other hand he was holding a copy of *The Sunday Times Magazine*, rolled up as if he was about to strike out at something.

The folks probably thought he looked a wee bit startled.

Sandy could live with that. As long as they didn't know he'd gobbed on his specs then Sandy could sure as hell live with the notion that the folks thought he looked a wee bit startled.

First things first. Sandy replaced the copy of Cassell's English–French French–English dictionary. He made like he was studying the shelves until the coast was clear then quickly wiped the spine of the book with the sleeve of his jacket.

Sandy then headed back to his table. He kept his back to Lady Muck and the hoity-toitys so's they wouldn't see what he'd done to his reading specs. He also inclined his head at such an angle so's the blob wouldn't slide off.

Sandy had it all figured out, though.

He would just act as if he was holding back a sneeze. That way, if Lady Muck and the hoity-toitys had their wits about them, they would realise the reason Sandy was facing in the opposite direction to which he was going was so that in the event of any mishap he wouldn't be sneezing in their direction.

Everything worked out fine. Despite banging into three chairs and two tables, Sandy made it back to the safety of his seat. All he had to do now was switch specs, return *The Sunday Times Magazine*, and take out a copy of something else.

Sandy took off his splattered reading specs, put on his seeing specs then went over to the rack.

There was a problem, though. Sandy's seeing specs couldn't make out the titles. It was all a bit of a blur. Sandy told himself that didn't matter, that wasn't important, all he had to do was put back *The Sunday Times Magazine*, grab something else and get back to his seat.

Sandy selected a copy of what he thought was the *Radio Times* and made his way back.

It was all over. He'd done it. Sandy sat himself down, took out his hankie and cleaned his reading specs.

The sense of relief Sandy felt once his specs were clean, positioned and primed for perusing was somewhat tempered, however, when that which lay before him came into focus.

'Dang and flaming blast it!'

Auto-Parts, flaming *Auto-Parts*. Of all the things he could've chosen, why did it have to be flaming *Auto-Parts*.

'Really!'

Sandy looked up. It was Lady Muck that had spoke.

Sandy glowered at her.

Lady Muck glowered back.

Sandy had to concede she was right good at the glowering. Obviously put in a lot of practice over the years. Right evil-looking and all. If she started anything, Sandy decided he would go for the shins. There was nobody as liked being booted in the shins.

Out of the corner of his eye, Sandy could see that her with the boots was on the phone again.

Oh God, that was it this time. Sandy was going to have to go a few rounds with Mavis. He was going to have to try and understand Mavis and at the same time be polite to Mavis. To be honest, he'd rather've faced one of Lady Muck's right hooks.

The sticky slippers squelched past the desk with barely a nod to her with the boots.

'Well,' said Mavis, 'it seems there's been a wee bit of a bother. Now, I was wondering if you could possibly begin to explain . . .'

Mavis was amazing. The poor wee woman was so shy and nervous that she swallowed the whole time she was talking.

Sandy thought about it. It had to be sore doing that. It was like forcing yourself to hiccup. Surely to God, you could choke going through all that carry-on.

Mavis had stopped talking. She was bright red in the face and swallowing thirteen to the dozen.

Sandy hadn't listened to a word she'd been saying, all he'd been doing had been staring her in the throat.

Jesus, the poor woman probably thought he was going to sink his gnashers into her!

'Aye, well, eh.' Sandy moved about in his seat. 'Got a wee touch of the cold you see.'

'Well then,' said Mavis, 'should you maybe not be back in your bed with a hot drink and a couple of aspirin?'

Sandy sniffed. That would do. Cue the violins. 'Oh,' said Sandy, 'it's a right cold house, my house, hen. The only day you'll ever get a heat out that place is the day you take a match to it.'

Mavis fell for it. She was struggling to hold back the waterworks.

'It's rare and warm in here, mind,' continued Sandy. 'I just like to come in and have a look through my paper.' Sandy indicated the copy of *Auto-Parts*. 'It does you good, hen, you know, to get out and about and mixing with folk.'

The trouble with the waterworks, of course, was that the waterworks were contagious, and as soon as the first tear rounded on Mavis' eyelash, Sandy felt himself going and all. If Mavis didn't sling her hook soon the pair of them were going to end up looking a right pair of jessies.

'Well,' whispered Mavis, 'if you could just try and keep it quiet then please, or well, you know. There's other people to think of.'

Mavis went away. The squelch of her slippers seemed faster than usual and Sandy wouldn't't've been surprised if she was heading up to the staff-room for a good greet.

Sandy got back to his magazine.

Auto-Parts, flaming *Auto-Parts*, what did he have to go and pick that up for.

There was nothing else for it. Sandy got himself up and took the magazine back over to the rack. On the way, he had a fly look over at Lady Muck and the hoity-toitys just to see how far through they'd got.

District Round-Up! They were only as far as District flaming Round-Up! Good God, what were they trying to do, memorise the thing?

This was getting bad. Sandy picked up a copy of the *Radio Times* and returned to his seat.

Drastic situations called for drastic measures. It was time to unleash the lethal weapon.

Sandy was going to let rip.

One-ah . . . two-ah . . . three-ah . . .

But it wouldn't come. Nothing happened. Sandy sat there, really straining, really trying, but nothing happened.

He tried again. Clenching everything. Then a really good shove and . . .

Talk about blood from a stone.

All that jumping about must've played havoc with his insides. There was nothing there. Not a puff.

Sandy gave it one last go.

It was only then that he noticed how Lady Muck and the hoity-toitys were up out their seats and ready for the off.

At last, at flaming last.

One of the hoity-toitys came over to Sandy. 'Excuse me,' she said, 'but are you feeling okay?'

'Aye,' said Sandy, 'doing away. This you off, is it?'

The hoity-toity looked at the other two before saying, 'Yes, need to get back and start getting the tea on.'

'Good,' said Sandy, 'good. Turned out nice, though, eh?'

'Aye,' said the hoity-toity, 'it's brightened up a wee bit. Pity about the rain, mind you. But, tell me, are you sure you're alright? Mean you've not got any pains or anything, have you? Pains in your arms or thereabouts.'

Pains, thought Sandy, pains in the arms. What was she on about? What, did she think he was having a heart- . . .

'No,' said Sandy, 'no, no pains. No, I'm alright. Fit as a fiddle.' Sandy gave a wee upper-body jig. 'Keeping fine yourself, aye?'

'Come on, Rita,' said the other hoity-toity, 'best be getting a move on.'

As soon as they were out of sight, Sandy went over to get a look at the paper.

He had a wee laugh to himself. The daft thing had gone and thought he was having a heart-attack. He'd have to remember that one.

Sandy sat himself down. He was still laughing to himself as he opened up the paper at births, marriages and deaths, looking to see if there were any decent funerals worth going to.

MOFFAT AND DONALDA

Folk never knew how to take Moffat.

'Seen anything of Tommy recently?' Moffat would ask Lisa. Lisa who didn't want to think about Tommy, let alone talk about Tommy.

'You still missing your dad?' Moffat would say to Carole. Poor Carole, who, two years on, was still under the doctor, still missing her dad.

And that was the way of it. Moffat liked to go on about things folk didn't necessarily like to go on about. The unemployed were quizzed about their prospects, failures were reminded of their failings and the troubled were expected to go on about their troubles.

Not that Moffat himself ever thought that he was talking out of turn, you understand. Not a bit of it. The way he seen it, the way to get to know folk was to get to know their problems, and the way you expressed your concern for folk was to ask them about their problems.

Now for all that all this, Moffat and his choice of conversations, had the habit of rubbing some folk up the wrong way, what Moffat *did* on the other hand was almost beyond reproach. See Moffat would do anything for anybody. It was never a bother to run you a message or look after your weans, never any trouble to help you out with a flitting or lend you a hand with your decorating. Moffat would always get a wee something for his time, of course. Folk would insist he kept the change when he ran a message, or they'd get him a quarter of his favourite cola bottles for keeping an eye on the weans. A packet of fags was the going rate for a flitting, while a sit-down tea would always be laid on if he was round helping out with the decorating.

Those that didn't have time for Moffat, mind you, were always quick to point out what they seen as an ulterior motive that all but explained Moffat and his favours – and that was the stone-cold gospel that whenever Moffat met you, you could be sure of one thing, Moffat was going to go on about you.

Moffat loved his gossip. Whenever he bumped into folk or was round visiting, Moffat would do his usual and interrogate them as to how they were getting on. Once all that was out of the way, Moffat would then move on to the subject of how other folk were getting on.

Everybody knew that Moffat talked about them. The saving grace was that Moffat never embellished or span out a story: he only ever repeated what he'd been told in the first place. And for that reason alone Moffat managed to keep his name in the good books. As folk said, 'He means well.'

As he was most mornings, Moffat was presently to be found at the foot of the stairs, cleaning out his lock-up, rearranging his junk so that he could pile in more junk. Moffat collected junk. Anything broken or finished with and Moffat would always be given first option before it went in the bucket.

It wasn't just his own lock-up Moffat tinkered about in either. If any of the weans got new bikes then Moffat took it upon himself to get things sorted out so's there would be room for the new arrival. Nails became brackets, bits of wood became shelves. Citing the example of it being possible to stand the entire population of the world shoulder to shoulder on the Isle of Man, Moffat maintained that providing things weren't so big that they wouldn't fit in the first place, then there was no limit to the amount of stuff you could pile in your lock-up. This analogy was enough to convince folk that Moffat knew what he was on about.

Of course, those that didn't have time for Moffat were quick to voice their own ideas as to why Moffat spent so much of his time down at his lock-up. The way they had it, Moffat was just making sure he was in pole-position so's to grab the ear of folk as they came in and out the close.

A door shut on the top landing. Moffat stopped what he was doing long enough to fathom out who it was.

It was Donalda, Donalda with Kerry and Leigh-Anne.

Moffat combed his hair with his hands and made sure his T-shirt was tucked in.

Moffat was getting himself into some state over Donalda. Donalda that was four foot ten in her stocking soles and who could best be described as a wee bit on the round side. Moffat that was six foot four and who could best be described as being able to hide behind a clothes pole.

When Donalda first moved in Moffat had given some consideration to the possibility that the pair of them maybe just might at some point or other end up the gether. It had to be said, Donalda had a lot going for her: a lass on her own; a ready-made family; no sign of a man. Moffat wasn't the only one thinking along those lines either. A few of them had been on at Moffat, asking him what he thought about Donalda. 'Nice lassie,' he would say. 'Seems a really nice lassie.' Then Moffat would probe a wee bit, trying to find out what there was to know about Donalda, who she was, what she did with herself, what was up with her man.

But nobody seemed to know that much about Donalda. On Tuesdays and Thursdays she went along to the bingo. Three mornings a week she did some work for the old folk. And that was about that.

Not that anybody ever had a bad word to say about Donalda, mind you. 'She's a cheery soul,' they said. 'Once you get to know her.'

That last bit always got to Moffat. 'Once you get to know her.' Moffat didn't know Donalda. And the way things stood, he wasn't about to get to know her either.

See they'd had a wee bit of a bother, had Moffat and Donalda.

It all stemmed from Moffat trying to find out about Donalda. Moffat had been down at his lock-up one morning when Kerry and Leigh-Anne had started playing out on the landing. As he did with all the other kids, Moffat had started playing along with them, and started talking to them. Till his dying day Moffat would swear on a stack of bibles the height of the steeple that nothing he said was in any way nosey or untoward. Not that it would've mattered, of course. The damage was done.

The next time Moffat seen Donalda, Donalda had that wee bit more to say for herself than usual. She was on about this one, she was on about that one, all the goings on, all the carry-ons, the whole kit and caboodle. Moffat could've done with a pencil and notepad.

As he always did, Moffat passed on what he'd been told.

A fortnight later Moffat found out that Donalda had just been having him on. Everything she'd told him had been a pack of lies. Worse still, everybody was in on it. Everybody knew what she'd been up to. In a way, Moffat supposed he should at least have been grateful for that, knowing that no harm could've come of it. No harm, that was, apart from the harm inflicted on the hapless Moffat.

Things weren't helped by the lack of sympathy winging its way in Moffat's direction. 'Well,' folk said, 'what d'you expect? Mean it's no nice quizzing weans about their folks. You no know you can get had up for that kind of thing?'

And the worst of it all was that all this had went and happened round about the same time that Moffat had gone and fallen for Donalda.

In his head, Moffat had still been sizing up the practicalities. After all, there was a lot to be said for being on your own: eating what you wanted to eat; watching what you wanted to watch; filling your time the way you wanted to fill your time. But that was the problem as well. Nothing unexpected ever happened to Moffat these days. For all that he was at folks' beck and call, Moffat was never under folks' influence – Moffat never got to share the benefit of folks' influence.

Then there was another angle. Being on your own meant that nobody ever got on your nerves. But the downside to that was that there wasn't a soul alive who could truly be said to care about Moffat. Equally, there wasn't a soul alive who Moffat could truly be said to care about.

But, as time wore on, the pros and cons of the practicalities seemed to count for less and less. Increasingly, Moffat became aware of his edginess and discomfort at the mention or sight of Donalda. He would get all embarrassed, all tongue-tied. He would lose track of whatever it was he was on about or whatever it was he was thinking about.

Then one day, a thought struck: if Moffat was ever to see Donalda with another man, it would pierce his heart worse than any bullet ever could.

The practical side counted for nothing. Moffat was smitten. Moffat was besotted with Donalda.

Kerry and Leigh-Anne were on the bottom flight now, racing each other down the stairs.

'Careful now,' said Moffat. 'Mind and take your time.'

Moffat positioned himself at the foot of the stairs, inviting Kerry and Leigh-Anne to jump all over him.

Kerry and Leigh-Anne duly obliged. By the time Donalda appeared, they were hanging from the back pockets of Moffat's jeans with their legs wrapped around Moffat's legs. This was Moffat's speciality, the Basil Fawlty.

'Right, hold on tight now. Mind and be sure and let me know if you're slipping.' Moffat took a loose grip on their wrists.

The kids said they were okay and Moffat proceeded to do the funny walk all over the landing. From the racket they were making, you'd have thought Kerry and Leigh-Anne were on the best ride at Disneyworld.

'Sh,' said Donalda. 'Keep it quiet, will you.'

Kerry and Leigh-Anne did as they were told. They were good kids, knew when to take a telling. Not that Moffat was ever in the habit of checking them, mind, or any of the other kids come to that, but he knew the good ones from the bad. You could always tell.

'Alright?' said Moffat.

'Doing away,' said Donalda. 'Surviving, I suppose.'

Moffat nodded. Inasmuch as he'd ever got off to a good start, then this was a good start. Moffat wasn't one to bear a grudge and as far as he was concerned their wee problem was well and truly where it belonged, in the past. He only hoped and prayed that Donalda felt the same.

With the kids still hanging from his back pockets, Moffat pushed his luck. 'Anything exciting been happening recently?'

Donalda just kind of shrugged. 'Nothing that springs to mind, no.'

Moffat cursed himself. Whenever he bumped into anybody or went round to see anybody, that was always the first thing he said. 'Anything exciting been happening recently?' It was like his catchphrase, his calling card. It wasn't supposed to mean anything, it was just something to get you going, something to break the ice.

'Can we get a helicopter?' said Kerry. '*Please?*'

'A what?' said Donalda.

'Eh,' said Moffat, 'it's just this thing I do with some of the kids. Hold on. I'll show you.'

Moffat told Kerry and Leigh-Anne to let go. Kerry and Leigh-Anne untangled their legs. They kept a good hold of his pockets, though.

'Right,' said Moffat, 'now, slowly, mind.'

Keeping his gentle grip on Kerry and Leigh-Anne's wrists, Moffat started spinning. This was them doing the helicopter.

Moffat kept his spin slow. He could do with the time to think, to think about what he was going to say to Donalda.

If he could only talk to Donalda then he could get to know Donalda. But he couldn't talk to Donalda because he didn't know Donalda.

That was the problem. You only ever said, 'Anything exciting been happening recently?' to folk that you knew – and Moffat only ever talked to folk that he knew. Donalda was the only person Moffat talked to that Moffat didn't know.

'Watch now,' said Donalda. 'Watch you don't get them dizzy.'

Moffat gave it another couple of gos, then stopped.

The kids untangled themselves and Moffat mopped his brow

with the back of his wrist, then combed his hair with his hands and tucked his T-shirt back in. The sweat was lashing off him.

Donalda took a brush out her bag and tidied up Kerry and Leigh-Anne's hair.

'Bonny bairns you've got, Donalda,' said Moffat.

'Aye, when they've a mind to be.'

'Will that be them starting the school next August?'

Donalda laughed. 'No,' she said, 'it was last August they started.'

'Away?' said Moffat. 'You're joking? Just goes to show you, though, eh? Time fair flies these days.'

Moffat knew full well that Kerry and Leigh-Anne had already started the school. He thought, though, that maybe getting on the old time flies routine could maybe be the spark that would maybe start some kind of dialogue between the pair of them.

'Aye,' said Moffat, 'I was just saying to Lisa the other day there, you know it's no so long ago since . . .'

Moffat was thrown into distraction. Donalda was struggling with the zip on Kerry's jacket. 'Is it stuck, is it? Here, let me have a go. I'm good with things like that.'

Moffat wiped his hands on his T-shirt and moved forward. 'Aye,' he said, 'blooming nuisances, some of these things. Now let's see.'

'It's okay,' said Donalda, 'I've got it.'

Donalda stood up. Moffat stopped. They were standing near enough toe to toe. Moffat had never been so close to Donalda. He wouldn't have known she'd had so many freckles, so many lovely freckles, almost a moustache of freckles. Moffat's wee heart was going like the clappers.

'So,' said Moffat, looking down, looking down on Donalda, 'is everything okay then – I mean alright with the house and that?'

Donalda nodded. 'No complaints.'

Moffat stood his ground. 'No problems, no? Settled in alright, aye?'

Donalda shook her head to the first part; nodded her head to the second.

Jesus, would this woman ever talk to him, ever tell him anything? Just something so's he could get to know her.

Moffat tried a different tact. It was a dangerous one, one that had landed him in trouble before, but, what the hell, like they always said, if you're going to die, you're going to die.

Moffat turned his attention to Kerry and Leigh-Anne. 'So,' he said, 'where you off to the day then?'

The chorus was loud and clear. 'Auntie Vi's,' they yelled.

Moffat turned back to Donalda. 'Now,' he said, 'is that your sister that stays up over Crawford Road way?'

'No,' said Donalda, 'it's their father's sister; and, no, she doesn't stay up over Crawford Road way.'

Moffat just stood there. The only thing moving was the sweat on his back. It felt like it was going up the way.

'Well,' said Donalda, 'come on then if you're coming.'

It was Kerry and Leigh-Anne she was talking to. It was Moffat who responded.

'Alright if I chum you down the road a bit? Just that I was supposed to be heading out for a bag of sugar.'

Donalda shrugged. 'Please yourself,' she said.

So Moffat wangled his way into walking down the road with Donalda and her bairns. Donalda with a hold of Kerry's hand, Moffat with a hold of Leigh-Anne's hand.

'Christ,' said Moffat, as they got out on to the main road, 'would you look at that? That's Carol-Anne went and got herself new curtains. You know that's the first time in five year I've walked down this street and no had to look up at those green monstrosities.' Moffat had a wee glance at Donalda. 'Did you hear about Carol-Anne, by the way? Supposed to be that she was . . .'

So Moffat told a few stories. His heart wasn't in it, though. He wasn't wanting to tell mere stories to Donalda, he was wanting to talk about things, things like the future, the possibility of their future.

And, surprise surprise, Donalda never came away with any stories of her own. To be fair to her, she nodded and said 'Aye?' in all the right places; she was obviously paying attention, but other than telling the kids to keep away from the kerb and not to kick the rubbish, she never said a proper God-damn word. Moffat couldn't understand this. Everybody was into gossip. Everybody went on about everybody else. Everybody it seemed apart from Donalda.

They reached the turn-off for the shop.

'Well,' said Moffat, 'suppose I better be going and getting my bag of sugar. Can't be having my tea without my sugar. Closest thing you get to poison.'

Moffat made a face. Kerry and Leigh-Anne laughed.

This was the 'Cheerio' bit. She'd have to speak to him. Even if only to be polite, she'd have to say something.

Moffat went first. 'Well,' he said, 'it's been nice seeing you again, Donalda. Be sure and look after yourself now. Maybe see you around some time.'

'Right,' said Donalda, 'say bye-bye then.'

The kids went, 'Bye!' Donalda said, 'Bye.' And that was that. They were away. No eye contact. Nothing.

Moffat and his disappointments dragged themselves round to the shop for their wee bag of sugar. Not that he was needing it, of course, but Moffat wasn't one for saying one thing then doing another.

Donalda, meanwhile, headed on down the road. She liked Moffat. He seemed a nice bloke. All those stories of his, Donalda could sit and listen to them all day and all night. In a lot of ways Moffat was just the sort of fellow she'd settle for, always keeping himself on the go, good with the kids, right friendly and all. Aye, Moffat had a lot going for him alright. But no, it wasn't to be, best not to give him any encouragement. Not after all she'd been hearing about him, anyway.

POP LIFE

It all stemmed from their problems. With Martin it was money, with Ray it was women and with Hilly it was . . . well, it was always a wee bit more complicated with Hilly.

See Hilly was the sort of bloke that would take offence; and that was about the size of it. All that was needed was for somebody to say something, something commonplace, something you'd hear any day of the week, and next thing Hilly would be heading for the door, slating the others for being nothing so much as 'spoilt bastards'.

That was what had gone wrong the last time, the last time the three of them had got together.

They'd been round at Ray's one night when Martin, as he always did, started going on about his latest financial crisis. In the course of this, Martin had happened to come away with the one about how the more you earn, the more you spend. Hilly made a joke of it at first. The joke being that if Martin had a million pounds in his pocket, then chances were the million pounds would disappear before Martin reached the end of whichever street it was Martin happened to be walking on – with nothing to show for it, no recollection of what he'd done with it. But then Ray made the mistake of agreeing with Martin, saying that once you reached a certain level of income you never seemed to be noticeably that much better off. That was enough for Hilly. He did his 'spoilt bastards' routine and stormed off.

It was a good six months before Hilly had anything more to do with either of the other two. Six months in which Hilly was seen to hang around with the Kelseys or the Kerrs, usually pissed or stoned, always laughing his head off.

Hilly was like that. When he was in a bad mood, he went out, he became more visible.

Ray was the exact opposite, when Ray was in a bad mood, he kept himself to himself.

For years Ray had had to put up with the others going on about their successes and their conquests as far as women were concerned. Every so often all this would get to Ray; and, every so often, it would be Ray's turn to slip out of the scheme of things.

Because he never really knew what he wanted from them, Ray was hopeless with women. Honestly, it was like watching a body trying to eat who didn't realise the food was supposed to enter via the mouth. Hilly and Martin told him as much. There was even a time when they figured it was as well to tell the truth as anything: they told Ray that no woman they knew actually liked Ray. But before they'd had the chance to develop that, to talk it through to an extent that would actually have been of some kind of benefit, Ray made some excuses and left. He never blew up or anything, that wasn't his style, he just, as Hilly put it, turned out the lights. Subsequently, the only times you'd ever catch sight of Ray were out late at night, out jogging, weights strapped to his wrists and ankles.

Back when they were younger, Martin had been the first to leave school. At a time when everybody they knew was signing on, Martin was changing jobs at the rate of one a month: dishwasher, labourer, that kind of thing. Even so, Martin was always short of money, always asking for loans. To his credit, he did pay back; but he was never the one to turn up at your doorstep and say, 'Here's that money I owe you.' No, Martin had to be hunted down, and you had to embarrass yourself by asking for what you were rightfully owed. Likewise, it wasn't unusual to be out with Martin, and for some complete stranger to come over and demand money from him. Such instances rattled Ray and Hilly. It was embarrassing, genuinely embarrassing. They weren't slow in saying so. Consequently, Martin would get slagged to bits, be made to feel really rotten; to such an extent that it would prompt Martin's hiatus. Martin, though, didn't storm off like

Hilly, or turn in on himself like Ray. No, that wouldn't have been dramatic enough. What Martin did was to run away. Martin fucked off. He would somehow manage to borrow twenty quid off somebody or other, then disappear off to the city, or away down south, or, on two notable occasions, over to the continent.

But it wasn't just the borrowing Martin did: Martin sold things. One time that was really annoying was when Martin sold his Bowie collection. He hadn't even sold it to a collecter, just some dud at a record fair for about a tenth of what it was worth. All he'd got in return had amounted to little more than a good night out. But that wasn't the point, the money wasn't the point, the point was *you didn't sell your records*.

For it was records that had brought them together in the first place. At school, they'd noticed the same names scrawled on each other's bags, books and desks. From there they'd got to talking. Soon, they were exchanging records and making up tapes for each other. It wasn't long before the three new friends were spending all their free time sat in front of each other's speakers, appraising their own collections, investigating their brothers' and sisters'; talking about nothing other than records.

Whilst everybody else of their generation seemed content to spend Saturday mornings hanging round up the town, giving it the best bored teenager routine, Martin, Ray and Hilly treated Saturday mornings as though they were on a no-frills, top-secret assignment. They'd head up the town, straight to the record shop, browse for exactly twenty minutes, make their purchases, then head straight back home with their disc-shaped carrier bags.

It was a truly amazing time; discovering all this great music, getting overwhelmed by it. And the great thing was it wasn't a case of one liking this, the other liking that; what one thought the others were thinking, what one said the others agreed with. Inasmuch as they ever could be the same, they were the same: they dressed the same; they did the same things; they were all in the same boat as regards money, women and opinions.

Then, just as they were getting their interviews with the careers advisory woman, punk rock happened.

Initially, it was great. More great records. Records, in fact, that were even better than a lot of the stuff they'd been listening to. It was a discovery again. Only this time round, it was a discovery they could call their own. This time, they weren't out hunting for records; this time, they were waiting for records.

Yet while Martin, Ray and Hilly were equally keen to embrace the new, they responded to it in completely different ways. For Martin it meant party, it meant always going out, having to try everything: every drug; every fashion; every possibility. Performance was what attracted Ray, being on stage – the forlorn hope being that women were only just waiting to fling themselves at the feet of the local axe-hero. For Hilly it became just as important to state what he didn't like as much as to state what he did like. So while Martin would be all excited, looking for a party, looking for the action, going, 'What's happening? What's happening?' Ray would be thinking about his bands, and what with being a bit unsure would waffle on something about, 'Don't know. Supposed to maybe be a gig in a couple of months. All depends, though . . .' Hilly, on the other hand, God bless him, was never too bothered with having to think about things. Hilly just started every second sentence with the then trademark words, the italicised 'I hate . . .'

And there you had it, the three friends: the hedonist, the hopeful and the hostile. Whenever Ray landed a gig the situation would transpire that Martin wouldn't turn up because he hadn't the money, while Hilly wouldn't turn up 'cause he thought the band were crap.

Responses that not surprisingly got right royally on Ray's nerves.

Not that Ray was ever the one to talk, mind, not when it came to getting on folk's nerves, anyway.

Thing was, Ray would always be leeching around in the hope of meeting up with women. He spent a small fortune treating Martin, going to this pub, that club, chasing parties here, heading round there. Not that it ever achieved the desired purpose, mind you. Martin was so restless, such a party animal, that by the time they got served somewhere, or got accepted somewhere, Martin would be on about where they would be going next, where they could be going that was better. Come the early hours of the morning, when everyone else was heading home, Martin and Ray would still be stopping off at the cash machines, stocking up for that elusive good time.

Ray was also into pestering Hilly to go out. A mission which was as doomed as any mission ever could be. See Hilly was never much of a mixer. Hilly's idea of a good night out was to sit in the same seats of the same pub with the same faces he always sat with, talking about the same things he always talked about. When Hilly was in company he didn't care for, he said so; when Hilly was in a place he didn't care for, he left.

Over the years things went on like this. The three friends got on with their lives but, increasingly, struggled to get on with each other. Martin married a rich man's daughter, Hilly married a lassie who lived three doors away. Ray never married. Ray could, however, lay claim to being the most well off, seeing as how he became an administrator for the region's education services. Martin worked for the health board in a self-advocacy project while Hilly earned his crust with a family-run removal firm.

Even allowing for the changes that entered their lives, and the fact that, by this time, they were hardly ever seeing anything of one another, Martin, Ray and Hilly continued to share a bond that came from them spending so much time together when they were growing up. When two of them bumped into each other, they invariably spent most of their time talking about the third – often to the exclusion of even talking about themselves.

On those rare occasions when the three did get together, it was only a matter of time before they broached the subjects they never liked to talked about, only a matter of time before one of them upped and opted for the early bath.

Even though the others weren't in the slightest bit interested, Martin would always contrive to go on about his money problems. He didn't get much sympathy. The fact that Martin never had anything to show for all this money that mysteriously disappeared was too much for Hilly. The fact that Martin admitted to nicking money from his wife, and denying money to his wife, was enough to send Ray off.

Ray was by far and away the wealthiest of the three. Ray knew this, and Ray didn't like it one little bit. The others never intended it as such, but whenever Martin went on about the ease with which Ray accumulated his wealth, or when Hilly went on about what he saw as the pointless possessions Ray had a habit of acquiring for himself, Ray felt they might as well have been having a go at his failure with women – he was rich because he was alone.

While Martin and Ray at least admitted to having problems, Hilly never would. There was nothing wrong with Hilly. If folk couldn't handle a few home truths then that was their problem. These self-styled 'home truths' covered everything from the mildly embarrassing right through to the downright ignorant. The mildly embarrassing was when Hilly was in the home of somebody he considered middle class. In such circumstances, Hilly would make a point of pilfering something, usually from the drinks cabinet, occasionally from the bathroom, but always something expensive, always something that would be missed. The downright ignorant side of Hilly had to do with his penchant for having a go at Martin and Ray, and folk close to Martin and Ray. See Hilly was a bit of a wind-up merchant, where nothing was ever practical, everything was a matter of principle. As long as Hilly was having a good time he wasn't the one to care. Martin and Ray couldn't stand it. It would always end up that one of the three would up and leave.

Then, following the 'the more you earn, the more you spend' incident, two whole years passed without the three of them being together. They only ever seen each other in the passing, down the town or going to the games. As for getting together, arranging something; well, they didn't really see the point. It was as though they'd gone through a bitter divorce; they associated each other with their problems and that was that. The memories just seemed to be bad memories.

As time wore on, though, it was the normally self-assured Hilly who came to realise just how much he missed the other two. Hilly had no fervour for socialising or meeting new folk. Hilly had such a dislike of most folk, anyway, that it was pointless him even contemplating going out and finding new mates. Sure, he got on alright with the folk at his work and with his family but somehow, something was missing.

And Hilly knew what it was. His two friends. Martin and Ray. Hilly wanted to see them again. Properly. He wanted the three of them all to get on with each other.

Hilly thought about it, about how they were all doing away fine on their own but how they couldn't get on when they were together. It was then Hilly had an idea, the same idea Hilly always had. When things weren't working out, then you went back to the way they were when they did work out.

Hilly contacted Martin and Ray. He told them that they should meet round at Ray's on the first Tuesday of the following month. The idea being that they would only talk about records. Seeing as how this was what had brought them together in their youth, there was no reason why it shouldn't continue to be the case. They would bring along their new purchases, play them and talk about them. On no account were they to talk about anything other than records.

In love with the romance of the idea as much as anything, Martin and Ray said yeah, they were willing to give it a go.

And that's what they did.

Unfortunately, though, the first occasion proved to be little short of a disaster. True to form, Martin hadn't brought anything. He said he hadn't had the money. Ray, meanwhile, had brought damn near everything. He'd even brought along stuff he hadn't yet played. Hilly was furious with him. After about two and a half seconds of each record, Hilly would go on about how crap it was, slagging it to bits, and slagging Ray for having more money than sense. Hilly himself was the star of the show, playing his records and enthusing about them.

The next time round was better. Throughout the month Martin had stayed in, listened to all the decent radio programmes, latched on to something that was brilliant and bought it. Ray and Hilly agreed, it was a classic. Ray himself had spent his lunchtimes hanging round the record shops, listening to what the kids were wanting to hear, and buying the best. It was mostly dance but it had a power and urgency that won over the others. Hilly, as was his want, took his cue from what the papers were raving about. Yet even he had to concede that what Martin and Ray were playing was as good in its own way as the stuff he normally listened to.

And that set the precedent. Martin listening to the radio, Ray hanging round the record shops and Hilly reading his papers. They held their monthly meetings, and they never talked about anything other than records.

At first they'd been concerned that what they were bringing along was good enough, making sure there wasn't some little reference that would draw the derision of the others. But, as time wore on, they got confident. They had a pride in what they were buying. Equally, they were keen to hear what the others were listening to.

Before long, they began to notice changes in each other. Martin had started off by coming along with just a couple of singles, but now he was appearing with a few singles *and* a couple of LPs. Not only that but people in the streets had been stopping Ray and Hilly to ask for Martin. Nobody was seeing much of Martin these days. They'd all assumed he'd gone a-wandering again. But no, Martin was around. Martin was doing fine. Simple plain truth was Martin wasn't going out because Martin didn't want to go out. He wanted to stay in and play records. Many's the time he'd got himself ready to go out but he always had to hear just one more record, then another, then another. It ended up with Martin having to ask himself the question: what did he want to do, did he want to go out, or did he want to stay in and play records? So Martin stopped going out.

The change in Ray had to do with his appearance. Whereas Hilly had always dressed classically (501s, white T-shirts) and Martin went for the latest Next or Top Man high-street fashions, Ray always looked as though he was going to a game in the middle of January. Now, following their Tuesday nights, Ray was taking a few chances, and it was paying off. He was looking alright. He was getting his hair cut every six weeks instead of every six months. His flat seemed different as well. It was more untidy, yet it was less filthy. It looked like he was staying there rather than just living there.

The big change, though, was with Hilly. Martin and Ray were always wary of Hilly, knowing that Hilly was perfectly capable of dismissing their purchases – and, by implication, themselves – with either a subtle shake of the head, or by going to the other extreme and bawling and screaming his socks off. But Martin and Ray were so into what they'd bought, so passionate about it, that they did something nobody else could ever be bothered to do: they argued with Hilly. Nobody ever argued with Hilly. Folk usually just ignored him, or laughed at him, nobody ever argued with him. But Martin and Ray did – and they won. They won him over. They got him to listen to what they were playing, *and* to listen to what they were saying.

On a couple of occasions they almost broke the rules. There was one time when Hilly was so excited he'd phoned Ray up at his work, telling him how he had to go out and buy something. Ray had said no, it had to keep, there were rules to be obeyed. Another time they'd all turned up with virtually the exact same records. Martin seemed uncomfortable. But he didn't say anything. Next time round, Martin appeared with the same number of purchases as he'd had the previous month. He said that yes, the notion had entered his head just to turn up with a batch of blank tapes, but that he'd decided the important thing was to own the records. That was what it was like when they were younger, that was the way he wanted it now.

The three friends still argued, of course; but now they only ever argued about records. They argued about what made a good record, whether something ephemeral could ever possibly be as good as something that was seminal. They argued about whether bad bands could make good records. They argued the case for 'Suspicious Minds' being better than 'Heartbreak Hotel'. They argued with passion, with loads of logic, even with blind prejudice – but they never held back, never kept their thoughts to themselves.

Hilly had long held the belief that the place for dance music was the dancefloor. Not that he was bigoted against it or anything, just that playing records that went beep-beep thwack-thwack in the privacy of your own home was about as pointless as playing 95 per cent of live LPs. But he came to understand, through force of sheer enjoyment as much as anything, that the records could stand on their own, that they were as valid and wonderful in their own way as the stuff he normally listened to.

As for Martin; well, it wasn't so long since Martin had all but stopped buying records. Occasionally, he'd've got something from the bargain bins, but he wasn't involved, he was purchasing out of a sense of obligation rather than want or need. Now he was buying things full price. Not only that but because he was taking his cue from the radio, he was ordering the likes of expensive imports and limited edition mail order. Martin's disposable income was still short in terms of its lifetime, but now at least there was something to show for it.

Likewise with Ray. Prior to the arrangement, Ray had been the one blanding out. When it came to music, what he'd been buying had been predictable – comfy compilations, bland bestsellers. He'd even bought a CD player. But, after a few meetings, he'd gone back to vinyl. Like he said, he'd got the taste again, and owning vinyl was like tasting chocolate.

It was as though they'd gone back to the old days, back to their youth. But they knew the only way to get the most out of records was to hunt them down, to be obsessive. See that was the great thing about records: you never just went out and bought the best, you had to discover the best. As much as the powers that be had tried to market so-called 'classics', records weren't mere things you owned, like accessories, and said 'I've got it', like you'd say you'd 'seen' a film or 'read' a book.

As agreed, the three friends continued to have nothing to do with each other, other than the monthly nights round at Ray's, and then they only ever talked about records – they never talked about themselves, they never gossiped, they never discussed what was happening in the news. Originally, this had meant that they wouldn't be bringing up their problems, letting their personal lives interfere with their friendship. The strange thing now was that they were all doing fine. But they didn't tell. Martin had bought a house, Ray was engaged to be married and Hilly had become a father. Most folk thought it was Hilly's parenthood that had turned him into a more reasonable bloke, but Martin and Ray liked to believe it was the time they spent together, listening to their records and talking about them, that had brought on the change that meant, for the first time, Hilly actually appeared to be interested in folk when he was talking to them.

Over the festive season there was no exchange of presents or even cards, instead the three friends compiled lists of their records of the year, compared them, and analysed those that were in the papers and those featured on the radio. During the summer they timed their holidays so's not to coincide with the first Tuesday of every month. There was no illness or problem that kept them from their appointments. They were never late, nobody ever left early.

The summer was always a lean time for new releases. In view of this, it was agreed to forego the norm and have an evening in which they brought along lists of their all-time favourites. Top two hundred singles, top hundred LPs. For the whole month they never went out. Wanting to be as sure of their lists as they could be, they stayed in and played and played and played.

It proved to be a great night. Easily the best yet. So many records they'd forgotten about. They'd had near-enough identical top fives but after that it was just classic after classic after classic. The lists were beyond dispute. It was almost scary that there were so many great records that they all knew off by heart, that they all knew so much about. Thinking about it, there had to be thousands. Those they'd listed had only been a fraction. The lists had been too limiting. Next time round – if there was to be a next time round, there was some debate as to that – they'd specialise. Not in terms of genre – that was crass – but in terms of period.

That night, they opened up, they shared their dreams. In turn, they fantasised about putting their knowledge into words or owning record shops; but, like when they were young, they only ever fantasised about it. Although they now had the talent and the financial clout to make it happen, they didn't want to be involved. Partly this was because it would break the rules of their friendship, but mostly it was because they realised they were still what they'd always been – they were fans. It was for this reason that none of them – excepting Ray's brief flirtation – had ever pursued the performing side: they didn't want to be stars, they wanted stars. In the same way that folk don't want to be gods, folk want to worship gods.

And so everything continued.

Until, that was, the evening one month short of the third anniversary of their first meeting.

Hilly didn't turn up.

Hilly was never late. He'd never been late for anything in his life. Hilly just didn't do things like that.

Martin and Ray waited. They didn't start. They wouldn't start without Hilly.

After about an hour, the phone rang. It was a guy who introduced himself as being Phil, Hilly's brother-in-law.

There'd been an accident, Phil said, Hilly had been involved in an accident up at his work.

It seemed important for Phil to take his time and explain as best he could everything that had happened.

It was ten days ago. Hilly had been doing a flitting over the old town. They'd been taking a chest-freezer down a flight of stairs when the guy at the top end had lost his grip. While the guy endeavoured to retrieve his grip, Hilly had tried to wedge the chest-freezer against the banister. But, somehow, the chest-freezer slipped, pushing Hilly down the stairs.

Phil said he wasn't sure what had happened after that, but the next thing anybody knew was that Hilly was flat out at the foot of the stairs. He must've lost his footing or something because the chest-freezer hadn't moved. It had stayed put, perfectly wedged between the banister and the wall.

Ray asked if Hilly was alright.

Phil took a deep breath. No, he said, Hilly wasn't alright. Hilly was in a coma. He'd been unconscious for ten days.

As much as Ray had been half-expecting something like that,

the actual words still managed to shock him in a way that amounted to nothing less than physical pain.

Ray asked when they could go up and visit. Phil said whenever, they could come up at any time they wanted.

Ray thanked Phil for letting them know. He said they'd probably be up later on.

Ray told Martin. They talked about what they should do.

They were both thinking along the same lines, but they didn't want to do it – they didn't want to make a tape up for Hilly. It seemed corny. It seemed sick. It seemed like interfering.

But the more they went on about it, the more it made sense. Really, it was the only thing they could do. That was what this night was all about. The records were more important to Hilly than Martin and Ray ever were. They knew that. Hilly was the one who always said he'd rather be blind than deaf. It was one of those challenges he always set the other two, like a childhood dare – would you rather be blind or deaf?

The deciding factor was when they got round to thinking about what would've happened if the circumstances had been reversed. It's what Hilly would've done. Hilly wouldn't even have thought about it, he'd just have gone ahead and done it.

Ray looked out the list of Hilly's all-time favourite records. They used that as their guide to make the tape up.

It was a truly horrible experience, listening to all these records, records that would normally have got them so excited, records, as Hilly put it, that made them feel so alive. After a while, they turned the sound as low as they could get away with, and busied themselves doing other things. Martin made a few calls, Ray went for petrol.

Even so, the process, by its very nature, could not be speeded up, and once they'd filled a side of a C-90, they called it a day, and headed up to the hospital.

They always said that the thing about folk in these situations was how normal they looked, how peaceful, but Hilly didn't look normal. He didn't look pained or distressed or harmed in any way, but in no way could you have said he looked normal.

There were four visitors already sitting round the bed.

Other than to say hello, Martin and Ray hadn't spoken to Hilly's mum for close on ten years, but she acknowledged them as though she'd only just seen them the day before. The passing of so much time just didn't seem to mean anything.

A bloke stood up and offered his hand. He introduced himself as being Phil, Hilly's brother-in-law, the guy that had phoned. Phil introduced the two women sitting by the bedside as being his sisters, Sarah and Julie. A second later he added that Sarah was Hilly's wife. Martin and Ray hadn't seen Sarah since the day of the wedding. If they hadn't been told her name, they wouldn't've recognised her.

Phil started to apologise for taking so long to let them know, but stopped when Ray shook his head to indicate that that didn't matter.

Martin took the tape and the Walkman from his bag. He asked if it was okay to leave them. The folk seemed a bit unsure but nobody objected. Martin explained as how the tape was made up of Hilly's favourite records. Everybody looked at Martin as though he was talking some kind of foreign language.

Hilly's mother told Martin just to go ahead. She put her arm around Sarah's shoulder and said, 'You know he loves his music, hen, you know he loves his music.'

Martin switched the machine on. The tinny beat could be heard coming through the earphones.

Ray went over and turned the volume up. It wasn't loud enough. It wouldn't've been loud enough for Hilly.

To look at it, it was like one of those uncomfortable scenes folk always laugh at when they see it on telly. Hilly wouldn't've laughed, of course. Hilly liked a laugh but Hilly hated comedy. He'd never seen the point of jokes and if he'd ever laughed at a film or sit-com then there was certainly nobody present when he'd done so. Knowing, he called it. Knowing meaning smart-arse, knowing meaning ironic. But, in practice, it always turned out to be the exact opposite. Folk that knew nothing about nothing pretending they did.

Martin and Ray were feeling distinctly ill at ease. Not for

themselves but for Hilly's family. They felt they didn't belong. They didn't know these people. The only person they knew was the one on the bed, and, at this precise moment in time, they felt as though they'd never really known him at all. They felt as though they'd only ever once met him.

Martin took the initiative. He suggested that maybe they should come back later. Ray agreed. He took out his business card and handed it to Sarah, telling her that if ever she was needing any help with anything, anything at all, then just to get in touch. He said it again just to make sure she understood that he meant it.

Martin and Ray left the hospital. Without so much as a word, they drove out to the docks. They didn't want to be indoors, in any kind of home.

It was neither wonder that at times like this folk had a habit of turning religious. There were no rules telling them how to behave. No precedent that told them how they should feel. Everything they felt was wrong. Guilt. Regret. Shame. Fear.

And, most of all, anger.

They started flinging stones and rocks out into the water, burning off their energy. This was the worst night of their lives, and it was compounded by the near ridiculous image of Hilly's family sitting round his bed watching him listening to a Walkman.

These people didn't understand.

Or, then again, maybe it was Martin and Ray who didn't understand.

See that was the problem. Their Tuesday nights were tantamount to a secret. And folk liked secrets. Its very success had to do not only with the way they avoided bringing up their problems, but the way it all had nothing to do with anybody else.

That was how no one had got in touch with them. Nobody knew about them. Nobody knew what went on. Hilly would never've mentioned these nights to anybody. Sure, okay, he probably said he was going round to see friends and play records, but he'd never've told anybody about what went on. Martin and Ray didn't, and if they didn't then there was no way Hilly would've. You could only talk to folk about such things, your passions, when they would understand, and nobody they knew, nobody Hilly would know, would understand all this.

For no real reason they could think of other than they wanted to, Martin and Ray decided to head back up the hospital.

They'd leave it a while, though. They wanted privacy. They wanted their secrecy.

They went back to Ray's and made up more tapes. They taped records from Hilly's list, records from their own lists that Hilly had regretted not including in his own, and the records they'd intended playing that night. This time, they taped with the sound up. They were positive about what they were doing. They were doing what it made sense for them to do. The only thing they could do. It was what they'd done for the first Tuesday of every month for the past three years and it was what they were going to do now.

It was the back of midnight when they returned to the hospital.

Sarah was still there, still sitting by Hilly's bedside.

She explained as how one of them always stayed over and slept on a Parker Knoll in an adjoining room. She didn't seem as wary as she'd done earlier. Truth be told, she looked too tired to be bothered. The Walkman lay on the bedside table, the earphones by its side.

Martin put the new tape in the machine. He fitted the earphones on Hilly, then switched it on.

Ray looked over at Martin. There were things that needed to be explained.

'You don't know anything about us, do you?' he said.

Sarah shook her head.

'It's a long story,' said Martin.

And, since there was nothing else to do, they told her the story: about how they first met; how they always fell out; their nights playing records.

When they finished Ray laughed. 'Do you realise,' he said, 'this is the first time we've ever talked about him and not slagged him off?'

The three looked over at Hilly. The music stopped. Ray switched the tape over. He turned the volume up a bit and closed the curtain round the bed.

Sarah told the story of how she met up with Hilly. It was a familiar story. The courtship was so typically Hilly, so single-minded, so matter-of-fact.

Just as Sarah was going on to explain what plans she and Hilly had been making for the future, the curtain round the bed was pulled back.

It was the doctor. 'Do you think you could maybe turn that down, please?' she said. 'It carries, you know.'

Martin apologised. He explained what they were doing.

'Still,' said the doctor, 'it's past one o'clock in the morning.'

Martin went over. He turned down the music.

The doctor tickled Hilly's toes then made a note on her clipboard. She said to Sarah 'Do you not think that maybe you should get some rest?'

Sarah looked at the other two.

'On you go,' said Martin. 'We'll stay here.'

'Are you sure?' said Sarah.

Martin and Ray nodded. They weren't going anywhere. The doctor smiled a thank you. She led Sarah away into a tiny side-room.

Alone at last, Martin and Ray looked at each other. Then at Hilly. They'd done all they could do. They'd played Hilly his favourite records, they'd played him the ones he'd regretted not having on his list, and they'd played him the ones they'd intended playing that night. It was pathetic. They were grown men, successful men, yet this was all they could think to do. Because of Hilly they'd changed so much, so much for the better, but now, when it was most needed, there was nothing they could do in return.

Martin took a piece of paper from his pocket. It was the list of Hilly's favourite records.

Martin studied it. He wasn't staring at it, he was studying it.

If there was an answer, if there was something that could be done, then this was where they'd find it.

After about five minutes Martin reached over and switched off the Walkman. He removed the earphones and placed them and the machine on the bedside cabinet.

Martin continued to study the piece of paper. A further five minutes passed before he finally spoke.

'I think you're wrong,' he said. 'I think you're wrong. And I'll tell you why I think you're wrong. No, listen, listen, you've had your say. See . . .'

Martin went through the list, talking about what they always talked about, the records. Ray pushed up his sleeves and joined in.

They talked about nothing other than records, slagging off the things they always slagged off, going on about the things they always went on about, how important it all was to them. *This* was what it was normally like. Tuesday nights, the three of them together, talking, talking only about records.

Before anybody knew it, it was four o'clock in the morning. They'd been going on like this for the best part of three hours when the doctor returned with another doctor. It was the change of shift, the handover.

The doctor tickled Hilly's toes.

She tickled Hilly's toes again.

She leaned over and shook Hilly by the shoulder. Gently at first, then quite vigorously.

'Can you hear me?' she said.

Hilly moved his lips. He didn't say anything but he moved his lips.

Martin went through and got Sarah. By the time they returned Hilly seemed less peaceful, more restless, almost groggy. For the first time, he looked genuinely ill and everybody seemed pleased.

Within the half hour, Hilly was sitting up, taking some fluids and responding to the doctor's questions. He was a bit doped and sluggish but, other than that, there didn't seem to be anything much wrong with him.

The doctor explained everything that had happened. Hilly took it all in. Yes, he knew who he was. Yes, he remembered what had happened. Yes, he understood that he was in hospital.

In fact, waking up in hospital didn't seem to bother Hilly – whereas the sight of Martin and Ray did. 'I just had this crazy dream about you pair,' he said. 'Going on and on. Havering the biggest pile of nonsense I've ever heard.'

Martin and Ray smiled, but it was Sarah who laughed. 'Then you could maybe introduce us all some time,' she said.

Hilly turned his head away. The very thought seemed to cause him nothing but shame.

It was then that he noticed the Walkman.

Hilly reached over. He picked up the tapes and the piece of paper.

'Your favourite records,' said Ray.

'We taped them for you,' said Martin.

Hilly seemed chuffed. 'So this is what brought me round then, eh?'

Martin and Ray nodded. Although, as they did so, they were thinking to themselves as how it wasn't the tapes, the music, that had brought Hilly round – no, if anything was responsible, it was them, the sound of their voices. Not that they'd ever dare dream of telling Hilly that, of course. After all, the three friends had an arrangement to keep: they'd only ever meet up on the first Tuesday of the month, and they'd only ever talk about records.

·

COMINGS AND GOINGS

Makes me out to be a basket-case. Tells folk that and all. 'Oh, did you not know, Kirsten's off her trolley these days. Kirsten's a skittzy. Kirsten's gone loopy lou.' Says I'll end up the tree-house; the tree-house he calls it, the flipping tree-house. Says I'll get my rubber-bedroom in the tree-house, get my gownie with the wraparound sleeves; up in the clouds with all the rest of the nutters.

Ken he does it. When he's away on his travels, ken fine he tells folk.

This is the new one; him and his travels. First it was him no coming back for his tea; now you never see him for days on end. Turn your back; all you hear is the door – ching ching – and that's him. Oh, you hear *of* him alright, it all gets back to me: 'been round at this one, round seeing that one, spending the night here, crashing over there'. You never know what to believe. There's no another woman: I ken that. Don't need anybody telling me there's no another woman. Bugger could never keep the smile off his face.

Then it's –

'Where you been?'

'Out.'

'Out where?'

And a look that says, 'How, what business is it of yours?'

Mean, 'What business is it of yours?' What business is it no of mine? No that I can say anything, of course, 'cause I'm off my head, I'm off my trolley, I'm loopy lou. Count for nothing. I'll end up like that. I will. Flaming will.

Makes me out to be a dragon and all. Makes out as how I'm flying off the handle at the slightest wee thing. And what was all that nonsense with the bloke from the council, him that was round seeing about the windows, what was all that about? Had him terrified of me. Said he was expecting some kind of mad wife-turning up; bawling and shouting the odds, giving it the screaming abdabs. Says, 'Your man was saying you'll no be too happy. Says to be sure and no have any sharp objects lying about.'

Was that no terrible? No a terrible thing to say about somebody? You wonder sometimes what folk are supposed to make of me.

'My wife says you were to have this job done the day or else.' That's what I'm supposed to've said. What does he have to go and say a thing like that for? Does he really want folk to think that I go on like that? Has he no the sense in him to act decent? I'm no that flaming stupid. Kent fine the fellow would never've got the job done in the one go. But, oh no, he's got to make it out like when I get back that I'm going to blow my top, that I'm going to go eppie, that there's going to be hell to pay.

You know that's the one thing I hate, the one thing I can't stand, him going round telling on me, telling all these strangers how I'm supposed to be so rotten to him. Bad enough when it's folk you ken, aye, but at least they ken you, at least they can make up their own minds, but when it's folk you've never even so much as met, when all they've got to go on is whatever he's been coming away with.

Can feel them looking at me.

What's he been saying? What's he been saying now?

That family of his, they've something to do with all this. Flaming filth of them: wouldn't know a bar of soap if it came right up and smacked them in the face. Half daft and all, the lot of them. They're all like that, the whole flaming lot of them. It's in the blood.

And all I get is, 'You knew what you were letting yourself in for, Kirsten', 'You knew what he was like', 'You knew fine well what to expect of him'. Christ, you'd think he was some kind of fly-boy the way they go on, nothing more than a laddie. Well, he's no, is he, he's no a laddie. He's a grown man. He's supposed to have some responsibilities.

Wouldn't be so bad if at least he was a wee bit fly, least then we'd maybe have some flaming money showing its face.

Christ, no, Kirsten, don't say that. That's the last thing you'd be wanting, flaming police at the door. Oh, they'd love that round here. That really would give them something to talk about.

God, I hope he's no gone and landed himself in any kind of bother. That's just about all I need. Mean how am I supposed to ken what he's up to? How am I supposed to ken who he's been seeing? Katherine was saying that and all. 'Do you think maybe he's on the drugs, Kirsten?' No, I can't see it, no him. Mean he's daft, aye, but he's no that daft. No that you could tell with the likes of him if he was on anything, mind, seeing as how as soon as he's out that door he's as high as a flipping kite half the time, anyway. Rest of the time he's just mooching: getting in your road, getting on your nerves, getting . . .

Behave, will you. Will you just learn, for once in your life, learn to bloody well behave and learn to act bloody decent.

If he'd only just give himself a shake, just give himself some kind of chance. Mean ken it's no all his fault he's no got a job but it's no as if he does himself any favours. Mean telling folk how he'll no do this, how he'll no do that. He's got to learn to go round and pester folk, keep on at them. It's no that when there's any of them in here wanting anything done, of course; oh no, when they're round and chapping at the door and it's, 'Oh, could Barry come up and do this; oh, could Barry come up and do that' and he's out that chair of his like a flaming rocket, all big smiles and holding in his gut like he's on a corset.

And what's this with him telling folk that I've been saying he's been with every woman in this close? What's all that supposed to be about? Aye, in his dreams. Wouldn't put it past some of them, mind, specially that Mandy. No, she can be awfy familiar at times, that one. Supposed to be that she served her time down the docks – one leg over here, other leg over there. Flaming fairy. All the same, that sort. Think they're something special 'cause they've a wee bit money. No lift a finger to clean the stair either. Oh no, that's beneath the likes of her. Say her house is the same – flaming filth. See when she goes out, though; oh, it's taxis everywhere; to see her you think she fancied herself as some kind of flaming supermodel, flashing all she's got like the tart that she is. That's all she is, too, a flaming tart. Say when she was staying over next the club she would send her laddie down the taxi rank damn near enough every night. 'Would you like to come up and see my mum?' Can you believe that? The neck of her. Say you see her down the market and all, giving herself to all the Pakis, them with the money. No, wouldn't put it past her. No that she'd get any off him, mind, any money. No a penny to his name. I know that. Maybe the odd tuppence he's pockled out my purse. No, no unless he has been getting himself into bother he's no money. Could see that family of his giving him handouts, right enough, but that wouldn't last. That mother of his, can just see her, 'Is she no looking after you, son? Is she no feeding you?' She's the worst, that one: she's just bad, just plain rotten. And there would be him, poor lamb, making out as how he's so hard done by. Flaming cheek of him. He's rotten to me. He's rotten to the kids and all. His own flesh and blood, treats them like flaming dirt. He'll no play with them. He'll no talk to them. All he does is ignores them and tells them how their mum's half-daft, and how they're the same and all.

No have nothing to do with Dad either, no even give him the time of day. Never spoke so much as a word to him in over a year. Dad says no to bother with him. 'Just pack his case and leave it out on the landing. Been nothing but trouble since day one.' Says I've just to bother with myself and the bairns. *But, Dad, it's no that easy.* It's easy enough saying it, aye, but actually doing it's a different matter. Mean half the time I never ken whether I'm coming or going, so how am I supposed to ken what's for the best; tell me, how am I supposed to ken what to do? Next thing you ken he could be coming through that door all lovey-dovey, all smiles and apologies, and that would be it all back the gether again. 'Cause that's what I'm wanting: I'm no wanting left on my own. I'm no wanting that. And that's what'll happen. And how am I supposed to get a man? Me, with two bairns; me, at my age? Bairns need a father. I'm no ending up like her up the stair. She never used to be like that. Kent her all my days and you see what's happened to her. She is daft, that one, going about all day with her gownie on. Flaming rattles with the pills. No, she's no the full shilling. Never used to be like that either. No, I could see that happening to me. I could. Just letting myself go and no bothering 'bout anything. Getting up to get them off to school then going back to my bed till it's time to go and fetch them. No, I'm no wanting that.

But what's there to do? Mean what can I do?

Oh, he's had me fooled alright, had me fooled a few times. 'Never again, hen.'

But there always is an again, isn't there, there always is another time. And I stand there and I believe him, take it all in like the sap that I am.

Never stand up for myself, that's my problem, just let him walk all over me. Many a lass would just get the locks changed and that would be that. End of story. No, no me, though; no, no Kirsten. 'Walking with a cloud on your head.' That's what Katherine was saying. I am and all. I know that. Ken fine I'm no myself. Ken I'm a wee bit down. And it's no just with him; no, it's more than that. I'm no in the mood for anything. I'm no up to it. Fit for nothing, nothing but the scrapyard. Can barely get myself going half the time. I just hate things. I hate this house. Hate having to look at it. Hate having to smell it. Hate having to have it. What have we got? Nothing. Nothing to call our own. Just rubbish other folk've thrown out. 'Oh, our table's broke, let's give it to Kirsten.' Hate this stair and all. Hate it. Hate this court. Hate it. Hate this flaming town. Just hate it.

And all I'm getting is, 'Don't blame yourself, hen', 'It's no your fault, Kirsten.' Christ, I ken fine it's no my fault, but that's no making it any better, is it? That's no solving anything, is it? Where's the flaming satisfaction in that? None. Not a bit of it. And it's no as if I can just up and go. See, he can do that. I've the bairns to think of. Oh, there's some as would just dump them with a neighbour, just go out and have a night on the tiles. No, no me, though; no, no Kirsten. Wouldn't trust any of them. Let their own kids run riot so what would they be like with mine, eh? Soon as you turn your back they'd be expecting to get away with blue bloody murder.

Has he any idea what all this is doing to me? Has he any idea what I go through? All the carry-on I've got to put up with? He's no idea, no flipping idea. If he'd half an ounce of decency, he'd just sit down and say, 'Right, that's it.' One way or the other. No him, though, of course, no him. Got to play a stupid bloody game. No sit down and talk to you like you're a human being, no bother with any of that, wouldn't even cross his mind. He'll no say what's the matter, what it is that's bothering him. No tell me at any rate. No, he'll tell a flaming stranger but he'll no tell his flaming wife. Get nothing out him. Just a big bloody wean. Puts on this voice, this sneery kind of voice. He'll no look at you; always has his head the other way, always mumbles. See, ken this, ken what it's like? It's like talking to a brick wall with him. Like talking to a flaming brick wall.

Merro? Bound to ken Merro: great big cunt with the long hair, chums round with the Pattersons and all that shower? That's him! That's the fucker. Always wears the cowboy jacket: Mellow Merro the Cowboy Calimerro. Anyway, like I says, I was down doing the bonding at the time, down Chalmers, and you want to ken what he done? You want to ken what the fucker went and did to me? Just 'bout frightened the life out of me that was all.

See I was just yapping away, right, having my break, yapping away with the boys, when I feels this tugging, this tugging at the back of my jeans, like. Next thing I turns round, and you'll no believe it, but there's this hook, right – the winch they use for lifting the barrels – and this thing's through the belt of my jeans.

So there's me, like; trying to get the fucker off, right, when next thing I ken my feet are flaming dangling: I'm off the deck, man, fucking flying, twelve foot up in the air, looking like some daft cunt out the circus. And there's Merro, cunt that he is, fannying about with the control panel.

Now see that's one thing I hate and all: I fucking hate heights, terrified of the fuckers. See when I go for an interview and they says to us, 'Now, Mr Kerr, how are you with heights?' Ken this, but I'm sure the buggers can smell the fear on me, fucking sure they can. Positive, in fact. Cause ken how you've got to say you're no, like, got to make out as how it's no a problem. Telling you, though, I am pure petrified of the fuckers.

No have nothing to do with water either, ken the sea or that, boats, like. Will I fuck. Aye, right. No, but you no think it's the look of the stuff, you no think that stuff just looks fucking terrifying? She was on at us to get the bairns learned and all, learned swimming and all that. 'Aye, right,' I says, 'in your dreams, pal. Let the bastarn school teach them.'

Oh aye, that's me left, by the way, left her. Next Tuesday, when she's away at her mothers and toddlers I am offski, and no before time. Here, you've no got Sandy's address by any chance, have you? No? No, never mind. Just as I was thinking of maybe going down and seeing him, ken, see what was happening down there. Mean what chance is there of getting a start up here? Bad enough for folk that've got qualifications and experience and all of that, but the likes of us, the likes of you and me, what chance've we got, eh? 'Bout as much chance of farting fivers. Was round seeing Ritzy the other night – ken Ritzy, eh? – and he was saying that was him turned down for the police *again*. You know every year since he's left the school he's applied for the police, he's applied for the prisons and he's applied for the fire brigade; and every year since he's left the school he's been knocked back by the police, he's been knocked back by the prisons and he's been knocked back by the fire brigade. Fucking sickens you. Was telling us the only wee bit work he's had in the last five year's been nothing but labouring. Now you ken yourself, that's all cash in hand, that's no proper work. Says to us, 'Barry,' he says, 'Barry, I want to work; I want to be doing something with myself, 'stead of just going round from scheme to flaming scheme all the time.'

Same with me, I'm the same and all. Ken I miss my work? I miss all of that. I actually miss getting up all hours of the morning and going out in all kinds of weathers. I fucking loved it, man. Getting all wrapped up, striding down the road, rain pishing down. Fucking loved it. Mind up the bonding, right, used to have to get up at six – up at six, right – then it was a coffee and straight down MacKie's for my paper and my morning rolls, my six morning rolls. And ken what I did, too? I scoffed the flaming lot of them, walking down the road I scoffed the flaming lot of them. See fresh morning rolls: oh, I'm slavering just sitting here thinking about them. Then we'd our break, right, had our break at ten, and we sent one of the YTSers over to the Pole's to get us them vanilla slices. Had two of them with my pieces and my tea. Here, you never had them, the Pole's vanilla slices? Oh, take it from me, man, fucking delicious they are. Should treat yourself one of these days. Then at dinnertime, right, at dinnertime, we all goes over the town, over to Carlo's, and, listen to this, I gets myself: a chipsteak supper; plus three buttered rolls; plus a bottle of American cream soda; plus my Twix; plus a Crunchie. Fucking brilliant. Every day I had that. Telling you, too; see by the end of the day I was starving. I had the weans's dinners and all. No, no kidding. 'You no wanting it, son? Well see's it here then, your dad'll eat it up for you.' As I always say, nothing ever gets bucketed in our house.

That's the thing with work – now don't get me wrong, you ken yourself, I was busy, I was humphing stuff left, right and centre, and some of them barrels was near a hundredweight, mind – but see your appetite: all you want to do is feed your face morning, noon and night. See I was fit then and all. All just went straight through me. Just fucking energy, you know, just fuel. You'll no believe this but I'm two stone heavier now than ever I was when I was working; and I'm no doing half the eating. Ken what it is, too – nothing but fucking laziness.

Worst of that, though, all the eating carry-on, was the deliveries, doing the deliveries with Comet. Oh, ya fucker, man, me and Walter, the Drop-Scene Dream-Team. Now don't ask me how but there's something 'bout being out on the road that makes you starving, don't know whether it's all that fresh air, the music blaring, eyeing up all that talent or what, but see all you want to ever do is eat a horse and go back for the jockey. No just that but see some of the places you had to cart stuff, up the top of flats and that. Thing was we were never supposed to stop and accept any food of folk – supposed to slow you down, like, eating

— but there was this one time, over in Abercruix it was, when this wee wifie turns round to us and says, 'You fancy a bowl of soup, lads?' Says to us her visitors had called off, like, so it would all just be going down the sink and that. And Walter, cunt that he is, he gives her all the spiel about how we've got to get going, how we're no supposed to take anything off folk 'cause of all that palaver about it slowing us down. 'Fair enough,' she says, and goes to take the lid off the pan to pour it down the sink. Oh, and see the smell: my gut feels like it's greeting. I goes, 'Excuse me,' I goes, 'what kind of soup is it?' 'Oh,' she says, 'it's fish soup.' Now, you tell me, you ever heard of such a thing as fish soup? No? Well, take it from me, my man, it is fucking brilliant, fucking scrumptious. So me and Walter, we gets a couple of bowls each and demolishes a loaf. Then, listen to this, the wee wifie turns round to us, cheeky wee grin on her face, and says, 'Better watch it doesn't slow you down too much, boys.' Fucking all-time classic.

Tell you what we used to do, right; what we did was to organise all our runs so's we could have our dinners up the Whitebridge, 'cause see, guarantee you, honest to God, you're ever up that way, there's a chip shop up there does the best chipsteak suppers in the world, and that's fact. See the portions you get: fucking like that, like that, fucking massive.

Aye, like I says, best job in the world, driver's mate. Best job I've ever had, anyway. Ken what I love and all? I love going into folk's houses, other folk's houses. I love that. Mean, fair enough, aye, there's some of them's just clarty bastards like my mother's — she is just one fucking tramp these days, by the way, never in my life will I darken her door again — but see rich folk's houses, some of them are just plain beautiful. I was always saying to Kirsten how she'd love to come out with us one day, just for a day out, like, just to see all the furniture, all the gardens, just to see what you could actually do with a house of your own. Mind one time, up the Cowrigg, I was standing next to this unit, in this guy's house, just a wee thing, like, nothing big or fancy or that, just a neat wee thing, and I turns round to Walter and says, 'Ken our Kirsten would love that for the weans's room.' And ken what the bloke turns round and says to us? Says, 'Well, son,' he says, 'there's one out there in the garage exact same, it's yours if you want it.' Aye, too right I did. Wouldn't take nothing for it either. Said we were doing him a favour taking it off his hands.

Picked up a lot of things like that. See there's a lot of folk move into wee'er houses and they've no the room they used to so they just want shot of stuff, and there's you with a van and think – aye aye, you'll take it off their hands. You know Walter's unit? That big mahogany one? That's how he picked that up. Got that from a bloke up the Braes. That thing's supposed to be worth a fortune, by the way.

See that's another thing with no having a job: there's nothing you can do with the house. Ken how long that paper's been hanging in the weans's room? Five year. Five flaming year. I am sick of the sight of that: every time I go in there. The whole flaming house is like that. Every day you see something else that's needing done. See the first thing I'd ever do ever I got money: I'd just do the whole flaming house: strip the lot, carpets, everything. That's another rip in the settee, by the way. See if you were to put that thing in a skip, it would still be there in the morning. No cunt would be seen dead lifting that. That thing shames me. Only thing decent in our house is the weans's unit I was telling you about. That's the only thing I'd keep.

Here, I'm starving, wanting a bit? You'll never guess what I did. I lifted a ten pence out her purse and found a twenty next the bus-stop outside Argees. Got myself five fruit salads and my Twix. Oh, I love my Twixes. Fuck off. What do I care? I'm as entitled to that money as she is. The way I look at it, she's got her pleasures, I've got mine. Here, ken what else I've been hearing? I've been hearing that all them up our close've been swapping their tablets. Now I'm no saying that our Kirsten's involved or anything, but ken this, see I wouldn't put it past her. No, she's been acting funny of late, awfy funny. To be honest, I think she could be on the drugs, I think she could. You know she's no spoke a word to me in five days. Five days she hasn't spoke so much as a word to me. Not a word. Tell me, that's no right, is it? Fuck, she's no right full stop. Fucking loopy lou. Fucking skitzzy.

That's her old boy round staying with us now and all, Henry the Headbanger. What, you mean to say you never noticed the changing of the seasons? Oh we get this every first day of spring, every first day of summer, every first day of autumn, every first day of winter: her old dear chucks her old boy out, and we've to put the fucker up on the settee. Makes you sick, so it does. I says to her, I says, 'Look, I'm not having this.' And you ken what she turns round and says to us, you want to ken what she says, want to ken what she has to say on the matter? Sweet fuck all. That was it. Sweet fuck all.

Ken I hate having that old bastard in my house more than I hate anything. Ken I won't sleep? I refuse to sleep with that fucker in the house. You can laugh all you like but I could just see me waking up in the middle of the night and the fucker being at my throat with the breadknife. That's a certainty by the way. What you think he gets chucked out for. The fucking mother's petrified of him. Ever looked at the cunt's eyes? He's no fucking right. Fuck it: the whole lot of them, they're no right. Our Kirsten's the same. Telling you, she's got one hell of a temper when she's a mind to. Oh aye, don't be fooled. She's went for me a few times, a good few times. But see her old boy; like ken how we've got to have all the doors open and the hall light on, 'cause of the kids and that? Well you see him, you see him stoating about at night, and there's me: sitting up on my pillows, arms folded, just watching the cunt, just giving him a look and going, 'You dare come in here and I'll fucking kill you, ya bastard. I'll fucking kill you.' I fucking would and all.

That's another thing: ken what she's been saying about me? Ken what she's been going round telling folk? She's been going round saying that I've been with every woman in our close. That no unreal? That no fucking sicken you? You ever seen the women in our close? Fucking woofers. Press the belly and ride the tide, man. Chuck a stick and they all run after it. Specially that Mandy; now that is revolting, that is. I wouldn't touch that with yours; Christ, I wouldn't touch that with the weans's. You want to see that house of hers, the inside of it: black, black with filth. You walk in the door, it's like sticking your head down the black hole of Calcutta: smell of piss, cat's piss; aye, probably hers and all. You know I'm sure them weans eat off the same plates as the cats, sure they do. Positive in fact. Them weans aren't right, by the way. God help them, but they are not right. That's the youngest been kept back a year at the school and all. Curly-wurlys, the lot of them. Oh, aye, meant to tell you, you heard the latest, the latest about Mandy? This'll give you a laugh. Our Paul was up the market one day, week past Saturday, right, and sees Mandy trekking through all the glaur, like. And you ken our Paul, ken what he's like, cheeky cunt that he is, he shouts over, 'Mandy,' he goes, 'Mandy, hen, you're ruining your good new shoes.' And you ken what she turns round and says to him, ken what she says to him? Turns round and goes, 'Shut your face, you. I've earned enough the day to buy myself ten pair of shoes.'

What you make of that then, eh? That's the kind of thing gives our close a bad name, slags like that. Fucking sperm-bucket. How would you want the likes of that living next to you, eh? No lift a finger to clean the stair either, not a finger.

Hey, no meaning to impose or anything, but don't suppose there's any chance of you putting us up for the night, is there? Just it's getting on, ken, and I'm no wanting to wake the bairns. Aye, sure, great. Couch does me fine. Cheers, mate, you're a pal. No wanting a mouthful of her, anyway. Fucking foghorn. Guarantee you, if the door doesn't wake them then she will. 'Where you been?' 'What you been up to?' Ken she scares me sometimes. Mind what I was saying about her old boy; well, don't forget, she's the same stock and all mind, same blood. She could snap just like that, and, like I say, between you and me, it wouldn't be the first time.

Hey, you'll never guess who I was round seeing the other night? Gav, Gavin Johnson. Mind of Gav? Aye, well it was him as gave us your address. Well he tellt us where your sister was staying and it was her as tellt us you were round here. Hey, Gav's doing alright for himself, though, eh? First time I'd seen the fucker in yonks. Here, ken what he was telling us and all? Donnie's deid, Donnie Williamson. Well, same here, likes, I've no seen him for years either, but all the same but; deid ken.

That's three of them gone out of this now. You no seen this recently? The old school photo. That was all our year. There's you, fucking parrot-faced git, Freddie parrot-faced junior. Here, d'you ken who that is, standing next Lapsley? No, on the left. That's right! Well done, sir. That's who it is. Guy Barnes. You know I could not for the life of me remember that name. Awfy quiet laddie, eh? What? You're joking? Guy Barnes is with the CID, the flaming CID. Fucking hell, man. Can mind of him being an awfy brainy laddie, right enough, but the CID? Bound to be on some money with them, eh? Must be what, what d'you reckon, what, twenty grand a year? At least, eh?

What, no recognise him? That's The Wheezer, man, Fergus Hutton. Bound to no mind of him, eh? Hear him a mile away, gasping cunt. Tell you one I couldn't mind but was that lassie there, d'you no mind of her? Aye, that's what Gav was saying and all. Now her there, Sheila Sutherland, the SS, the serious shag, Gav was saying that she's supposed to be something with the BBC these days. Aye, gen up.

Mind of her then, mind of that one? Come on then, what's the name, what's her name? Aye, Christ, I ken she's The Little Green Snotrag but what's her actual name? No, no mind? Helen, Helen Allardice. No ring any bells, no? Nah, me neither. Tell the truth, it was Gav as minded. Mean I kent The Little Green Snotrag but I'd never've minded the name.

Lassies in this are dogs but, eh, fucking dogs. Aye, ken they're only five year old, but you seen her recently? Looks 'bout forty, man. Her and all. She could pass for fifty. Ken she stays up the stair, up the stair from me and Kirsten? Kirsten hates her, can't stand her, no speak to her at all. Fucking pills she's on, you would not believe it. That's another clarty bugger, that one there. Tojo, Tommy Jones. That cunt has not changed one bit. Ken I seen him the other day there and I'm sure he had on the exact same jumper as he's on in that photo. No, Christ, swear to God, look at the fucker, it's about ten sizes too big for him. They're saying he's supposed to be on the drugs these days and all. Needles, everything. Fucking looks it. Fucking weirdo. Should see his skin, that right yellow, ken bright yellow. See him at night, man, fucking glows. Fucking belisha beacon.

Nah, but I fucking love this, man; talking about the old days. Ken that's all what I've been doing? Just going round and seeing all the folk in this photo. See on the back I've got all the names down. I've ticked all the names I've been round and seen. See? Same with my work. Been going round and seeing all of them and all. Just talking about all the old days and all what we was up to. Great, though, eh? I love it. See the way I look at it is it's the only way you can mind yourself of all what you've done with your life.

See that's the trouble with me and Kirsten: we never go on about things. Only things we ever talk about end up in rows. Mean I'm no saying it's all her fault, like, ken that, there's faults on both sides. Mean I ken I've no been myself, ken that. Mean I'm fucking down. Mean half the time I never ken whether I'm coming or going. Ken I can't look at my bairns anymore? Can't face them. I just don't know what to do with them. They just get on my fucking wick. I've fucking had it up to here with them. Never get so much as a second to myself. Every time you turn round: she's there; the bairns're there; her old boy's there. And I'm just thinking, 'I don't want this. Just give me peace. Just give me some time to myself.' Thing is, but, I'm no going to get that when I'm staying there. Lot of folk've been telling us it would be alright if I was working, and granted, I'll grant you, that would help, that would make a difference. But all you hear about these days is folk getting divorced, folk with jobs and all. Aye, right, I ken that, ken you've got to work at it. But that's five year, but. She can't turn round to me and say I've never tried. In five year I've never even so much as looked at another woman; I'm down that job centre every other day; I've got my name down on the books with Rodney's, with Stephen's, with Lawrence's, with all of them. I'm round there all the time and all. Any time I have been earning, I've gave the money straight to her, just handed it over. Any money we've had's went on the house. Try telling her that, though, see trying to tell her that. See, the way I look at it is, ken this, you'd be as well talking to a brick wall. You'd be as well talking to a flaming brick wall.

SOME KIND OF FOREPLAY

Your bed should be lengthwise and located midway along the shortest wall.

Like so.

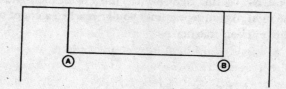

(fig. 1)

Now, to begin with, take off each other's socks. Roll them up. Not too tight, not too loose. Think of bean-bags.

Now, with one rolled-up sock in one hand, the other rolled-up sock in the other hand, one of you move to corner A, while the other moves to corner B.

Then, facing the shortest wall, lie on the floor, with your feet up on the bed, so that you approximate a Z-shape.

Like so.

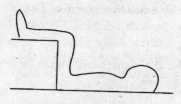

(fig. 2)

This is your position for the duration.
Okay?
Now let's begin the twelve tasks.

Task 1

Throw the sock in your left hand off the ceiling. Catch it with your left hand. Count one. Repeat until you've reached a count of five consecutive 'clean' catches. Note: *all catches must be in 'mid-air' with no 'deflections' allowed*.

Task 2

As Task 1 but use the right hand. Throw with the right, catch with the right. Again, repeat until you've reached a count of five consecutive 'clean' catches.

Task 3

This one's called Juggling.
    Discard the sock in your right hand.
    Now, throw the sock in your left hand off the ceiling and catch it with your *right* hand. Count one. Then throw the sock off the ceiling with your right hand and catch it with your *left* hand. Count two. And so on until you've reached a count of ten.

Task 4

Tighten the socks. Tight as you can.
    Now, throw the sock in your left hand off the facing wall and catch it. Throw with the left, catch with the left. Count one. Repeat until you've reached a count of five.

Task 5

And the same for the right hand. Again, repeat until you've reached a count of five.

Task 6

Tasks 6 and 7 are all about getting your angles right.

Task 6 is called Cornering.

Take your tightest sock. Tighten it. Discard the other one. Now, depending on which is easier (i.e. depending on which hand you favour), either, a) throw the sock so that it hits first the near-side wall then the facing wall, or, alternatively, b) throw the sock so that it hits first the facing wall followed by the near-side wall. You can throw with either hand and catch with either hand.

You need only complete this task once.

Task 7

Task 7 is called Sliding.

Again, depending on which is easier, either, a) throw the sock so that it hits first the ceiling followed by the near-side wall, or, alternatively, b) throw the sock so that it hits first the near-side wall followed by the ceiling. As with Task 6, you can throw with either hand and catch with either hand. Likewise, you need only complete this task once.

Task 8

Task 8 is all about Power.

Take your tightest sock. Tighten it. With whichever hand you like, throw the sock against the far-side wall and catch it. You can catch with either hand.

You only need complete this task once as well. Please remember, though, as stated earlier — *all catches must be 'clean' i.e. caught in 'mid-air' with no 'deflections' allowed.*

Task 9

This one's called Overhead Doubling.

A sock in each hand, throw both socks off the ceiling at the same time and catch them. Throw with the left, catch with the left. Throw with the right, catch with the right. No 'gathering' allowed.

This task need only be completed once.

Task 10

This one's called Facing-Wall Doubling.
As above, but throw both socks off the facing wall.
Task 10 need only be completed once.

Task 11

The near-side wall.
Throw the sock in your left hand off the near-side wall and catch it. Count one. Repeat until you've reached a count of five consecutive 'clean' catches.

Task 12

As Task 11, but with the right hand.

And that's you completed a circuit. The twelve tasks comprise a circuit.
For beginners, a couple of circuits should be enough to get you going.

LIFE ON A SCOTTISH COUNCIL ESTATE VOL. 3 CHAP. 2

Me and The Tank are trying to cheer ourselves up. We're eating chocolate, drinking coffee, smoking fags and trying to mind everybody we ever went to school with that wore glasses. The door goes. It's Stuart. Oh! God! No! Stuart thrives on folk being depressed. The day he's going on about this lassie that he's met over the past week that's already seen sense and binned him. Stuart's always been like this. Any time you ever skint your knee, he had to go and skin his knee. Any time you ever lost a cowboy or an Indian, he had to go and lose a cowboy or an Indian. Any time you were off the school, he had to go and go off the school. And now he thinks 'cause I've gone and lost the greatest love of my life, he's got to go and lose the greatest love of his life and all. We are now, in the world of Stuart, bonded. The door goes. It's The Big Man! Time was when The Big Man could cheer us all up with just one flick of his wallet. These days, though, he's one seriously depressed muchacho. Poor bastard got rifted out of his airline pilot gig when significant traces of cocaine and cannabis, LSD and MDMA, and Irn-Bru and square sausage were discovered following a random test of his urine, blood and faeces. His explanation, that he needed something to see him through being twenty thousand feet in the air in charge of a hunk of metal put together from the cheapest components money could buy, was translated for press purposes as being 'stress brought on by a succession of family bereavements'. Nowadays, The Big Man cleans the balls up Megabowl. This is all he ever goes on about. Cleaning folk's balls. Especially folk that bring in their own balls, 'cause you can never get their balls clean enough. Oh no, they stand over the top of you, watching you, demanding that you clean out the machine before you put their balls in. And you've got to spit on their balls and give them a good wipe and polish afterwards. Spit. Wipe. Polish. Spit. Wipe. Polish. Spit. Wipe. Polish. Spit. Wipe. Polish. And folk'll no spit on their own balls. Oh no, you've got to spit on their balls for them. You've got to admire them, you've got to patronise them, you've got to stand there and say nice things about their balls. 'What a lovely pair of balls you've got there.' Their balls that are the exact fucking same as everybody else's fucking balls. 'Oh, that's a rare set of balls.' To all intents and purposes, balls that are identical. 'Lovely balls, sir. Lovely balls.' Goes on about the state of folk's balls all the time . . . But, no the day. No the day he's on about this lassie, this lassie that mans the reception up at Megabowl. The Big Man is trying to fix me up. The Big Man's heart is in the right place, he just doesn't understand fuck all. 'Who does she look like then?' I says. The Big Man shrugs. 'That's the thing,' he says. 'She doesn't really look like anybody.' 'Oh, come on,' I says, 'if she's any good, she's got to look like somebody.' I count out on my fingers: the crucial five. 'She's got to look like Maggie, she's got to look like Katie Puckrick, she's got to look like Nicole out the Papa adverts, she's got to look like her out of *Cardiac Arrest*, she's got to look like . . .' The door goes. It's Wee Harry. He's about as depressed as the rest of us. 'I've lost it,' he says. 'Lost what?' says The Tank. 'It,' says Wee Harry. 'Everything.' The door goes. It's Wendy. She points at Wee Harry and goes, 'See everything that wee cunt's just told you, it's a pack of fucking lies!' Wendy and Wee Harry start shouting and bawling at each other. Something to do with their cat, their cooker, and a pair of Wee Harry's red underpants. The door goes. It's Edwin and English Edgar. They look rough as fuck. 'What's up?' I says. 'No fucking drugs,' they say. The door goes again. It's Carmel this time with the exes, my ex-girlfriend and my ex-psychotic big brother. 'Look,' says Carmel, 'you're acting like a right pleb. Come on, grow up, will you. For the last time – she is not your type.' My ex-girlfriend looks at me. 'True,' she says, 'I'm not your type.' My ex-psychotic big brother looks at me. He shrugs and says, 'She's not your type.' I give a deep sigh. Everybody's looking at me. Everybody's looking at me like I'm responsible for every fucking problem that's ever been. They're all nodding to themselves. They're all saying the same thing. 'She's not your type.' 'She's not your type.' 'She's not your type.' 'She's not your type.' 'She's not your type.' 'She's not your type.' Okay, I'm thinking to myself, peace. Christ, I must be getting old. Time was when I'd just've stormed off round the library. Aye, there's a lot to be said for getting old. I'm just about to stick out the hand of friendship when the door goes. Fate! Fate! Fate! Now I've always been a staunch believer in fate. I believe in fate like some folk believe in Elvis. Even though I'm being all reasonable about things, there will be no handshake till I've checked out this door. I rushes out to see who it is . . . It's . . . It's a bin-bag!!?!!! A full open bin-bag. I leans forward. 'SURPRISE!!!' Fuck me sideways, as out springs Hamish. Christ, I'd forgotten all about Hamish. I gives him a big eccie hug. 'Where you been, my man?' I says. 'Eh,' says Hamish. 'Saughton.' 'Saughton,' I says, 'what the fuck?' 'Well,' says Hamish, 'ken how nowadays you can only take two hundred and fifty bar out of a cashline machine in a day?' 'Aye?' I says. 'Well,' says Hamish, 'eh, it was me that caused them to introduce this new measure.' 'Christ,' I says. 'Ken,' says Hamish, 'but, telling you, I was partying like fuck till they got me.' Hamish, man, what a fucking hero. 'So, anyway,' says Hamish, 'to celebrate my new-found freedom I thought I'd bring along these.' Hamish produces from within the bin-bag two Willie Lows poly-bags, full to the gummels. Two Willie Lows poly-bags, full to the gummels, that look like they've seen better days. In fact, two Willie Lows poly-bags, full to the gummels, that look like they've been lying in the freezer since last September. Oh noh, I says to myself. 'Noh,' I says. 'Well,' says Hamish, 'they were just lying there.' I opens up the poly-bags. As I suspected, the most vile, horrible, pathetic excuse for a pharmaceutical ever.

Mind you, it does give me a sneaky plan.

A VIEW TO A HILL

My favourite place in all the world is the window. Try if you will and imagine a sink without a window. I've seen it. It's horrible. Some folk even have toilets without windows. Not where I come from. No, where I come from we live our lives at the window. We stand there, hands on hips, listening to our music, watching the world go by, lending an eye and an ear to beauty.

Ultimately, I think it's all to do with getting things in perspective. After all, if you think about it, really, what is a telly? Just a window, eh. Books? Windows of the imagination.

My family are, and always have been, nothing less than window-daft. My mother stands at the window while my father has his chair nearest the window. Over the years my father has become so adept at looking over his shoulder you'd think he'd trained as a taxi driver. If there's any commotion going on out in the street, my mother has no qualms about standing there and watching it. This was her window. This was her view. There were never any net curtains in our house.

When I turned five, the family moved to a new flat, a newly built flat. Around that time, windows meant putty, and back then putty was by far and away the most exciting word in the known world. (Funnily enough, a few years later, it was superseded as such by the somewhat different word nymphomaniac.)

With the industry of looters, me and my pals staged twilight raids on building sites, collecting putty, timber and nails. We each had nail collections. Mine's was well over a hundred. I stored it in a sock. When wielded, it became the most lethal weapon you could dare to dream of.

Mind you, it wasn't just outside the building was going on.

Back in the sixties, inside, things were just as active. You couldn't go round to visit one of your pals without discovering that their living-room now gave airspace to bead curtains or louvre doors, in order to accommodate something that went by the name of dinette. Equally, folk would be busy seeking out planning permission so's they could make a hole in a wall and call it a serving hatch. It was the corners I felt most sorry for. You weren't allowed to have an empty corner. Time and time again, you'd go into somebody's house and discover a fully functioning bar now occupying what had previously been an otherwise harmless corner. Thankfully, our family was never so inclined. Forced by conformity, our sole contribution to acknowledging the times was to bedeck each of our precious windows with its very own set of blinds. We had to get them. Every room of every flat in our block was blinded. Some folk even had the temerity to have them multicoloured. We were plain off-white. For as long as I live, I'll never forget our blinds. I'll never be allowed to. It shames me to say it but there are only three things I can recall liking the taste of from my childhood: rubber bands; the tops to ball-point pens; and the toggles with which you adjusted blinds. A hairy taste that, to this very day, still dictates my palate.

Whenever the family visited other homes, we would head straight for the window. My mother ostensibly to admire the obligatory ledge ornaments, my father to rush and acquire the nearest seat – or rush to acquire the nearest thing that would suffice as a seat (footstools were big in the sixties). I was even more brazen. I would make my excuses and disappear off to spend hours at the toilet. Finding all the windows en route, I'd stop off to chew on any available toggle. Failing that delicacy, I would delve into my trouser pockets and find solace in my trusty collection of ball-point pen tops and rubber bands. (It goes without saying that I collected ball-point pen tops and rubber bands – as in, I found them, I stole them, I collected them. Hairy pen tops in my left-hand trouser pocket, slimy rubber bands in my right-hand trouser pocket.)

Don't ask me about the decor of any of these rooms, or, for that matter, any of the other rooms I've ever been in. I simply won't know. Ask me about the window: you've a friend for life. In fact, try as I might, I could not, in all honesty, tell you the colour of my present carpet,* but I could tell you all what's going on across the road alright. Mind you, that is a trouble with staying through here. That's your view, what's across the road. The windows are so small in these old tenements you might as well be wearing blinkers. I was brought up with windows the size of shopfronts. Now, when you're standing there, full on, you get this feeling you're just being nosey. My mother isn't happy when she visits. With hands on hips, she's broader than the window. Who's that? she says. Who's who? I try to muscle in. Frightened she'll miss something, she won't let me. She's pointing to something I can't see because there's no room to see past her. My father, meanwhile, keeps adjusting his seat (for these purposes, one of my floorstanding speakers) in a vain attempt to get a decent view. But, to his eternal frustration, when he looks over his shoulder, he's eyeballing nothing more exciting than the small of my mother's back.

Like my parents, I keep my phone by the window. I sit there, one cheek and one foot on the ledge, knee bent like an alp, always making time to comment on what I see.

And, like my parents, my choice of windows reflects my moods. With me, living-room's okay, kitchen's sad, bedroom's secretive. If I am leaning out of an open window then chances are I got off with someone the night before.

It's always been like this. When I'm in the huff about something, I stand at the window. When I'm happy about something, I stand at the window. As a child, whenever I had the mumps/scarlet fever/measles/chicken pox, etc., I was never so ill I never made it to the window. To this day, when I get up to go to the toilet through the night, I stop off and stare out the window – usually for ages.

Now, what all this is leading up to, all this obsession with windows, is the failure of my most recent job interview, and the

* By the way, I checked this out. I thought it was blue. It is, in fact, browny-grey.

subsequent masterplan I have since formulated, a masterplan which should, if there's any justice in this world, go some way to ensuring my long-term financial security.

Let me explain.

I was up for a teaching post at the university. My interview was at eleven o'clock on a bright Tuesday morning on the seventeenth floor of the university's admin building. At the given time I was shown into the designated room. There, I was introduced to Professor Thomas Lynch, Professor Raymond Fergusson, Doctor Andrew Stoppard, Doctor Jane Wagstaff and Caroline Aitchison from the student body.

Funny how a scatterbrain like me remembers the names, eh – especially when you consider that behind this esteemed gathering was a window the size of a cinema screen.

Wow!

I dare say I answered their questions. I probably even thought about my answers. I usually do. Actually I take ages to think of answers. I'm very thoughtful. Trouble is I tend to fill in the time between question and answer by talking a lot of shit. And, as my pal Wee Al will testify, it's the shit folk tend to remember, not the answers.

That window was amazing. The size of it. And, this was the truly amazing thing, not a bit of it was less than filthy. I looked the interview panel in the eye. I concentrated on their name tags. It didn't do any good. Honestly, I'd have been as well to've sat with my back to them.

Afterwards, I complained. I'd been put off my stride. I put forward what I considered to be a thoroughly appropriate analogy. You wouldn't, I said, in all honesty, expect to interview a prospective chef in a kitchen that gave the appearance of being a permanent home to fifty-seven cats and rats, now would you? Sorry, they said, the window had to be like that. They weren't allowed to clean it. Their insurance company deemed it to be too dangerous an endeavour.

So, for the time being, my career in an artificially lit lecture hall has been put on hold.

In fact, you never know, all being well, maybe for ever.

The thing is, as I implied earlier, I now have a new career plan. It actually came to me following my interview, when I was back home, sulking at my kitchen window. From now on, I am going to be a photographer. Now, before we proceed, let me make this as clear as Isle of Man whisky: I have absolutely no interest in photography or, for that matter, any of the other visual arts, whatsoever. I may spend all my time staring out windows, but that's only because I'm interested in – and formed by – what I see, not what you see. But, to get back to the career plan, for this one exception, I am going to make allowances. I am going to take a photograph, one solitary photograph, and I am going to live off the proceeds for the rest of my life.

Think about it.

When you're that high up in the university tower, there is only the one thing that you can see. And it's not the castle, it's not the folly, it's not the old high school or the Queen's bed and breakfast. No, it's that hill, that hill in the middle of the town.

When you travel into the town, by road or by rail, and you're staring out your window, the first thing you see is the hill, the hill in the middle of the town. From at least ten miles away you can clearly identify it. There is one road in particular (and no, I'm not telling you which) from where the view is truly, if not spectacular, then appropriate. Like having a window on the town.

There exist no postcards of this view. In fact, there are no postcards of the hill at all. Believe me, I've looked. I've studied the windows of souvenir shops, searched through the newsagents and combed the various cardracks. All I found was an unappealing and inappropriate shot of a sun-drenched crag.

There can be no rational justification for this. Surely it can't be size. I'd be surprised if you didn't get postcards of the tower in Paris, the pyramids in Egypt. Is there something maybe then against the natural world? Against hills? Yeah, funnily enough, I think that's what it is. Hills are meant to be picture pretty, not powerful. But, and here's where I get on my soapbox, to accept that notion is to accept a lie. Basically, it's geography without the perspective. Something that makes about as much sense as a room without a window.

So, starting with the hill in the middle of the town, I'm going to try and do something, I'm going to try and put things in perspective. 'Cause I'm getting pissed off with this, folk not putting things in perspective. It happens all the time. This is going to be my example, my metaphor, my political allegory.

Everybody visits the hill. Everybody loves it. But they don't get the perspective.

No, they need a memento.

They need perspective.

They need their window.

My photograph.

In next to no time, my tourists will return home. Humbled by their new-found sense of perspective, they will proceed to make the world a better place.

In next to no time, on a more personal level, I will be minted.

From the proceeds, I will buy a big house. Decent-sized windows in every room. No blinds this time. No toggles. I think I'm over that now. My family will come round. Bold as can be, we will celebrate, drinking a toast to all those who pass and all that we see. I will give my mother a budget and free reign to purchase appropriate ledge ornaments. I will strategically place mirrors so's my dad will not have to strain his neck. Who knows, and maybe it's about time, I may even invest in a swivel chair.

SCHEMING YOUR DREAMS

Like a lot of folk who lack confidence in their appearance, Maureen always made a point of getting in first: always bringing herself down, she'd savage her every feature. Thing was, you couldn't disagree; Maureen would just go on about it all the more. You couldn't agree either. You couldn't just say, 'Jesus, Maureen, so what, so what if you've got the biggest nose this side of the Wicked Witch? Who cares if you could draw a decent map of Scandinavia on your forehead?' Maureen had an answer for everything. 'But,' she would say, 'what if it was your nose? What if it was your forehead, eh? Trying to tell me you wouldn't be bothered? Aye, right.'

Changing the subject didn't help. You said something, Maureen would automatically disagree with you. See Maureen had this thing about folk trying to make a fool of her. The way she seen it, Maureen was a freak, therefore Maureen was fair game. Needless to say, any stand-off attitude that existed as regards Maureen was merely a reaction to all this, all this confrontational paranoia carry-on, and had next to nothing to do with the way she looked. But see trying to tell her that.

School was a horrible time for Maureen. My abiding memory'll always be the physics and chemistry labs, picking partners for all our experiments. Maureen would go over to the furthest corner. She would just stand there, being really intimidating, just waiting, waiting to see who would be left over; or, even worse, waiting to see which pair the teacher would nominate her to go and join to make up a threesome.

Scant consolation for all this, all this social outcast persecution nonsense, was to be found in the normally esteemed world of sports. To add to all her other hang-ups, when she turned fourteen, Maureen shot up from just under five foot to just over six foot. Consequently – so Maureen would have you believe, anyway – sports were easy. All she had to do was try, maintain her wee bit effort, and Maureen trounced everybody. Maureen won races at a canter. She went on to represent her school, her town, her district, her region and her country at netball, basketball, volleyball and hockey.

Maureen's final year at the school – like the rest of us she stayed on for a sixth year – was a leap year. More importantly, in the sporting almanac, it was therefore also an Olympic year. As usual, the nation was fair gripped by the achievements of those representing the home countries. In terms of mass popular appeal, though, no amount of medals or records matched the minor success of a young west coast lass by the name of Caroline Findlay. Young Caroline only managed fourth in a fifteen-hundred metres semi (just missing out on a fastest loser position that would have seen her through to the final), but her gap-toothed grin, boyish good looks and gritty determination made her the only worthy winner as far as the northerly five million were concerned.

Doubt, though, was to preside over young Caroline's racing future. Unlike all these East Europeans and Americans, who were basically professional athletes in all but name, Caroline's chosen career had to come first. For the next four years competitive running would be taking a back seat. Caroline was off to uni to study medicine.

The tabloids mirrored the national disappointment. 'Exiled to academia', ran one headline. A couple of MPs got in on the act. 'A scandal,' they said. The *Daily Record* set up a think-tank. Comprising publicity-hungry/genuinely concerned (delete as appropriate) representatives from the media, politics, sport and the business world, the think-tank pressed for the introduction of a campus-based course that would benefit the likes of young Caroline. Based on the American system, a dual-degree course that would combine the facilities for sporting excellence with whatever else it was you wanted to study.

Surprisingly, they got what they wanted. The newly established Balfron University (publicity hungry/genuinely concerned – delete as appropriate) stepped in and announced that, starting from October, such a course would come into being.

Time was of the essence. Other students were needed to fill out the numbers. The powers that be scouted round the national youth netball, basketball, volleyball and hockey teams. Lo and behold, they discovered all these same names appearing again and again. One of the names, of course, was that of Maureen MacIntosh MacIntyre, our Maureen.

With the media giving it laldy, Maureen and her fellow students appeared on five different telly programmes in the one week. On the last of them, the Friday night sports preview, Maureen got to say her piece. Typically, she was keen to play down any notion of her being in any way superfit or gifted. 'We're just freaks,' she snapped, turning her face away from the camera. 'It's not fun, you know, when you don't have a social life, when your legs go up to your armpits and when you can't walk down the street without your knuckles having to brush the pavements.'

A nation cringed. There was nothing worse than some ungrateful brat feeling sorry for herself.

Whether as a consequence of this or not, nobody really knows, but the course turned out to be a pretty major flop. Caroline Findlay never reached her former glories. In fact, none of the high-profile track and field athletes reached any kind of glory. To be fair, the national netball, basketball, volleyball and hockey teams didn't do too badly, but suffered from a total lack of public support or even interest. Certain sections of the media even tried to stir up some scandal. The tabloids went on about sex and drugs parties up on the remote Balfron campus. Self-inflated broadsheet columnists questioned whether it was right that tax-payers' money should have to stump up so that young kids could travel over to Singapore one week then Chile the next to do what exactly? Play a wee game of what? Volleyball? Aye, right. It was never like that in their day. Football in the streets. That was the way. Lamppost and wall were the goals.

When Maureen graduated, exactly three years and three months to the day after details of the course had first been revealed, all media interest in the students had abated, the sponsors had withdrawn their funding and the only publication which even bothered to note that the course had been discontinued was the university prospectus – and that was a four-line footnote.

Luckily, though, for Maureen, when she left uni, the nation was in the grip of a new buzz-word. It seemed like everybody that was anybody was getting off on this thing called aerobics. Like most buzz-words, nobody really knew what aerobics actually meant. Funnily enough, Maureen did – she even had a certificate to prove it.

Maureen found herself taking charge of a few classes. Soon, more through the accident of hard work rather than the design of planning, Maureen had established her own company, Maureen's Workout.

By the time she'd reached her mid-twenties, Maureen was effectively working seven days a week. On the first six she laboured, taking a total of twenty-odd classes – including, at one time or another, Wise Thighs, Tums and Bums, Tone Your Bones, Skip to Slim, Step by Step, Motions with Maureen, Mornings with Maureen, Mondays with Maureen, etc. etc. – while, on the seventh, Maureen supposedly rested, going over all her paperwork, designing her publicity, and reading up on the latest literature.

On the plus side, Maureen had become both very wealthy and very fit. But, on the down-side, Maureen was still patently miserable, and also, nearly always, tired to the point of exhaustion.

Even though she'd the sort of figure her clients longed for – and, incidentally, the sort of bank balance I would personally kill for – Maureen was still grounded by this notion of herself being a freak. All these folk that attended her classes, they weren't freaks, they were just fat. They could laugh at themselves. Hell, they *did* laugh at themselves. It was all just a joke when they squeezed into their leotards.

Apparently, Maureen really punished them with her regimes. I can quite believe it. Maureen, standing out front, in front of the wall of mirrors, going for it like the drill sergeant from county hell.

Even so, her clients loved her. See you weren't just going for the time-honoured burn with Maureen; no, you were settling for nothing less than combustion.

It was all fairly straightforward, all these classes, but the cumulative effect of taking twenty-odd a week, and the correspondent travelling and timekeeping, meant that Maureen was not only very fit, but also, nearly always, very tired indeed.

Other things didn't help.

Aside from her exercise, Maureen didn't lead too healthy a life. Parking her car in out-of-town lay-bys between sessions, Maureen tended to cat-nap during the day. They were lovely, wonderful, peaceful wee sleeps but the upshot was that Maureen didn't sleep too well at night. Likewise, Maureen's diet was appalling. She seldom sat down to a meal, preferring instead to binge when the need arose on chocolates, cakes and the odd scoffed-in-a-oner loaf.

And, Maureen smoked. A good forty a day.

And, as they say, Maureen liked a drink.

Of all the supposedly life-affirming things Maureen had come across, drink was by far and away the one that had made the most sense to her. She'd discovered it at uni. She loved what it did to you; the way it got you going, really loosened you up. When she was drinking, and in company, Maureen's looks were always the last thing on her mind. She was too busy being totally hyper. All she wanted to do was dance, laugh and get off with someone. Usually, she did.

With a drink in her, Maureen was one of Balfron's great characters. When Maureen was around, everybody had to get up and enjoy themselves. Everybody had to party. But when sober — usually hungover — the fragile Maureen would stay in her room; feeling sorry for herself, feeling embarrassed by herself. When she had to go out, to classes, for food, whatever, her head would be down. She'd go past folk, folk she knew, totally ignoring them, then she'd sit on her own in the lecture theatres, convinced that everybody was slagging her off, going on about the freak that couldn't handle her drink. Like school, Maureen was of the opinion that everybody at uni hated her. They didn't, of course. Granted, a lot didn't like her, a lot thought her a pain, but, as to the reasoning, well, like I say, like school, Maureen had it all wrong. Folk weren't repelled by Maureen, folk merely reacted to Maureen.

More recently, in the aerobics days, Maureen moved on from campus parties to spending her nights out with her sisters and sisters-in-law at singles nights (aka meat markets) and over-25's discos (aka grab-a-granny nights) down the Aberforth (aka Jurassic Park), dancing away to the sounds of the sixties, the sounds of the seventies, and, every so often, if you were really lucky, even a couple of hits from the eighties or nineties.

Medallion man was fair in his element when he was introduced to Maureen. He would hold in his corseted stomach. 'A fitness instructor? Aye? Play a wee bit rugby myself: prop forward.' Or, 'A fitness instructor? Aye? Ran a couple of marathons a few years back. Under three hours it was. No bad, eh?'

There was one question they always wanted answered. One secret Medallion Man always wanted divulged. 'Tell me,' he would whisper, 'but I've always wanted to know this – what's the proper way, I mean the best way, to do your press-ups and sit-ups?'

'Oh,' Maureen would tease, 'that'll cost you.'

And it did. Maureen would get plied with drinks, and, more often than not, Maureen would get a bag-off for the night. After all, you couldn't demonstrate such manoeuvres on the hankie-sized dancefloor of the Aberforth, now could you?

Maureen bagged off with loads of guys. A few lasted a while, maybe a couple of weeks, but, ultimately, conversations about press-ups and sit-ups had no effect other than reminding poor Maureen that poor Maureen was nothing but a freak. Maureen would crack up. Take my word for it, not a pretty sight.

As much as Maureen could get off with guys easily enough,

Maureen could never quite get to grips with loving them. That was the problem. That was what was missing. It might surprise you to learn how, at heart, our Maureen was a romantic soul who firmly believed that true happiness was only to be found in fidelity and the sanctity of this thing called marriage. Maureen knew this guy was out there, the guy who would give her the confidence in herself, the guy who would lend hitherto only dreamt-of dignity, joy and content to the words husband, wife and family.

That's not to say that, over the years, a few proposals hadn't already come Maureen's way. 'Cause they had. The proposers, mind you, had always seemed more interested in the state of Maureen's bank account than in the state of Maureen's ovaries. When Maureen happened to express how much she'd like to start a family, her supposed suitors all but took to their heels and ran. 'Ah, well, eh,' they would say. 'Plenty of time for that. Now, what I want to know is, have you never thought about trying your luck in the video market? Just small-time, like, flogging them off at your classes and that? Worth a try.'

Maureen was loaded. Before we'd paid off our washing machine, Maureen had paid off her mortgage. Being self-employed, Maureen never took holidays. Her only overheads were tax-deductible petrol and tax-deductible hiring of halls. Maureen never spent money on clothes. Through a deal with a local sports shop – they got mentioned on all her promo material, bits of Maureen's body modelled for theirs – Maureen got freebee jogging suits, T-shirts, underwear, leotards and footwear. Her going out wardrobe consisted of four identical wee black dresses. That was all she reckoned she'd ever need.

Equally, on the financial side, Maureen's prospects were excellent. Provided she kept in shape, and doing twenty-odd classes a week there was no reason why she shouldn't, Maureen could go on at this for ever. Older instructors were becoming all the rage. The fact that, like the rest of us, Maureen was born in a baby-boom meant that she would have a generation growing up with her, the biggest generation yet.

Maureen's classes were almost always exclusively female. Just the way Maureen liked it. Occasionally, you'd get the odd guy turning up. Fancying this was as good a place as any to get a free shag, he'd set himself up as some kind of wit, coming away with wisecracks all the time, adopting the totally uncalled-for role of class joker. Maureen hated them, guys like that. Being Maureen, she saw an immediate parallel with drink. Drink was serious business, and so was exercise. You either went out to get blootered/to get fit and have a good time in the process or you shouldn't bother going out at all: there was no two ways about it. Maureen hated jokers, guys who thought that, through being sarcastic, being cheeky, they were setting everybody at ease. Oh no they weren't. They were in the road, in the road of Maureen's good time, in the road of everybody else's good time. What their tiny little shell-likes never quite seemed to grasp was that fun wasn't something you created, fun was something you under-took. It wasn't something you bore witness to, it was something you were entitled to. Damn it, it was a God-given right.

Maureen made a poster of that last bit. 'Fun, damn it, it's a God-given right!' The sports shop she got the clothes from were so taken they paid to use it as a slogan on a series of limited edition car stickers given away with a certain brand of training shoe. Maureen was quite the thing when it came to promotion and publicity. There was none of this namby-pamby 'Why not come along and give it a try?' nonsense, Maureen favoured aggression. She liked to appeal to those who, against the odds, were struggling to be assertive. They always made the best clients.

So, anyway, the last place Maureen would be expecting to meet the guy that would eventually sweep her off her size $9\frac{1}{2}$'s would be at one of her classes. Then one day, at one of her step sessions – Step Lively, to be exact – who should turn up? This guy. This guy that was good-looking to the point of gorgeous. This guy that was quiet to the point of shyness. All the women were drooling.

Obviously, this being a class, and Maureen being sober, she could hardly even bring herself to look at him, let alone fling herself at him.

After the class, Maureen had her quickest ever shower, then

joined the others in the community centre's canteen for some juice and a blether. Usually, Maureen never stayed long. She would always be wanting to get away to her car and drive off somewhere for a couple of fags and one of her sleeps before heading off someplace else.

This time, though, Maureen hung around. She was waiting to see if the guy was going to join them. Alas, he didn't. But he did appear. He did show face. And what a face. It wasn't just his body this guy was into looking after. He was freshly shaven. His hair, a French crew-cut, glistened with gel. 'Bye then,' he said, nervously, barely coming in the door. 'See you all next week then.'

'God,' said Maureen once the guy was out of sight, 'I think I've just died and gone to heaven.'

'Haven't we all, love,' said one of the other women, 'haven't we all.'

That week, Maureen didn't have any nights out. Instead, she wallowed in homely self-loathing, self-pity and alcoholic self-abuse. While, during classes, Maureen was just the thing – very assertive, very confident, just right for the job – outside of class, and with a drink in her, Maureen was, to quote her best friend, her sister Jenny, 'a major threat to the national sanity'.

Maureen hit the bottle. She hit it hard.

She was thinking about all those girls, all those women – schoolgirls, students, colleagues, family – who'd all, at one point or another, announced to the world those immortal words, 'Oh, I'm never getting married. Oh, I'm wanting my career. Oh, I'm wanting to be successful.' Aye, right. And as soon as the first Mr Average had come along and one-kneed it they were off to the altar quicker than you could scream, 'Two-faced lying bastard!'

Maureen was successful. Maureen had a career. But Maureen was successful – glug! glug! – and Maureen had a career – glug! glug! – because – glug! glug! – Maureen was a freak. Anybody with half a brain could've worked that one out.

Like she always does when she's getting herself into one of these kind of states, Maureen was soon on the phone and pouring her heart out to the aforementioned sister Jenny. (Who, incidentally, by the way, just happens to be my wife, just in case you're wondering where all this comes from.)

Like she always does, Jenny told Maureen to chance her arm, to go for it, to go for this dreamboy. After all, what did she have to lose?

Like she always does, Maureen started inventing problems. What if he already had someone? And, anyway, what difference did it make: how could a dream like him be expected to fancy a nightmare like her? After all, Maureen was just a freak.

Jenny got Maureen to shut up. 'Listen,' she said, 'mind what I always tell you: *everybody can be swayed*. Never forget that.'

Like she always does, Jenny took over.

She got Maureen to go on about her dreams and her fantasies appertaining to this bloke, then to think about planning and scheming in such a way so's to make these dreams and fantasies come true. Even if nothing came of it, there was nothing wrong with dreaming, nothing wrong with trying your hand. Dreaming was as good a way as any of getting by. Jenny used a sporting analogy. A long-jumper imagines his run-in and jump. When he's settling into the starting blocks, a hurdler imagines himself sprinting between then going over the hurdles. The idea being to make the reality as much like the dream as possible, to achieve that degree of relaxation and euphoria through mental preparation. Through scheming your dreams.

Maureen, though, kept bringing up problems. She had this rule: never go out with guys from your classes. It was cheap. Like a rep on an 18–30 holiday, she knew she was some kind of prize. It was as close as the bozos' ever got to bagging off with teacher. No way.

Jenny told Maureen: 'Rubbish!' That was just rubbish. If this guy was as special as Maureen was making him out to be, then Maureen had to get her shit the gether and go for it.

Maureen still wasn't convinced. She said how she was never really in the proper state to get to know him, not in the class, anyway. Maureen needed her dose of Dutch courage. Sober, she wouldn't have known how to approach somebody, let alone fling herself at them.

'So,' said Jenny, '*plot*.' Think about what you'd most want to happen, then try your damnedest to make it happen. If Maureen was going to make moves for this guy, then obviously Maureen was going to have to arrange some kind of night out, wasn't she?

So, the following week, after class, in the community centre canteen, Maureen summoned up her energies, remembered all she'd been told, and, in a roundabout kind of way, hesitantly broached the subject by suggesting that maybe since they'd all been doing so well they all deserved some kind of reward.

The class were in the throes of an adrenaline hit. They were as assertive as they would ever be. Praise be to God, they took the bait. None of them had been out for ages. They could do with getting pampered for a change. Somebody suggested a girls' night out. What a great idea.

While they were all still in the grip of this enthusiasm, Maureen got on the phone to the Aberforth, letting them know that a party of fifteen or so rampant women would be appearing next Wednesday.

That was it booked. There was no turning back. Not that any of the women were entertaining second thoughts, mind. 'Let them make their own bloody teas,' they said, referring to their offspring. 'Let him wash the bloody dishes for once,' they said, referring to their spouses. ''Cause I'm getting dolled up and I'm going out.'

There was only one of their number still to be accounted for. One perfect body to be accounted for.

As he'd done the previous week, Mr Clean-Shaven, Mr French Crew-Cut, Maureen's dreamboy, popped in to say his cheerios. 'Well then,' he said, in that wonderful way of his, 'see yous all next week then.'

Maureen was just about to blurt out something when one of the other women spoke for her. 'Hold on a minute, sunshine,' she said. 'Listen, we're having this night out, up the Aberforth, next Wednesday. Fancy coming along?'

The guy hardly stopped to think about it. 'Yeah,' he said, 'suppose I could. Yeah. Great. Look forward to it.'

Maureen's heart was giving it serious cartwheels. Jenny had planned it to perfection.

'Excuse me,' said one of the women, just as the guy was about to take his leave. 'Sorry, but what did you say your name was again?'

Of all people, the guy looked at Maureen.

'Davidson,' he said. 'Mungo Davidson.'

Mungo? Mungo Davidson?

Wow!

Maureen Davidson. Mungo and Maureen Davidson. Mungo and Maureen. Maureen and Mungo.

A couple of days later, a truly sozzled Maureen was back on our phone. It wasn't going to work. This was too good to be true. Mungo and Maureen was too good to be true.

'Rubbish!' said Jenny. 'It's going to work out just fine.'

That Saturday, Jenny went round early and dragged Maureen out her bed then dragged her round the shops. They got Maureen a wonderbra and a new wee black dress. At Jenny's insistence, Maureen got her hair done. Normally, she only ever got her ends seen to, but, in the one go, Maureen got more chopped off than she'd had shod in the previous ten years. Maureen always had this thing about her hair. If there was one thing, she said, that was worse than being patronised, it was when a part of you was being patronised. That was what she'd got when she was younger, all her rellies coming up to her and going, 'My, what beautiful *hair* you've got. Hasn't she got beautiful *hair*, eh?'

Up until the last moment, however, Maureen still wasn't sure whether or not she was going to go up to the Aberforth. This wasn't unusual, mind. Maureen was like this near enough every time she went out the door. Stop. Start. Stop. Start. I'm going. I'm no going. I'm going. I'm no going.

I'll tell you what would've happened, what would've swung it, what usually swung it.

And it wasn't the drink. No, it was Abba.

Maureen would've put on Abba's *Gold* CD, programming tracks one, two and three. The songs that always gave her the confidence to go out. The unabashed joy of 'Dancing Queen', the fumbled share of 'Knowing Me, Knowing You', the opportunism of 'Take a Chance On Me'. Maureen would've put the three songs on repeat while she got herself ready.

Empowered by the sentiments, energised by the sounds, everything would've been positive, the intentions would've been clear: get rubbered, fling herself at Mungo. If that failed, get rubbered and have a laugh and a joke with the girls. Either way it would turn out to be a good night.

In the event, none of this really mattered.

None of this really mattered because, once Maureen reached the Aberforth, Mungo was straight into flinging himself at Maureen.

The king and queen hit the dancefloor. Maureen's hands got to know Mungo. Mungo's hands got to know Maureen.

There was never a question of whether they were taking a chance.

Before ten o'clock, they were in the back of a taxi, chewing each other's faces off.

Maureen had never been home so early. Maureen had never been home so sober.

It was a dream that became a scheme that became the dream. Mungo was the perfect lover. You name it. Considerate. Patient. Athletic. Inventive.

And, unbelievably, a first: he never once stopped to request technical tips vis-à-vis the old bit press-ups or sit-ups.

He did, however, afterwards, draw constant attention to the fact that Maureen was a fitness instructor. This seemed a big thing to Mungo. After all, Maureen's body was plastered all over the town: on the bus-shelters, on the sides of buses, on the fly-posters outside the car-parks. It was all those posters – bits of her body – done for the sports shop that he was on about.

Then there was that embarrassing cabinet with all of Maureen's medals and trophies. There had to be close on a hundred. Where did they all come from? Mungo wanted to know.

Maureen explained. Netball. Basketball. Volleyball. Hockey.

'You really are something, aren't you?' said Mungo. 'Got any scrapbooks?'

Yeah, Maureen had scrapbooks. Half a dozen of them. Proper scrapbooks. Scrapbooks she'd got out of John Menzies that came with 'Sports' already printed on the front of them. Three videos as well. Clips from the telly, and stuff her family had filmed.

Maureen was getting agitated. What was the guy playing at? Wanting to watch videos of volleyball matches against Bulgaria where those involved in the match outnumbered those involved in the crowd by a good two to one?

The guy was seemingly gobsmacked. He wasn't teasing her, he wasn't childishly amused, he was gobsmacked. Mungo was gobsmacked.

He was surprisingly knowledgeable, yet he still wanted to know more. He kept on asking questions. He wanted to know about all the matches: how they'd went, how Maureen had felt about them.

Then it hit Maureen – to use a family expression, it hit Maureen with all the subtlety of a kick in the stovies.

The reason for all this.

There had to be a reason, of course. After all, she'd went for him because he was gorgeous. She wouldn't've bothered with him if he hadn't've been. So there had to be some reason why he'd went for her. And the reason was to be found in all this. All the medals. All the trophies. All the videos. The fact that Maureen's name repeatedly appeared in four different papers every single week of the year caused Mungo no end of wonder.

All this stuff that had never mattered to Maureen, all this stuff that had frankly embarrassed her, he was in awe of. The guy was actually, genuinely, interested.

The guy was a heid-the-ba.

Of all things, the guy was starstruck.

Of all things, he had to be flaming starstruck. The poor bugger thought Maureen was some kind of star.

It took Maureen a while to work this one out, a while to get upset by it. The fact he'd been asking such specific questions meant that Maureen had had to think about her responses. Yeah, she could remember that game. That was the time . . . Yeah, of course she'd been in Berlin before the wall come down. The funny thing was . . .

All the guys she'd been out with before, all the guys from uni, from the singles nights, from the over-25 discos, they'd never went on about this stuff. Maureen wouldn't've let them. She was good at sports that were designed for freaks. Tall folk with no social lives and long limbs and short bodies. She'd even played in goal at hockey. That was the one that really hurt. She was the tallest ever goal-minder to play for one of the home countries. That was the one that would go down in the history books. The number of shots she'd saved 'cause of that extra few inches of arm or leg? Hundreds. But she'd've swapped the lot for just one chance to play outfield, to show the world that she could pass, dribble and shoot with the best of them. Just one chance.

'What's the matter?' said Mungo.

Maureen was more pissed off than anything. She wasn't up to anger.

'Just all this stuff,' she said. 'You know, all I ever wanted to be was just ordinary. To be an ordinary height, to look ordinary, to grow up to have an ordinary, normal family with ordinary, normal kids and do ordinary, normal things.'

Mungo laughed. 'Why?' he said.

'Just because. You know, everything in my life has been dictated by the way I look. I've never had a say in it, in my own life I've never had so much as a say. Because of my height. Because of the way I look. Think about it, you're only here 'cause of that.'

'No I'm not.'

'Yes you are. 'Course you are. Okay, you're really sweet and everything, and I've had a really great time, and, yeah, I'd really like to see you again and all that, but you're going on at me like I'm some kind of celebrity. I'm not. I'm a freak. All this is because I'm a freak. I'm good at crap sports that nobody's interested in because I'm a freak. I'm successful at business because I'm a freak. Ultimately, you're here because I'm a freak. Don't you see?'

Mungo shook his head. 'Well,' he said, 'if you want to put it like that, if you want to take it that far, then yeah, I suppose so but . . .'

'Look, I'm sorry,' said Maureen. 'Look, I have problems with this, okay. See I've never believed that anybody could just like me for being me. There's so much baggage that comes along with being me. I just don't believe that if you and I had met under ordinary, normal circumstances, that you and I would be here just now.'

Mungo shook his head. Maureen lowered hers.

They were quiet for a bit, a good four or five minutes. It was Mungo that finally found the courage to break the silence.

'Tell me,' he said, 'when was the first time you seen me?'

Maureen looked puzzled. 'At the community centre,' she said. 'At the class. Where d'you think I first seen you?'

Mungo laughed. 'Don't know really. I suppose that's what I expected you to say. D'you know when I first seen you?'

'At the community centre? At the class?'

Mungo smiled. 'No,' he said, 'I'll tell you where it was. In fact, I'll tell you all about it. I was out jogging one day – four weeks ago last Tuesday, to be precise – out the Blantyre Road. I do a lot of jogging, four times a week, usually. That's how I keep myself fit. I enjoy it. I like my jogging, as they say. Normally, mind, I don't go quite so far. Don't ask me why on that particular day I did go that far, 'cause I don't know. Maybe it was 'cause it was such a beautiful day. Honestly, I don't know, I really, truly don't know. Fate, maybe. Who knows. Anyway, you know that sunken lay-by next the entrance to the cement works? The one that's surrounded by all the trees? That big long one? Yeah? Well, that day, there weren't any lorries parked there, there weren't any caravans parked there, there was only the one car. And in that car was the most beautiful sight I've ever seen. A woman sound asleep. You know, up until that moment I thought I was doing great. Believe it or not, I thought I was happy. Out jogging for miles and miles, imagining myself doing the marathons – London, New York, Tokyo – overtaking millions of folk. Daft, eh? Oh, I thought I was brilliant. Then I seen that woman in the car. You know I felt like I hadn't lived. I felt like I'd missed out on everything in life. I have to admit it, I went back. I wanted to stop and look at her. I'd never seen anybody or anything so content. I'd never seen anybody so pleased with theirselves, so satisfied, so at ease with theirselves. See the smile on her face, just beautiful. I thought to myself how I wanted to share that, that feeling. I wanted a part of it. There was a sticker on the back window of the car, a sticker for this sports shop. It had this daft slogan, "Fun, damn it, it's a God-given right". I liked that. I'd never've thought of it in that way. I got it into my head that the woman worked there, that the woman in the car worked in that sports shop. Crazy, eh? When you think about it that is crazy, really crazy. You know that week I was blushing all the time? Couldn't stop myself. I'd be walking about and I'd feel my face going red. I couldn't stop thinking about this woman. For the first time in my life I was in love, and, boy was it great. To think, too, I was in love with a woman I'd only ever seen sleeping in a car. I remembered the name of the sports shop. (There was no way I was going to forget it.) I went in there every day for a week, looking for this woman. I kept buying things and taking them back, saying this didn't fit, that wasn't right. I made out how I was really sorry about all this. I said that I was a rep, how I travelled about all over the country. If they had any stickers or something, I could stick one on the back of my car, give them a wee bit free advertising. The boy behind the counter, though, he said he hadn't any stickers, he'd never heard of any stickers for the shop. But, I said, I seen one the other day, last week in fact, I'm sure I seen one, on a car, in a lay-by. There was a woman in there, in the car. I think she was asleep. The boy started to laugh. I'd never been so excited in all my life. "Oh," he said, "I can't tell you anything about stickers, pal, but I've a good idea who the daft bugger in the car might've been . . .'

SHAFTING AUNTIE CATHERINE

Every Tuesday night after training, Raymond 'Raisins' Weir would disappear for the best part of a couple of hours before finally meeting up with the rest of his teammates round at The Merry Goose.

New guys to the club were always fair intrigued by this, this now you see him, now you don't routine. 'Where's he off to?' they would ask. 'What's he up to?' they wanted to know.

But, thing was, nobody would ever tell them. Those that knew would just sit around teasingly giving it the time-honoured nudge-nudge wink-wink routine.

So the new guys, emboldened by their youth, would just come straight out with it: they'd ask the man himself. 'Hoy, Raisins,' they'd say, 'where you been? What you been up to?'

By means of response, Raisins shied away from conventional explanation; preferring instead to opt for what could only be described as a biological mutation.

It would start with a slight flush, a slight reddening of the cheeks. Next, there would be silence, total silence. All attention would be focused on Raisins. And when all attention was focused on Raisins, Raisins had but one recourse.

Raisins would burst out at the giggling.

And when you say burst, you really mean burst. The shoulders would be going, the tears would be flowing and folk at nearby tables were seen to cover their glasses so's not to be contaminated by any flying bogies or sputum.

The upshot being the new guys, in spite of these best endeavours, were never *told* what went on with Raisins and his missing couple of hours. The town being the town, however, they did, of course, *find out*. From what they heard, from what they seen and from what they surmised the new guys managed to conjure up a theory – and when they put forward this theory nobody denied it; in fact, a few even nodded to confirm it, confirming that, in between Tuesday night training and meeting up with the others round at The Merry Goose, Raisins was away at the shafting; to name names, shafting someone that went by the name of Auntie Catherine.

Surprised? You bet they were.

Up until then the new guys would've had Raisins down as being a bit, well, simple. A man of simple pleasures, and a man of undoubted simple intellect. A decent enough boy on the wing, like, good at holding the play up and relieving the pressure on the defence – which was all you could ever really hope for from a ball-player in these kind of games – but probably the last person you'd be thinking of when you were contemplating matters carnal. When you thought of Raisins you thought of the bloke who worked as a greenkeeper up the golf course, you thought of the bloke who helped out with the floats for the Gala Day, and you thought of the bloke who not only played, but, each and every night, practised, the banjo.

As for women? Well, Raisins always had about him that good old bachelor persona. 'What would I be wanting with a wife?' he would say. 'Pah, nothing but moaning and complaining all the time.' Raisins had a joke for every occasion. His marriage joke was as follows:

D'you know what the definition of a bachelor is?
A man that never makes the same mistake once.

So, anyway, the new guys, their interest by now well and truly whetted, would next be wanting to find out exactly what sort of woman could ever possibly be interested in Raisins: a creature who, to all intents and purposes, was borderline technical imbecile, had about as much going for him in the looks department as your average sluice, and – as a quick glance in the showers was to confirm – was found not to be blessed with any admirable deformities.

'So,' asked the new guys, 'who's this Auntie Catherine character then?'

'Oh,' folk would say, 'that's her that drives the pink Morris Oxford.' 'Oh, that's her that painted her house purple.' 'Oh, that's her that's always in the paper complaining about the council and her parking tickets.'

Auntie Catherine was Catherine Ferryman. Near enough everybody had a tale or two to tell about Catherine Ferryman. And those who hadn't? Well, clearly they hadn't been paying enough attention. To those in office – the council, the police, the local MP – she was a major pain in the bahookie; to the general public, she was the sort of person who although you didn't really want to know personally, you were always keen to know about.

The history between Raisins and his Auntie Catherine, as pieced together from confided gossip, sparkling innuendo and overheard scandal, had all the trappings of a series of grossly exaggerated lies.

Funnily enough, though, it was all true.

Auntie Catherine had been married to Dennis Gillies – Raisins' uncle on his mother's side – when Dennis had tragically lost his life in a motoring accident up the Whitebridge Road. Part of Raisins' duties over the mourning period, as allocated by his domineering old dear, involved collecting the deceased's clothes for delivery round to the local Oxfam.

But when he went round, on that fateful Tuesday evening, Auntie Catherine suggested to Raisins that anything he was wanting, any of the clothes, he should just take away for himself. Raisins, though, was never one for bothering much with the cut of his cloth or the coordination of his colours. In fact, all he ever wore was what his mum and dad got him for Xmas – jumpers and trainers; what his mum and dad got him for birthdays – jeans; and what his mum and dad brought him back from their holidays – T-shirts. While the rest of the family coughed up with the socks and underwear, the blessed council supplied its greenkeepers with British Standard summer jerkins and British Standard winter jackets. So Raisins had politely perused Uncle Dennis' wardrobe, politely declined – explaining it was all 'a bit loud' for him – and just started filling up his bin-bags.

Auntie Catherine was having none of it. These were looks, she said, these were complete looks. You couldn't separate this shirt from that tie from those trousers. If things were going to be put away, then they were going to be put away properly. By way of explanation, Auntie Catherine instructed Raisins to try on a few of the looks. Maybe then he would begin to appreciate the clothes, maybe then he would even want to take some of them away for himself.

Raisins wasn't what you'd call keen. But, what with the circumstances and everything, he felt it best just to go along, just to, as they say, humour her. After all, it couldn't've been easy for the poor woman, what with her being in mourning and all. So Raisins tried on a few of the outfits. Auntie Catherine tucked in this bit, tugged out that bit. It was just the exact same as how his old dear treated him – pampered him – but, somehow, seeing as how this was Auntie Catherine, things were just that little bit different.

See, thing was, for as long as he could mind, Raisins had always had a bit of a shine for his Auntie Catherine.

Partly, this stemmed from Auntie Catherine's status within the family. What with that high-falutin voice of hers and her decision to have a career instead of children, Auntie Catherine was very much the outsider. Not one of us, you see. Not only that but, unlike the rest of the family, Auntie Catherine didn't come from the town; to make matters worse, she actually came from the other side of the country – the dreaded west coast – from a wee village just outside Oban. Then there was the name business. In the seventeen years that she was married to Dennis, Auntie Catherine always retained her maiden name, always calling herself Ms, never Mrs. And, she was always Catherine, never Cathie, never Cath, never Kate. She was very strict about that. As she was about loads of things. Like the way she dressed her Dennis. Even when he was just going round to the shops, Dennis had to be done up in double-breasted suits, dark shirts and bright,

self-coloured ties. The shade of Dennis' hair was dictated by
Catherine. When the first grey one appeared, Grecian 2000 was
added to the weekly shopping list.

Now Raisins himself could never by any stretch of the
imagination be called a rebel, but he always had a soft spot for
those who were, and, what with the way she carried on, not
forgetting the way she got treated – 'Folk who're born in the
west should stay in the west,' as Raymond's mother had it –
Auntie Catherine was definite rebel material.

Then there was the other aspect.

More than any woman Raisins had ever yet come across,
Auntie Catherine carried herself like the stars you see in films and
magazines. As the women of Raisins' family put it, Auntie
Catherine was always 'dolled up', always 'plastered' with make-
up. In terms of her own clothes, Auntie Catherine went in for
really tight jumpers with really tight knee-length skirts. And she
always wore belts – big wide belts, wee thin belts, chain belts,
imitation snakeskin belts. All of which combined to emphasise
what the women of Raisins' family spitefully dubbed Auntie
Catherine's 'figure'. In family circles, this word was afforded the
same hushed tones as 'expecting', 'language' and 'women's
problems'.

And now this woman – this self-same woman who, incidentally, Raisins had been thinking of when he'd first 'discovered
himself' – was kitting Raisins out in all these daft clothes.

There was one particular pair of trousers Auntie Catherine was
very keen for Raisins to try on, a pair of high-waisted fawn loons
that were near enough a second skin round the hind-end but
which could easily've hid a small dog under each of its flares.

The tightness of said trousers meant Raisins couldn't actually
get the zip up.

Auntie Catherine gave it a go. She told Raisins to breathe in
and pull. At the same time she would attack the zip.

And this was what they did. Until, that was, Auntie Catherine
became aware of a certain something that wasn't exactly helping
matters – a certain bulge, so to speak.

Auntie Catherine looked up at Raisins.

Raisins looked down at his Auntie Catherine.

Auntie Catherine shook her head.

Raisins shook his head.

Then – surprise surprise – Raisins did what Raisins always did when he was the focus of any kind of muted attention.

He burst out into his ten little piggies at the tea-time trough of a giggle.

And he giggled. And he giggled. And he giggled.

Now one of the things yet to be mentioned concerning Raisins and his giggling was that it was damn near impossible to take offence at, because it was damn near impossible not to join in.

And so it proved with Auntie Catherine.

She giggled. And she giggled. And she giggled.

As to exactly who it was that made the first move that eventually saw the pair of them ending up in the sack together; well, despite what a lot of folk would've liked to believe, it was actually Raisins who made what he termed, 'the first grab'. And while Raisins was never what you'd call the world's greatest at telling the truth, the one thing everybody knew about Raisins was that Raisins was totally incapable of bullshitting. This version, his version, had to be the truth.

So, anyway, that was the history of Raisins, Auntie Catherine and their Tuesday night shafting. An arrangement that had lasted three years now: three seasons' winter training with the work's team, three seasons' summer training with the pub team.

It was an arrangement that really couldn't be said to be doing anybody any harm. Raisins' family, of course, weren't exactly over the moon, but seeing as how they were still at the hushed tones stage vis-à-vis 'language', 'expecting', 'women's problems', etc., then there was about as much chance of them kicking up a fuss as there was of them guesting on *Jerry Springer*.

There was, however, one bunch of folk, mind you, who were far from enamoured. An assortment of normally decent, hard-working individuals, famed for their stoicism and their strong stomachs, who found the whole scenario disgraceful, disturbing and, ultimately, an insult to their very manhood.

And who were they?

Why, the dockers, of course, the guys that worked down the docks.

For the past fifteen years Catherine Ferryman, Ms Ferryman, had ran the Port Authority pay office, a job which did not by its very remit endear Catherine to the workforce. From half eight till half four, five days a week, Catherine was to be found behind her wire mesh explaining away back taxes, the difference between overtime rates and excess hours rates, the difference between being sick and being absent, and so on and so forth. On the other side of Catherine's mesh would be some foul-mouthed, foul-smelling stevedore, complaining as how his pay packet was seventy-odd quid less than he was expecting.

Among the dockers it was generally believed that Catherine Ferryman was in need of nothing so much as a good seeing to, and, when her Dennis sadly passed away, there were more than a few who bathed themselves in after-shave in the hope that they would be called upon to oblige.

Catherine was having none of it. Week-in week-out, she declined invitations to country and western nights, karaoke nights, hypnotist nights and – on more than one occasion – some 'brother-in-law's caravan up at Kinghorn'.

A book was set up as to which of the dockers would eventually be first to play hide the sausage with Catherine. Twenty-three men put money on themselves. Twenty-three of them! And we're talking big money here, by the way, we're talking pay packets.

So you can well imagine the reaction when word first hit the Port Authority of the Tuesday night goings-on.

'Raisins?'

'That twerp?'

'That banjo-twanging bumpkin?'

'Christ, if all she was wanting was a weekly ride then what did she no come crawling to me for?'

Initially, the dockers gave Catherine the benefit of the doubt; figuring that maybe, what with the grief and all, the lady was still in a state of shock, a wee bit vulnerable, not entirely of sound mind. Given time, she would doubtless seek out the alternatives. After all, folk who were into sex without commitments – as sex with Raisins surely had to be – were the sort of folk who were into fooling around, weren't they?

So the dockers set out to woo Ms Ferryman, to alert her to these alternatives.

Stripped to the waist, they held barrel-lifting competitions in the waste-ground round the back of the pay office. There was plenty of attention – let's not forget this was the docks – but none, alas, from Catherine.

The dockers persevered. They queued up at the photocopying machine. They sent photocopies of their knobs round to the pay office, complete with strange coded messages.

One of these strange coded messages bore the following inimitable legend:

Why have Raisins when you can have Melons?

The sender was one Melvin 'Melons' Taylor, a mountain of a man but, in recent times, not a man blessed with the best of happiness. First, about four years previous, Melvin's wife had left him. Then, sixth months on, on a weekly custodial visit up to McDonald's, Melvin's beloved kids had tried to poison him. Then came the divorce. And now, for the past three years, this.

Melvin tried everything to win the favours of Ms Ferryman. In the barrel-lifting competitions he'd lifted twice as much again as his nearest competitor. Melvin bought and sent flowers to Catherine. He composed poems for Catherine. He even begged.

But it was all to no avail.

Because, when it came to the male of the species, Catherine was quick to put a dampener on any amorous attentions by letting it be readily known that she was quite happy with things being the way they were: she was quite happy with Raymond, and she was perfectly happy with her Tuesday nights, thank you very much.

Upon being told this, Melvin would, understandably, be beeling. To calm himself down, he'd head off home and spend as many hours working on his weights, pumping his iron and popping his pills till the veins on his forehead resembled nothing so much as his old granny's knitting basket.

As they say, Melvin liked his weight-training. When he wasn't actually using them, Melvin's weights were such that they had to be supported by a specially constructed titanium frame. Had this not been the case then, when lowered, the weights would've made kindling of the floorboards, en route to inflicting God knows what kind of damage on any poor bugger that happened to be lounging about downstairs.

Melvin was big. Six foot six, seventeen and a half stone, the cocktail of steroids he consumed for breakfast, for dinner, for tea and for supper had removed every hair from his body, granted him a nice pair of breasts and left him with a vocal intonation that brought to mind none other than the nation's favourite bubbly American, the lovely Sandra Dickenson.

Not that Melvin was bothered, mind you; 'cause Melvin was only bothered about being big.

Following the break-up of his marriage, Melvin had got involved with the work's team. For Melvin, football was therapy. Melvin wanted to hit folk, kick them, maim them. As for playing the actual game; well, in most teams Melvin would've been deemed unsuitable: too big, too immobile. Like most folk who spend their time lifting weights, all Melvin was really good for was lifting those self-same weights. The dockers, though, prided themselves on being hard. And, in these kind of games, on the kind of pitches they played on – and where referees were well-known to be susceptible to the odd bit of intimidation – hardness had a proven track record of equalling success.

So Melvin got his game. He held down one of the centre half positions, the one that was known as stopper. A wee shove here, the odd sliding tackle there. Melvin was quick to sus that if you were apologetic afterwards, expressing concern for your victim, then you could get away with three such challenges before you got a booking, five before you got sent off. There were loads of other things you could do and all, things that never merited any kind of punishment. As one of his colleagues explained: 'Think about it,' he said. 'When was the last time you seen somebody getting ordered off for, say, grabbing the odd bit loose flesh and giving it a twist; bending back somebody's fingers; pulling somebody's hair; standing on somebody's toes?'

Melvin's belated success as a stopper happened to coincide with the Port Authority reaching the final of the annual J.B. Fowlie & Sons Memorial Trophy – a sort of work's cup – for the first time in three years. If they came out victorious this time round then they would be out on their own as having won the trophy on more occasions than anybody else, a feat they could really brag about when it came to putting one over on their fiercest rivals – the team that went by the name of Recreation & Amenities. The team whose star winger just happened to be that banjo-twanging bumpkin, Raymond 'Raisins' Weir.

Indeed, it was to be Recreation & Amenities that the Port Authority would be facing in the final of this year's J.B. Fowlie & Sons Memorial Trophy on Sunday the 13th of June, at Ochil Park, normally the 1500-capacity home of Dennybridge Juniors.

Over the years, the Fowlie final had become recognised as a major attraction on the social calendar: a big day out for all the participating players, their families and the families of fellow employees, with a near-capacity crowd always guaranteed.

There existed, however, for this particular final, one potential member of said crowd whose loyalties were the subject of much debate around the Port Authority: and Catherine Ferryman was reminded on an almost hourly basis as to who her employers were, who her colleagues were, and about which side she was technically on.

The discerning Catherine, of course, had no intention of giving the final a second's thought, let alone gracing it with her presence. Like she said, if she couldn't find anything better to do with herself of a Sunday afternoon than stand amongst supposedly sensible people who chose to kit themselves out in, of all things, *crêpe*, and who paid to have the faces of their children painted amber and black, then she'd reached a very sad stage in her life indeed.

No, Catherine wasn't interested, not in the slightest.

Or at least that's how it was right up until the morning of Friday the 11th of June, two days before the final, when Wee May, Catherine's assistant in the pay office, who busied herself each and every lunchtime creating a piece of headgear so ridiculous it would've shamed ladies' day at Ascot, confided to Catherine that, come Sunday's final, Raisins was going to get himself seriously wasted.

'What?' said Catherine.

Wee May went on to explain.

The behaviour of the aforementioned Melvin 'Melons' Taylor had increasingly been causing concern among employees of the Port Authority. In the lead-up to the final, Melvin was known to be pumping himself with yet more and more steroids. But while his pectorals continually endeavoured to approximate polished ivory balloons, Melvin's brain was seen to be in danger of losing its somewhat tenuous grip on what passed for reality.

This wasn't entirely news to Catherine, mind. The bovine one was never her idea of a likely Mensa candidate in the first place.

But then Wee May insisted that Catherine take a minute to go look outside.

Catherine said she was too busy to go look outside. She asked May just to tell her what was going on.

Wee May shook her head. She told Catherine it was best to go see for herself.

So Catherine went outside.

And Catherine looked for herself.

And this is what she saw.

Standing next to the old dock-wall was a stripped to the waist Melvin. Melvin was holding a can of spray-paint. Emblazoned on the old dock-wall, in six-feet-high blood-red lettering, was a message, a message that hadn't been there earlier that morning:

Why have Raisins when you can have Melons?
                              signed Melvin 'Melons' Taylor

Catherine gulped.

Melvin stood there, grinning, grinning at Catherine, smirking at Catherine. He pointed up the hill, up to the golf course, then repeatedly punched his open palm with his spray-can crushing fist.

Now, you see, to explain a bit of sociological background, there's a stage men go through when they've been rejected by a woman. A stage that involves the somewhat irrational belief that the only course of action open is to eliminate the man said woman has gone ahead and flung herself at the feet of. Most times, mind you, this stage doesn't last that long: common sense will prevail; somebody new will appear on the horizon; a realisation will strike – hey, if the woman doesn't like you then you were really just wasting your time in the first place, weren't you? Anyway, life's too short to go about in a bad mood.

You'll often hear guys going on about the time this stage happened to them – usually it only happens the once – and looking back with a bunch of your mates can often prove to be a rich source of mutually amusing embarrassment, seeing as how rejection tends to be the forerunner of a) some sort of daft self-mutilation – fists through old-style telephone boxes being a favourite – or b) foul and abusive behaviour in the public domain – the accepted norm being to walk really fast down busy high streets bawling and screaming at yourself.

It was well-known around the Port Authority, however, that poor Melvin was stuck at the bit that went 'KILL!'. To him it was simple: if Raisins was suddenly to become deformed to such an extent that he could no longer perform on Tuesday evenings then that would leave the way free for the musclebound Melvin to access the charms of the bashful Ms Ferryman.

Even his colleagues were saying it: Melvin was cracked. True, the dockers prided themselves on being hard, but, here, Melvin was priding himself on being psychotic. There was talk of dropping him from the team. The trouble with that notion was that the guy who ran the team just happened to be the cousin of the local councillor who dealt Melvin his steroids. And since Councillor McGibney was currently away with three of his colleagues on a fact-finding tour of the Channel Islands, then there was no chance of the concerned parties getting together for a clear the air and calm the waters discussion. In other words, as Melvin made mighty clear, if Melvin was to be dropped from the team, then Melvin was going to sing like Al Jolson could only ever have dreamt of.

Melvin was popping pills like nobody's business. He'd even got himself a second supplier: the head of the PE department of the local high school was dishing out brand new blue ones. In terms of the forthcoming final, the even better news was that the brother of the head of the PE department of the local high school – the local fire officer – had just been named as referee for the final of this year's J.B. Fowlie & Sons Memorial Trophy.

This, not unnaturally, prompted Melvin to think in terms of corruption and blackmail. He suggested to the head of the PE department of the local high school that maybe it would be a good idea if the Port Authority were to, shall we say, receive the benefit of any fifty-fifty decisions that arose during Sunday's final. Or else maybe a few parents might just get a bit upset when a series of anonymous phone calls tipped them off as to just how their sexually ambiguous sprogs were managing to do so well in inter-district athletics meetings.

Not surprisingly, the head of the PE department was quick to agree. He got on the phone to his brother, the refereeing fire officer, telling him how if the Port Authority didn't get the benefit of any fifty-fifty decisions in the J.B. Fowlie & Sons Memorial Trophy then maybe the local paper would get wind of how Reflexions Niteclub, Tropix Disko and Kamera 2000 Danserama managed to secure fire safety notices when they were all regularly overcrowded and had about one half-decent half-hour fire door between them.

Not being one to court unwanted publicity, the brown-trousered refereeing Fire Officer said he would see what he could do: not that he could definitely promise anything – especially over the blasted phone – but he would definitely try and see what he could do, alright?

Catherine Ferryman, meanwhile, following the incident with the dock-wall, had taken time due to her and left her work early. It was Friday the 11th of June, two days before the final, and

Catherine was heading up to the police station, en route to demanding a meeting with the Chief Inspector.

Not, you understand, that that was particularly unusual, mind, Catherine heading up to the police station, demanding to see the Chief Inspector. The bold Ms Ferryman always had a bee in her bonnet about something or other: ever-present noise, brand new eyesores and, of course, her ever-expanding wad of parking tickets.

With all the subtlety of an outraged Exocet, Catherine stormed in.

'Mr Lindsay,' she said, 'I wish to report an assault.'

'Please, Catherine,' said the Chief Inspector, a world-weary divorcé who was secretly turned on by Catherine's appearance, but somewhat turned off by Catherine's demeanour, 'call me Bob.'

'Mr Lindsay, there is a psychopath out there. An individual by the name of Melvin Taylor. I have his personal details.'

Catherine handed over Melvin's work file and sat herself down.

'Now, Catherine,' said the Chief Inspector as he perused the document, 'you know as well as I do, this is highly confidential information. Under no circumstances should you have removed it from your office. Now if something like this were to fall into the wrong hands . . . Well, you tell me, how would you like it if somebody was sitting here looking through your file?'

'Mr Lindsay . . .'

'Call me Bob.'

'Mr Lindsay, this individual is planning an unprovoked attack on my nephew, one Raymond Weir, this Sunday, at Denny-bridge Juniors football ground during the final of the J.B. Fowlie & Sons Memorial Trophy. His intent being to maim poor Raymond, to maim poor Raymond to such an extent that he will be incapacitated for the foreseeable future.'

'Ah-ha.' The Chief Inspector brightened up at the mention of Catherine's well-known banjo-plucking paramour.

Catherine continued.

'Mr Taylor is a well-known abuser of anabolic steroids. I demand that you immediately pay him a visit, apprehend him, charge him, then incarcerate him and throw away the key.'

Catherine sat back, folding her arms.

The Chief Inspector leaned forward, displaying his palms. This was no good. What did she think he was? Judge Dredd or something? That he could just turn up and go, 'K-pow. Take that, ya fucker!'?

'Now, Catherine,' said the Chief Inspector, 'think carefully, and answer me honestly if you would, has this Melvin character ever made any verbal threats against you personally?'

Catherine shook her head.

'Have you ever been present at all when any verbal threats have been made against Mr Weir?'

Again, Catherine shook her head.

'Could you perhaps give me the names of anybody who *has* been present when verbal threats have been made against Mr Weir?'

Catherine thought for a second before wearily closing her eyes and saying, 'No.'

'Well, would I be right then in assuming that what we are dealing with here is what is commonly known as hearsay?'

'No, Mr Lindsay,' snapped Catherine, 'what we are dealing with here is not what is commonly known as hearsay, what we are dealing with here is what is commonly known as fact.'

While Catherine went on to describe the incident with the dock-wall the Chief Inspector took time out to order some tea and biscuits.

Really, the Chief Inspector could be doing without all this. See, when all was said and done, Bob Lindsay was one for the quiet life. Actually, when he came to think about it, when he really came to think about it, Bob Lindsay didn't want any kind of life at all, all he ever wanted was a routine. That was what it used to be like, back in the good old days, being a bobby on the beat, just routine: bit of bother round the pubs on a Saturday night; go round hassling a few dopeheads of a Sunday; check the domestics on a Monday; break-ins on Tuesdays; graffiti Wednesdays; hassle the chip-shop kids on Thursdays; and there was always a good rowdy party to keep you going on a Friday.

'Are you listening to me?' said Catherine.

'Catherine,' said the Chief Inspector, 'in a field of five thousand all talking at once, I would have ears only for you. Trouble is, there is no evidence of wrong-doing. Your Mr Taylor may be a danger to the public – I don't doubt you for a second – but as to yet he has committed no crime. His behaviour may well be threatening and unpleasant, but there is nothing tangible. The procurator-fiscal would laugh us out the office.'

Catherine near-screamed: 'Steroids!'

Calm as you like, the Chief Inspector raised a conciliatory finger. 'I was just coming to that. Now the area of controlled substances is a tricky one. As you know, possession is nine-tenths of the law. Should we come across Mr Taylor in possession of controlled substances then yes we may be able to do something, but the trouble with your steroids is . . .'

Catherine got up out her chair. She'd had enough. 'Well,' she said, 'pay him a visit then. You get given good enough money, so, for once, why don't you go out and earn it, eh?'

And with that, Catherine took her leave. Her swivelling hips causing the Chief Inspector no little pleasure. Mind you, her slamming of the door probably initiating some kind of afternoon migraine.

Nevertheless, after the tea and biscuits arrived, and the Chief Inspector found himself standing at his window, supping his Earl Grey and biting on a Hobnob, the sight of the wilful and wonderful Catherine pouring herself into her car then driving the wrong way out the constabulary's car park – totally buggering the highly efficient one-way system – was enough to prompt an attack of the torch-carrying guilts. The Chief Inspector felt obliged to do something. He got on the phone to his desk sergeant.

'Mike? That you, yeah? Look, sorry to be bothering you, pal, but tell you what it is, I believe one Melvin Taylor – hold on a sec, what was it again? 84 Downbrae Gardens – has been a bit out of sorts of late; threatening behaviour, that kind of thing. Any chance you could maybe, as they say, pay him a visit?'

Mike, the desk sergeant, wasn't one for mincing his words. '*Melons?* You must be joking. Look, sorry, Bob, pal, no can do. Mean middle of January, yeah, no problem, but middle of June, man, we're up to our eyes. You know what it's like, this time of year, half the bloody force is in Gran flaming Canaria. Mean I know the guy you're on about; telling you, the original brick shithoose that one, I'd be needing a squad of us before I was even thinking about heading round there.'

The Chief Inspector laughed. 'Oh well,' he said. 'No harm in asking, I suppose. Sorry to've bothered you.'

And with that, the Chief Inspector and the desk sergeant said their cheerios and hung up. The Chief Inspector returning to his Earl Grey, his Hobnob and his Superintendent Lestrade novel. The desk sergeant getting back to his Diet Coke and *Driller Killer IV* on the Mega-drive.

The pink Morris Oxford, meanwhile, was back on its travels, this time heading up the hill to the golf course.

Intervention had failed, it was time to try evasion.

Totally ignoring the 'club captain only' sign, Catherine parked in the first available space. Then, without so much as a by your leave, stormed into the club pro's shop and demanded of the guy behind the counter as to where she might find Raymond.

'Just a minute, doll,' said the guy behind the counter, the club pro, an embittered soul who'd once held the distinction of leading the Open on the second day for all of forty-seven minutes; but who, on this, of all days, the second Friday of June, the seventh anniversary of that momentous event, was presently earning his crust from trying to flog a set of Colin Montgomerie 'Beat The World!' irons to a bloke that wanted change out of fifty quid.

Catherine snapped, 'Had I a minute, doll, I would quite happily wait a minute, doll. I do not, however, have a minute. Tell me, please, and tell me now, where is Raymond?'

The embittered club pro looked at Catherine, then at his watch. It was exactly seven years to the minute. Seven years to the minute since his greatest achievement, the greatest moment of his life. A moment any golfer would've dreamed of. A moment he would now, in hindsight, gladly have swapped for castration any day of the week. Your fifteen minutes of fame? You can take it. You can stuff it.

'Well?' said Catherine.

'Yeah,' sneered the embittered club pro, 'I'm going to tell you. Round about now, I would expect you to find your Raymond on the sixteenth fairway. Okay? Try the south bunker, the one nearest the reservoir. Thank you, and good day.'

'Thank you,' said Catherine. 'Now, how do I get there?'

'Well,' said the guy, frustration giving way to sarcasm, 'you see that elevated piece of grass over there? The one with those guys standing on it? Well that's called the first tee. That little flag you can just make out at the other end, that's called the first hole. If you keep following those round you'll eventually end up at number sixteen. South bunker. The one nearest the reservoir. Once again, thank you, and good day.'

Catherine, too, said, 'Thank you.' On her way out, however, she succeeded in slamming the door so hard a life-size cardboard cut-out of John Daly fell over, causing, in turn, the collapse of a shop-soiled display of reduced-to-clear Arnold Palmer graphite woods.

Catherine was off.

Adopting a gait that brought to mind none other than Maureen O'Hara striding it out in *The Quiet Man*, she proceeded to make her way round the course.

Mind you, traversing this souped-up putting green was proving to be a might more dangerous than separating John Wayne and Victor McLaglen ever was.

Cries of 'Fore!' seemed to anticipate Catherine's every movement.

'Fore!'

'Fore!!'

'FORE!!!'

It was as though all these ridiculously coordinated gents were using her for some kind of target practice.

So irate was Catherine she grabbed a hold of one of their balls – one of their *golf* balls – and flung it in the direction from whence it had come.

Not long after, some daft bloke in a buggy drove up to Catherine, wanting to know exactly what the hell she was playing at.

Catherine explained exactly what the hell she was playing at. She was looking for the sixteenth fairway. The south bunker. The one nearest the reservoir. She was looking for Raymond. It was urgent.

'The sixteenth fairway?' said the guy, his anger giving way to anecdotal amusement, the guys in the clubhouse would love this one. 'Okay,' he said. 'Hop in. Anything for a quiet life.'

The guy gave Catherine a lift over to the sixteenth fairway. He pointed her in the direction of the bunker she was looking for, the one nearest the reservoir.

Catherine thanked the colourfully-clad gent for his time and kind heart.

'No problem,' said the guy. 'But, please, lady, in future, unless you're playing, keep off the fairways, alright?'

Seeing as how the man was so nice, Catherine promised she would, then went over to what he had said was the south bunker, the one nearest the reservoir.

Now to those who know about such things, this particular sandtrap is fairly notorious in Scottish golf circles. Not notorious in the fearful sense, you understand. In fact, anything but. For one, it faces completely the wrong way. More importantly, in order for the bunker to come into play, you need to hit the world's worst first shot followed by the world's worst second shot. The ex-Open champ who'd designed the course was said to have been on a bit of a bender when he drew up the plans. It didn't say much for the local committee that a par five with no trees, no bushes and no rough, that was about as wide as it was long, was never at any stage in the proceedings deemed to be a tad on the friendly side.

In other words, if you wanted a bit of peace and quiet, the

south bunker on the sixteenth fairway, the one nearest the reservoir, was the place to be.

Clad in only his cut-off jeans and a pair of cheap shades, Raymond was found to be spreadeagled in the bunker. Sound asleep.

'Raymond,' said Catherine, kicking the slumberer's legs, 'Raymond, wake up. We need to talk. Listen, you're not playing in this match, this football match. There's a man out there, a man called Melvin Taylor, who's vowed to do you damage. I'm not having it. You're to phone and say you're not going. Okay? Capeesh?'

Upon waking, Raisins' first reaction was to cover his nipples.

Upon covering his nipples, Raisins' next reaction was to wonder what the hell his Auntie Catherine was doing there.

Upon realising what the hell his Auntie Catherine was doing there, Raisins' immediate response was to say, 'No. No way, man.'

'What?' said Auntie Catherine. 'What do you mean, "No"?'

'Away you go,' said Raisins. 'This is the highlight of the season. I'm not missing my game, not for you, not for anybody.'

Catherine explained. The photocopy. The graffiti. The steroids. The threats.

'Ach,' said Raisins, 'all that's just kiddology, all that kind of stuff, all just trying to psyche each other out before the big final. Nothing to worry yourself about.'

'Raymond, listen, listen to me, this *is* something to worry about. This man is ill, he's sick, he's out to do you harm. Raymond, I don't want you playing. I'd never forgive myself.'

A solitary tear trickled down Auntie Catherine's powdered cheek.

Raisins lay back in the sand and stretched. He started to laugh. 'Pah,' he said, 'women. You're all the same, eh? Worrying yourselves over nothing. Mountains out of molehills. Anything so's you can get het up, eh?'

Tickled by the thought of it – the very thought that some big, fat oaf could get close enough to tackle him, let alone maim him – Raisins' laugh turned into a giggle.

And he giggled. And he giggled. And he giggled.

Only, this time round, Catherine didn't join in. No, this time round, it didn't seem funny, it just seemed stupid.

Frustrated at his unrepentant inanity, Catherine kicked sand over Raymond, then informed him, in no uncertain terms, that Tuesday nights were now a thing of the past.

Catherine headed back to her car, the sound of manic giggling ringing in her ears.

Catherine had tried intervention. That hadn't worked. She'd tried evasion. That hadn't worked either. All that was left now was mercy.

Catherine drove round to 84 Downbrae Gardens – the home of Melvin 'Melons' Taylor.

Melvin had been working on his upper abdomen when the door went. The disturbance caused him to lose track of his repetitions, whether he was supposed to be breathing in or breathing out.

So you can understand as how it wasn't a happy Melvin that answered the door.

No, it was a seriously pissed off Melvin – clad in only a g-string, his hairless body covered in baby-oil – that answered the door.

Mind you, when he saw who the guilty party was . . .

Melvin gave a gasp of a grunt.

'I believe,' said Catherine, 'you have some explaining to do.'

Melvin grunted.

Then Melvin grunted again.

Because, as far as verbal communication went, grunting was about as much as Melvin could presently muster; seeing as how, as from that morning, Melvin was now incapable of articulate speech. The blue ones – Melvin's latest steroids – had been wonderful for vein definition but, rather unfortunately, had made rubber bands of his vocal cords, causing his normal bubbly Sandra Dickenson to give way to a high-pitched Minnie Mouse which appeared audible only to next door's pet rotty, Tyson the Third.

'Well?' said Catherine.

Melvin grunted.

'I'm asking you not to play in this match, this match on Sunday, this football match. I believe you harbour intentions to maim my nephew, Raymond Weir. I beg of you not to do this.'

Melvin grunted. He pointed to himself. Melvin smiled. He pointed to Catherine. Melvin grunted again. He pointed through the house.

Catherine shook her head. 'Not while I've still got a finger to call my own, sunshine.'

Not being of a mind to chase lost causes, Catherine about turned. There was about as much chance of getting mercy out of this God-forsaken freak as there had been of getting sense out of Raymond. Catherine went down the stairs, slamming the close door so hard that Tyson the Third, next door's pet rotty, charged down his lobby, anticipating some kind of police raid.

So, anyway, that was the Friday, the Friday before the final, the Friday of failures.

On the Saturday, the day before the final, Catherine gave it one last go. After hours of mental to-ing and fro-ing, come tea-time, she finally plucked up enough courage to go round and see somebody she hadn't spoken to in three years, Raymond's mother.

As ever, it was open-house round at chez Weir. Raymond was away out at a pre-match meal and team talk but two of Catherine's sisters-in-law were round, as well as a couple of neighbours and a brood of kids that could, for all Catherine knew, have just wandered in off the street.

As best she could, in between the telly, the radio and battling kids, Catherine tried to explain the situation. The past, the present, the likely future.

But it didn't register: not one bit, didn't arouse any parental concern whatsoever. All it did was provide ammunition to have a superior smirk at Catherine.

Raymond's mother made it only too clear that she wasn't bothered about Raymond and the possibility of his being assaulted. ('He's old enough and daft enough to look after himself,' was her view of things.) No, as far as she was concerned, the heart of the matter was the villain of the piece, and the villain of the piece wasn't Melvin Taylor; no, the villain of the piece was the cradle-snatching Catherine Ferryman – because if it wasn't for the cradle-snatching Catherine Ferryman then none of this would've happened in the first place, now would it?

But, said Catherine, all that was in the past, Tuesday nights were over, finished, kaput, done with – and quite frankly were none of anybody's business barring her's and Raymond's. What mattered was the present, the future. The fact that this monstrous psychopath was out to maim young Raymond.

During her explanation, Catherine happened to mention that she'd seen Melvin in a g-string. Catherine had been struggling to liken Melvin's body to one of The Gladiators, some sort of grotesque bodybuilder, only more so, hideously more so. But Raymond's mother and her visitors were more interested in how Catherine had acquired such a working knowledge of Melvin's anatomy. Answered the door wearing only a g-string? Aye, that'll be right.

Just as Catherine was about to give up, the men came in. They'd been out back inspecting the greenhouse. Like the women, there were five of them – Raymond's father, a couple of brothers-in-law, a couple of neighbours.

The story was repeated. Surely to God, at least one of them would take on board the seriousness of the situation.

But, oh no, if anything, the men seemed to find it amusing.

'Telling you, hen,' said the proud father, 'he'll need to go some to catch our Raymond.'

'Ach, away you go, hen,' said a macho brother-in-law. 'It's a man's game. He's got a referee and two linesmen out there to protect him.'

'Christ, hen,' said a know-it-all neighbour, 'you expect the odd bit of needle leading up to a final. Wouldn't be the same without the odd bit of needle.'

Convinced they hadn't been listening, Catherine repeated everything. Every last detail.

But, this time, when she got to the bit about the dock-wall, Catherine became aware that the telly was no longer on; likewise, the radio was off; and where were the kids?

There was a look of the utmost smugness on the faces of Raymond's mother, his father, all the visitors.

They hadn't been listening to a word she was saying.

With a calmness that belied the intent, Catherine was asked to leave.

She lowered her head. It was all over.

The Weirs had waited years for this: to fling Catherine Ferryman out their house. Their big victory: to put a stop to Catherine Ferryman. Their moment of triumph: to publicly humiliate Catherine Ferryman.

Catherine was led to the door – manhandled – by Raymond's father and one of the brothers-in-law.

As they marched her down the garden path, the women came out to the doorstep.

'Trollop!' they shouted. 'Slag! Cradle-snatching tu'penny flaming whore!'

As she got into her car, Catherine gave them the finger – and, boy, did she mean it.

Catherine drove straight home.

When she got there, and finally got her feet up, Catherine surprised herself by doing something she hadn't done in ages. For the first time in three years, Catherine had a good greet. For the first time since her Dennis had died.

God, she missed Dennis. Why couldn't people see that? Sure, they'd lost a brother, they'd lost a member of their family, they'd lost a friend, but Catherine had lost a husband, a husband she was devoted to, a husband that had meant everything to her.

This thing with Raymond, it had all started with the clothes. Those stupid bloody clothes. Catherine hadn't been well. Really, she should've went to see the doctor. Got some pills or something, some help at least. She'd been confused, she'd been alone. All that giggling. Just like his uncle. All those clothes. All those daft bloody clothes. The first time had maybe been a mistake – sure, a truly daft mistake, she'd been aware of what she was doing alright – but the subsequent arrangement had suited them just fine, every Tuesday night after training. Everybody needed a cuddle now and then. It was good for her. And there was no doubting it was good for Raymond. Imagine it, being brought up in a house like that. No wonder the poor lad had no wits about him.

And now he was going to get battered, or get maimed, or get his legs broke. And, yes, when all was said and done, ultimately, yeah, it was Catherine's fault.

Catherine continued to greet, to let it all pour out. But it was a funny kind of greet. Not a mourning one, not like the one for Dennis. No, this was more like the hiccups, or the giggles, more of a nuisance than anything, an inconvenience. Catherine made her tea; but didn't stop greeting. Catherine did the crossword – finished it – but didn't stop greeting. Catherine had a bath; but didn't stop greeting.

Strange.

The following morning, the Sunday morning, the morning of the final of the J.B. Fowlie & Sons Memorial Trophy, Catherine rose late, about ten. Unusually for Catherine, for the first time she could remember really, she'd slept right through, a good eleven hours. By the time she'd washed, had a look through the papers and had something to eat, it was near enough one o'clock – an hour before kick-off.

Catherine had made up her mind. She was going.

As much as she wanted revenge on the Weirs, she would gain no satisfaction from anything that happened; but she wanted to go. She knew she was responsible, but she wouldn't feel any guilt. Not anymore. No, it was others who should've felt the guilt. It wasn't her who'd poured the drink down Dennis' throat that night of the accident. No, she'd been away for the weekend, away home, back up to Tarduff, visiting a sick aunt. Dennis had stayed put, he couldn't get time off his work. A free man for the weekend. That was the joke – the family's joke – just like the old days, before Catherine had took over. That night, he'd got drunk. He'd got mortal. *No. They'd* got him drunk. *They'd* got him mortal. He'd driven home from the club. He'd crashed. He'd died. The family had blamed Catherine. She was over a hundred miles away. She'd said she'd phone at eleven. Dennis had wanted her to phone, begged her to phone, to let him know that everything was alright. It was the first time they'd been apart in fourteen years. Dennis was driving home to take the call. It was the family who'd got him drunk. They wouldn't give him the money for a taxi. That was their idea of getting their own back, their idea of a joke. How could anybody have thought that was funny? How could anybody have thought that getting somebody drunk then watching them drive was funny?

There was no post-mortem, no inquest. The family hadn't wanted one. Nobody else was involved. Nobody got word to Catherine till she came back. For two days her husband was dead and nobody got word to her.

Swines. Nothing but swines.

The sun came out as Catherine drove to the ground. She parked her car – for once, legally; for once, carefully – then followed those bedecked in the amber and the black, the colours of the Port Authority. Inside, Catherine found a place for herself near the front of the terracing, just behind the face-painted kids leaning over the track-side barriers.

What with the good weather, all the colours and everything, there was a definite air of everybody being up for enjoying themselves, an atmosphere more akin to a carnival than a football match. Folk were shouting to each other, holding conversations when they were fifty yards apart. Every face had a smile on it.

All that was to change, however, all that good-natured *bonhomie*, when the two teams came out for their warm-up.

The air was stifled with an aghast hush.

Every smile disappeared from every face as every pair of eyes homed in on one pathetic excuse for a human being.

Melvin.

'Melons'.

Taylor.

Melvin was snarling at the crowd. He was pointing at Raymond then, like he'd done up at the dock-wall, punching his palm.

Even those around Catherine, those that were supposedly supporting the Port Authority, were rushing down to take their kids away from the track-side barriers, lest their weans should catch an eyeful of this baleful monstrosity.

'Would you look at that?' they said.

'That's no real.'

'That's disgusting.'

'That should be in a flaming zoo, that should.'

While the rest of his colleagues strived to model themselves on the sort of folk you wouldn't want to meet in a dark alley, Melvin was merely the prototype for the sort of person you just wouldn't want to meet.

Melvin had shaved his head – a nailbrush mohawk. His legs were so big that clearly his shorts had been cobbled together from a set of pillowcases. Likewise, his upper body was so developed that, had Melvin had a neck, then the number of his fit-to-burst shirt would've been up round about it.

'Ah-ha,' said a friendly familiar voice, 'I take it that's your man, Catherine – your so-called serious psychopath.'

Catherine looked round. It was the Chief Inspector, Mr Lindsay, Bob as he liked to call himself, all done up in his ill-fitting uniform.

'And you, the appointed leader of Central's finest, are just going to grin and stand there, I suppose, eh?'

The Chief Inspector nodded. Too damn right he was. Okay, he was maybe on double-time overtime – this being a Sunday and all – and a Chief Inspector's double-time overtime was nothing to be sniffed at, but the bottom line was he of all people shouldn't be here. Christ, he was supposed to be the boss. Okay, he was maybe a nice boss, and one of the things about being a nice boss was that you let folk – namely your underlings – have their holidays when they wanted them; but you'd think, though, that after all these years they'd have the wits about them to work it out so's that everybody wouldn't go on blasted holiday at the same flaming time, but, oh no, every last PC Plod and WPC Plonda's got to get the first fortnight in June. Never mind if there's epidemics of burglaries, never mind if there's riots in the streets, never mind if there's fifteen serial killers out there on the loose, never mind . . .

'Well?' said Catherine.

'Eh, aye,' said the Chief Inspector, regaining his calm. 'He's a bit of a bruiser, I'll grant you that.'

'And you wouldn't consider his behaviour threatening?'

The Chief Inspector shook his head.

'How can you tell?' he said. 'Really, how are you supposed to determine intent? From the look of somebody? Civil Liberties would be down on us like a ton of bricks. The bottom line as such is threatening behaviour is not a legally enforcable indicator of malice aforethought.' The Chief Inspector was reminded of one of his favourite party tricks. 'By way of example,' he said, 'let me demonstrate.'

The Chief Inspector went, 'A-hem.' He then turned to face the crowd and gave a great big smile.

The crowd duly responded.

'Lindsay, ya bastard! You put my brother away!'

'Lindsay, ya bastard! You're a dead man, by the way! I know where you drink!'

'Lindsay, ya bastard! Think you're tough, eh? Christ, my bairn's done shites that're bigger than you!'

The Chief Inspector turned his attention back to Catherine. 'See,' he said, 'now that's your stereotypical standard threatening behaviour — undoubtedly — also damn anti-social to boot. But, basically, it's all good harmless fun. Any attempt to reprove would probably just have the effect of aggravating the situation. Who's to say that your man out there isn't just best left alone? Maybe just a little exuberant, eh, showing a wee bit bravado, psyching out the opposition.'

'"Exuberant"?' said Catherine. 'Look at him, his eyes shake. He's sick. He's a sick boy. That isn't exuberance — that's psychotic. That isn't bravado — that's intent. Look at him, will you?'

The Chief Inspector looked. This one was a tad scary, mind. He could see now what Mike the desk sergeant was meaning about needing a squad of guys. Trouble was there was only the two of them in the ground, two policemen, the Chief Inspector himself and a peely-wally greenhorn with the given name of

White who was patrolling up the other end. There was supposed to be a dog, but the only officer entrusted to handle Tyson or Rocky or whatever it was called these days was — surprise surprise, you guessed it — currently sunning himself in the ever popular early summer resort of Gran Canaria.

'So,' said the Chief Inspector, 'all things being equal, what would you want me to do then?'

'I don't know,' said Catherine. 'Something: anything. You're supposed to be the expert. Go over and appeal to his better nature, I don't know, appeal to man's better nature, but do something.'

The Chief Inspector gave a shrug of resignation. Really, at the end of the day, when all was said and done, he wasn't equipped for this: the unexpected, the complicated. See what everybody seemed to forget was that policework was routine. Hell, it was supposed to be routine. Policemen didn't prevent crime — that was like expecting ambulance drivers to prevent accidents — they cleaned up messes. When folk read their books or watched their films they quite happily accepted that all policemen ever did was turn up afterwards and sort things out, solving mysteries, recovering stolen property. Yet when they wanted help, nine times out of ten, what the great general public really wanted was crime prevention. For something to stop. For something never to've started.

The warm-up over, the teams trooped off the park.

Catherine turned to the Chief Inspector. 'You're not going to do anything, are you? You're just going to stand there, eh? You're just going to stand there and let this happen.'

'Catherine,' said the Chief Inspector. 'I'm sorry, I can't do anything *until* something's happened.'

'I know. I know. And then you'll come down on him like, what is it you always say again, like a ton of bricks, eh? The good old ton of bricks. Think, will you, think. For God's sake, for once, for once in your life, try and stop something before it's started.'

Ever willing to please the public, and Catherine in particular, the Chief Inspector tried to think. Not something he was accustomed to, mind, not when he was on his feet, anyway, not when he was working. No, thinking was something that derived from patience, and patience was something you reserved for the likes of crosswords . . . or books.

Books?

Yeah, books, detective books. The Chief Inspector's favoured reading material. Such detectives were proper policemen, solitary blokes that didn't anticipate problems – solitary blokes that cleaned up messes. Always too busy dealing with crime to be bothered with crime prevention.

Like if Lestrade – the Chief Inspector's current favourite – was confronted with all this, what would he do? He wouldn't go by his eyes, that's for sure, he wouldn't go by what he was looking at. That was too obvious. No, he'd go by his ears, what he'd heard.

So what had Catherine said?

'Appeal to his better nature.'

Appeal to a steroid-bloated psychopath's better nature?

Aye, right.

That wasn't all she'd said, though. She'd also said, 'Appeal to man's better nature.'

Appeal to man's better nature?

So what was man's better nature? What did man value above all else? What did the Chief Inspector value above all else?

Peace. Quiet. Routine.

And what did the Chief Inspector's underlings value above all else?

Gran Canaria, apparently.

But, hey, wait a minute; really, just exactly why were they all away to Gran Canaria at the same time?

Because some daft, peace-loving, quiet-living, routine-fixated fruitbat of a Chief Inspector had allowed them all to go to Gran Canaria at the same time, that's why.

No, that was stupid, that was missing the point, this could be important: the point was why did they all *want* to go to Gran Canaria at the same time?

Because, folk being folk, somebody must've suggested them all going to Gran Canaria at the same time.

!!!

Who then?

The Chief Inspector was reminded of something else, something else that was said. Something he'd said, or thought he'd said – as often happened with these things, he couldn't remember which: 'Policework was all about cleaning up messes.'

Okay then; how about: to prevent a problem, clean up a mess?

!!!

So what was Melvin's mess?

Where did all this come from?

The Chief Inspector thought. Again, the Chief Inspector remembered something. Something close to home, a bit too close to home.

Okay, that was two lengths of the detective's triangle. What was the third?

What was Catherine's mess? What had she to do with all of this?

Why was she like that?

Something clicked.

'Hold on,' said the Chief Inspector, 'I think I've got it.'

'Got what?' said Catherine.

But it was too late. The Chief Inspector was off. Barging his way through the crowd, he leapt over the track-side barrier then, displaying a sprinter's turn of pace, raced across the pitch.

The crowd was buzzing. Old Lindsay might've been getting on a bit, but, at full pelt, was clearly still a fearful sight.

What the hell was he up to?

Had he seen something taking place up the tunnel?

Was he going to batter fuck out of Melons?

Nah, no way, man.

Nobody could batter fuck out of Melons.

Mind you, the way he'd pelted across that pitch.

No see him?

Time passed. The crowd grew restless. The kick-off was delayed for fully fifteen minutes. The paying public wanted their entertainment. To make matters worse, there was a possibility they were missing out on the main attraction; a rammy between Lindsay and Melons? Nice one.

Catherine was praying with her fingers crossed.

But when the two teams eventually came out for the start of the game, the first figure she saw was the one that always looked as though it'd just landed.

Acclaiming what they perceived to be the victorious Melvin, the crowd started up a chant. 'Lindsay got his head kicked! Lindsay got his head kicked!'

Catherine uncrossed her fingers. Some things just never worked.

Whatever the Chief Inspector had attempted had obviously failed. Melvin was centre-stage, strutting about like he owned the place, like he was the only one that mattered.

With the crowd singing, 'Que sera sera/Whatever will be will be,' the referee blew his whistle and the game got under way.

During the opening exchanges, Catherine switched her attention back and forth between Raymond and Melvin. Whenever they were near each other her heart leapt to her mouth. But something was wrong. Amazingly, the only time they ever looked like they were going to clash, Melvin seemed more interested in kicking the ball than in kicking Raymond.

Indeed, it was from that monstrous clearance that the Port Authority went on to score the first goal. Buoyed up by those around her, Catherine almost cheered. Anything that used up time and kept the ball out of play merited a cheer. Anything that meant Melvin would be kept away from Raymond.

The chant of 'Lindsay got his head kicked! Lindsay got his head kicked!' started up again.

The Chief Inspector was making his way round the ground. His pace funereal, his hands clasped behind his back, very much the patrol policeman, all the time staring into the crowd, as though he was trying to memorise every last detail of every last face.

When, eventually, the Chief Inspector reached as far as Catherine, he looked up, smiled and mouthed the word, 'Okay.'

Catherine didn't feel so much reassured as vindicated. Something had been going on. Something was being seen to.

The game continued.

A fight started up. Two players were ordered off. Shortly afterwards, there was a scuffle that saw two being carried off.

But, against all expectations, none of these incidents involved Melvin. There were tackles going in that could best be described as crude, but Melvin was keeping out of it. But when you came to think about it, that wasn't entirely surprising. Melvin was too big to be doing any running about. In fact, what he was doing was next to nothing. Most of the time he was just standing there. Really, to be objective, he just looked stupid. Had Catherine not known what she knew she could easily've laughed at him. Melvin was as out of place as a panto dame at a Kirov ballet. Sure, he was a presence alright, a towering presence, but by no stretch of the imagination could you have called him a participant. Even Catherine would've fancied her chances at getting away from him.

The referee blew the whistle for half-time. Catherine was looking for the Chief Inspector, hoping he would reappear and reassure her that everything really was alright, but the Chief Inspector's walking pace was so slow, so deliberate, that he was only now just reaching the opposition end. It would be ages before he got back round.

The person who did come over was Wee May, Catherine's assistant in the pay office.

Wee May was wanting to know what had gone on between Melons and Lindsay. But Catherine couldn't tell her: she didn't know if anything had gone on, if anything was going on, or if anything would be going on. All she knew was that everything was, seemingly, 'Okay.'

Disappointed at the lack of gen, Wee May and her extravagant headgear went back to her pals.

Catherine looked for the Chief Inspector. He was still at the other end. This time, though, he was stopped and talking to folk in the crowd. Familiar-looking folk. Catherine could make out

Raymond's mother, Raymond's father, the brothers-in-law, the sisters-in-law, the neighbours.

Oh, to be a long-distance lip-reader.

The teams came out for the second half, with the Port Authority now defending the goal at the end populated by their support, the end Catherine was standing at.

Melvin came trundling down to the edge of the eighteen yard box. Catherine could see the veins sticking out on his arms and legs. Melvin indulged in some showboating, pulling up his shirt and flexing his muscles.

Even those that would normally be impressed by such things, those that booked twelve months in advance to see the Chippendales, the Wee Mays of this world, even they turned their heads away. Likewise, parents were seen to cover the eyes of their children, hoping to stave off that night's nightmares.

Surprisingly, as the second half kicked off, it was the Port Authority who took the initiative. Playing to their strengths, they kept the ball high, playing it long, shooting on sight, hoping for deflections, their aim to get a corner.

It paid off. Following a series of scrappy set-pieces, they eventually managed to score. Two-nil to the Port Authority.

Spurred on by their poor showing thus far – and life-threatening threats from their supporters – a truly rattled Recreation & Amenities pressed forward. During the next fifteen/twenty minutes the Port Authority were under constant pressure.

The ball went out to the left, to Raymond. Raymond skipped past one tackle then another. He was into the box. He just had Melvin to beat.

Melvin went flying in.

Raymond went crashing down.

The crowd were booing.

They were outraged.

But no, they weren't outraged because of the severity of Melvin's challenge. No, they were outraged because Raymond had dived.

And it wasn't just supporters' prejudice.

Even Catherine had seen that Melvin, hopeless as he was, had actually succeeded in playing the ball. He hadn't touched Raymond.

The referee awarded a penalty. He was motioning Melvin over. It looked for all the world as though Melvin was going to be ordered off.

But, as the crowd and the rest of the Port Authority players were only too keen to point out, the stand-side linesman had his flag raised.

A confab took place between the referee and the stand-side linesman. Really, it was more like an argument. The players, meanwhile, proceeded to have a handbags-at-ten-paces shoving match in the box. Only one man wasn't involved. A man who looked like he was too busy shitting himself.

Who else but Melvin.

Following the heated confab between the referee and the stand-side linesman, the referee's decision stood. It was a penalty. Melvin was booked for his troubles, but, clearly against the referee's original wishes, he wasn't sent off.

Recreation & Amenities converted the spot-kick, bringing the score back to 2–1.

Catherine had mixed feelings about Melvin not being sent off. Ultimately, of course, that was what she'd have preferred, but Raymond's dive was so blatant, such a deliberate attempt to cheat, that Catherine couldn't help but feel sorry for the hideous one. No one, however loathsome, deserved to be a victim of cheating.

From then on, it was all Recreation & Amenities. Their leaner physiques still up to the task of running up and down the full-size pitch. The sagging Port Authority, their muscles visibly turning to fat, seemed content just to blast the ball any which way they could.

Just when it looked like the Port Authority's resistance was about to crack, the referee blew the full-time whistle.

The Port Authority had won, for a record twenty-second time, the J.B. Fowlie & Sons Memorial Trophy.

Catherine was embraced by several of those around her. She

embraced them back. Folk she knew by sight, folk she passed the time of day with, but, never in a million years, folk she'd imagine herself wanting and needing to hold on to.

Wee May came over. She practically leapt on Catherine. Not that Catherine was bothered. The relief that it was all over. The relief that Raymond hadn't been hurt.

'A-hem,' broke in a friendly familiar voice, 'sorry to interrupt but is everything alright? See we've had a series of reports concerning the normally redoubtable Ms Catherine Ferryman, claiming she's actually been seen to enjoy herself.'

'What did you do?' said Catherine, untangling herself from a bouncing Wee May. 'How did you manage to stop him being such a bloody psychopath?'

The Chief Inspector pointed to the pitch.

Catherine looked. Melvin was being presented with the J.B. Fowlie & Sons Memorial Trophy.

'Sorry,' said Catherine. 'I don't get it.'

'Well,' said the Chief Inspector, 'I'll explain it to you. Remember that file you showed me? Well, when I was looking through it I happened to notice that the entry in Melvin's marital status column had been changed. So, like you said I should, I appealed to his better nature, to man's better nature. You know, it's a theory of mine that when you're down like that, when your world's fallen apart, there's nothing men – or women, come to that – need more than they need respect.' The Chief Inspector gave a knowing look to Catherine. Catherine blushed. From here on in, the Chief Inspector maintained eye contact. 'Contrary to popular belief, Catherine, we don't need a replacement – another woman/another man – we need a vocation, we need routine; but it's not just routine, we need to feel that what we're doing and who we are has some worth. You can't be selfish about these things. So, bearing all this in mind, I got Melvin's manager to make Melvin captain for the day, a decision heartily endorsed by all his teammates. And, I might add, a decision which rather touched the big fellow. Anyway, in order to maintain this new-found respect your pal Melvin had to set an example, the perfect example. He never put a foot wrong, did he? Look at him, the big, daft bugger; you know, right at this moment, I doubt if there's a happier soul alive.'

Catherine could hardly believe it. Miraculously, the solid seventeen and a half stone that was Melvin was being carried shoulder-high down to the Port Authority end.

Catherine shook her head. 'No wonder it took you so long.'

The Chief Inspector laughed. 'Nah, to be honest, that only took a couple of minutes. The main trouble was getting the officials to conduct a fair game. You wouldn't believe the number of deals that were getting struck over there.'

'Well, funnily enough,' said Catherine, 'actually I would; and I'll tell you something for nothing, you never got to that referee. That was never a penalty.'

'Aye?'

'No. Raymond dived. Saw it with my own two eyes.'

The Chief Inspector made a mental note. If the Fire Officer's candidacy for captain of the municipal golf club were to prove successful then maybe it would be worthwhile paying a check of his own to some of these nightclubs, these overcrowded ill-equipped death-traps.

The crowd made their way out the ground, singing, as they went, 'Always look on the bright side of life.'

'Well, Catherine,' said the Chief Inspector, 'I take it you've enjoyed your day out?'

'A change,' she said. 'A change. And you?'

The Chief Inspector nodded. 'Oh, pretty much the same. Nothing like a good bit of routine to get you going. That's what policework's all about, you know. You've no idea how much I enjoyed that, walking round, hands behind the back, keeping an eye on everybody, looking after them.'

'You like your routines, don't you?'

'Oh, aye,' said the Chief Inspector, 'love them. Like I always say, I don't want a life, I just want a routine. Just want to be doing the same things at the same times all the time.'

'And you never ever want to be doing anything else?'

The Chief Inspector stopped for a second. Actually, if he was being totally honest with himself, he did, he did want to do other things. Normally, he could hide these feelings, delude himself, hide them behind routine. But, following on from the bit of news the Weir family had given him – this most exciting bit of news that had quite frankly (and totally unprofessionally) prevented him from thinking about anything else for the past forty-five minutes – these age-old feelings had bubbled to the surface like the most obvious of clues.

'Well, I must admit, now you come to mention it, there is one thing,' said the Chief Inspector. 'One minor blip on my weekly calendar.'

'Oh,' said Catherine, 'and what and when would that happen to be?'

'Well,' said the Chief Inspector, his grin as broad as Melvin's, 'to tell you the truth, I've never really been one for being particularly busy on my Tuesday evenings.'

FINDING OUT ABOUT LAIRDY

Lairdy was one of those guys that never mentioned things.

Like you would get the instance of somebody coming in and maybe saying something along the lines of, 'D'you hear about the fire over the town last night?' We would all go, 'No, never heard a thing. What happened, like?' And the boy would go on and proceed to tell us all what he knew about it. At some point or other, though, as sure as sure could be, we'd get Lairdy piping up – and it would transpire that not only had Lairdy known about the fire, but Lairdy had been out watching the fire, Lairdy had seen the engines arriving and Lairdy had stayed put until the whole shebang was well and truly dealt with.

And he'd never thought to mention it. Happened all the time. Anybody came in with any wee bit news about what was going on round about the town, and Lairdy would just say, 'Aye, I heard something about that myself.'

We would say to him, we would say to Lairdy, 'Why d'you no tell us?'

Lairdy would shrug. 'Never thought about it,' he would say.

We would quiz him. We'd go, 'So what was the fire like then?'

Lairdy would just look at us as if we were all half-daft. 'A fire's a fire,' he would say. 'Just flames, you know.'

Now it wasn't as if Lairdy was ever in the habit of being stupid or cheeky, that he was into winding folk up; the simple plain truth of the matter was that Lairdy just never mentioned things, he never wanted to go on about anything, just wasn't his way. And, like I say, whenever he confirmed a story, he never elaborated or went on about it.

But see we all knew he could've: if he'd a mind to, he could've alright. Damn right he could.

The way I seen it, it was like having a telly that didn't work – you always felt like you were missing out on something. Just something to fill in the time, like, mean we weren't expecting world exclusives or juicy revelations or anything of that sort, but a wee bit diversion every now and then wouldn't exactly have done us any harm. A change from the usual diet of moaning and moaning, anyhow.

Now don't get me wrong, I liked Lairdy. Lairdy was alright. In all the time that he was here, I never once heard a bad word said against the fella. By the same token, you never heard of Lairdy taking the huff or having a go at anybody. Lairdy liked a laugh when we were all having a laugh. Lairdy never let anybody down at the job. For want of a better word, Lairdy was normal.

Even his quietness, there was nothing wrong with that. To be brutally honest, there's nothing worse than some mouth going off all the time, playing pinball with your lugs, forever telling you all what they've got to say about everything and anything.

But the thing with Lairdy was, he seemed to know about things that were interesting, genuinely interesting. Things you wanted to know about. But he just wouldn't let on.

Bearing all this in mind, all what I've been telling you, the time we go on about when we go on about Lairdy was the night of Rab Sterland's retirement do.

To let you understand, Rab was a foreman that used to be on our shift, but that had been ages ago, long before Lairdy was ever taken on. Chances were Lairdy wouldn't have known Rab from Adam, and vice versa come to that. So you can appreciate the wee bit surprise we got when we dished out the invites and Lairdy turned round and said, 'Aye, sure. No problem. I'll be there.' And to think, we'd only really asked him out of a sense of politeness.

When word got out that Lairdy was putting in an appearance, a few of the younger lads changed their minds and said they'd be coming along and all. The prospect of getting Lairdy on a night out, and plying him with drink, was proving too good an opportunity to let pass.

So, anyway. We'd gone ahead and booked the function suite up the Grange. It was fifteen quid a skull, and for that you got a buffet supper with a disco and bar till one. All in all, about forty were expected, us guys from the work accompanied by what passed for our various better halves.

We made a point of stressing as how we wanted everybody there for eight. With too many of these kind of affairs you just get folk turning up, showing face, then buggering off. You can also get the problem with some of them when they decide to get tanked up beforehand then come along half-cut and go ahead and ruin it for everybody else. Our idea was to make a night of it. Get everybody in from the start, keep them there, and get a bit of atmosphere going that we could all be a part of.

It was eight o'clock we asked for, and it was eight o'clock on the dot when Lairdy arrived.

Lairdy and guest.

Heads turned. I wouldn't be surprised if a few even spun.

To say the lass on his arm was a looker would've done her a chronic injustice. To say she was stunning to the point of staggering would've been no word of a lie. If the pair of them had about turned and walked straight back out, it wouldn't have mattered diddly. Just to've clapped eyes on this vision had been a rare privilege that would've sent yours truly for one to God's acre a very happy and contented man indeed.

Up until that moment, nobody'd really made much of a fuss of introducing their companions. At best all you'd got was an apologetic shrug, or a vague nod, as if to say, 'Well, this is her, I suppose.' The mumble that followed could've been anything.

You have to remember, though, that quiet as he was, Lairdy was always polite. So when Lairdy introduced his companion as being Kaye, his wife, we all felt compelled to make a decent job of introducing our motley crue.

Once all of this was out of the way – and we discovered that eight of the women present were either Jackie with a 'k' or Jacqui with a 'q' or Jaki J-a-k-i or Jakki J-a-k-k-i – it was time to move on to the business at hand, the serious business of having a good night out.

The Grange had done us proud. There was a good spread and

everybody promptly bombed round and helped themselves, then we all sat back down at this big, long banquet-type table that had been set up for us and got well and truly stuck in.

As is the way with these things, one end of the table was soon busy having a right good time, while the other end of the table was busy wondering why.

I was at the wondering end. Lairdy was at the fun end.

Not that Lairdy himself was responsible. Not directly, at any rate. No, it was Lairdy's wife, it was Kaye that was causing all the fuss.

The word spread down the table – Kaye was saying this, Kaye was saying that.

And what Kaye was saying was – interesting.

Soon, the disco started up, prompting the now traditional male rush to the bar and the toilet. All the excuses of the day to avoid having to shake your time-honoured groove thang.

The only bloke to set forth and trip the light fantastic was – you guessed it – Lairdy. Lairdy leading Rab Sterland's wife, Lorna, up onto the dancefloor.

At which point, eight of us from the work, the eight guys off the shift, just happened to casually saunter in the general direction of the seat so recently vacated by Lairdy.

And I got there first. I got the seat. The seat next to Kaye.

Not that the others were put off, mind. No, they just went and grabbed themselves the nearest available chairs and hauled them over. It ended up with the near-farcical situation that if the poor lass had been in a hurry to shift, she'd've had a full-scale obstacle course to contend with.

From the look of her, Kaye was going to be one of two things: she was either going to be elegant and sophisticated, or, to put it bluntly, she was going to be thick.

Wrong. Wrong on both counts.

What Kaye was was just a really nice person, really friendly, really down to earth. She kept her eye on you the whole time she was talking to you. I've always liked folk like that, folk that want you to listen to what they're saying, folk that want you to understand what they're saying. Kaye wasn't one of them that talks just 'cause they love the sound of their own voice.

And, boy, could she talk. Talk? Kaye herself had a better way of putting it. She said that back when she got her jags, the doctor had made the mistake of using a gramophone needle.

So there was us, me and the eight guys off the shift, paying more attention than we'd ever been paid to; transfixed, huddled round, asking questions like it was some kind of press conference, requesting clarification when we wanted to find out more.

And why not?

See we'd been deprived of all this. This was the side of Lairdy we knew existed. This was the source. This was Lairdy unplugged. This was what we'd been wanting all along. This was Mrs Lairdy.

Our assorted wives and girlfriends, meanwhile, were circled round the dancefloor, giving it plenty, clapping and cheering just like they were at the Chippendales. All of them wanting the next dance with Lairdy.

What they seen in him, I didn't know. To his credit, I suppose he must've been able to dance or else he wouldn't have went up there in the first place. Either that or he got a kick out of making a clown of himself.

A few comments were said to be doing the rounds to the effect that Lairdy's hands were wandering beyond the norm of accepted dancefloor etiquette. The general consensus on that matter, though, as much as we were bothered at any rate, was a resounding shrug.

So what. Who cared. We had other things to occupy our minds. Namely, Kaye coming away with all these stories of hers.

The only thing I can think to compare all this with would be some kind of religious experience, some kind of audience with a guru or something wherein you get everything explained to you – everything you've ever wanted to know, everything that there is to know – and, lo and behold, it all makes sense.

After a while you forgot how Kaye looked. Noh, well, hold on, that's as big a lie as any lie. You don't forget things like that. What I mean is it was what she was saying that we were all taken in by, all her news, views and opinions. It wouldn't have mattered how she looked.

We found out all about her, all about her and Lairdy, how they'd travelled here, there and everywhere but never seemed to settle. We found out everything that was going on round about the town. You name it, we found out about it. Kaye explained to us things we'd never quite understood. We heard all about things we never even had an inkling of.

Kaye took an interest in us as well. She wanted to know who we all were and what we all had to say for ourselves. I can't even begin trying to explain to you just how good it felt having somebody listening to you like that, taking an interest in you, wanting to find out all about you. We even found out things about each other we never knew. Listen to this one: two of us discovered that our grannies had been born in the same wee town. Think about it, they probably knew each other all those years ago. Christ, imagine not knowing that.

Just as we were getting round to hearing all about the planned redevelopment of the old paper mill, somebody grabbed a hold of me, reminded me that it was getting on, and how we were supposed to be making this presentation to Rab. We'd all chipped in and got him this carriage clock to mark his retirement.

In keeping with the spirit of the proceedings, however, we all felt it would be far, far better if Kaye were to do the honours. She was up for it, so on we went.

I got the DJ to cut the music – loud jeers from the female contingent at this point, I might add – and tried to get everybody to shoosh so's we could get a move on.

There was a problem, though. As luck would have it, my blasted camera wouldn't work.

Not that Rab was complaining, mind you, seeing as how he'd already got a kiss off Kaye for each of my three failed attempts.

It was then Lairdy took over. He asked if I wanted to use his camera. 'Noh,' I said, moving out of the way, fearful of this expensive-looking brute he was offering, 'on you go, just you go ahead and take the photos.'

So, Lairdy did his David Bailey. Kaye showed a good bit of leg and placed Rab's hand on it.

'Again,' shouted Rab, 'again. Another one.'

We were all of us laughing like I don't know what.

After the presentation we all went over and shook hands with Rab, telling him how much we'd miss him, to look after himself, all that kind of stuff.

Lairdy, meanwhile, was using up the rest of his spool, taking snaps of all the wives and girlfriends. We couldn't exactly see what was going on over there but from the racket they were making, the old imagination could fair let itself run riot as to what they were up to, as to what was going to appear in those photos.

Kaye stayed with us. She was really good to Rab. She told him how him and Lorna had to come round for tea some night, round to her's and Lairdy's. She told Rab that he wasn't to sit about wondering what to do with himself, he had to get out there, had to keep himself on the go.

Kaye then started giving it the three cheers for Rab bit. Rab was fair overcome. You could see he was holding back the tears.

The night kind of petered out after that. The younger ones – including Kaye and Lairdy – had to get away to let their sitters home. When Rab and Lorna left a few of the older ones took that as their cue and started heading and all.

Rab and Lorna were really pleased at the night. I could tell they meant it. I was pleased for them. Lorna – Holy Lorna, as Rab usually called her – said it was 'good to see all the young people behaving for once and not falling over drunk making nuisances of themselves'. To be honest, I hadn't noticed that, I hadn't noticed how little we'd all been drinking. Later on, the boy behind the bar told me how the takings for the night had been chronic. He made a joke of saying his boss had been wanting him to go round searching everybody for hip flasks.

Everybody was pretty much unanimous about the night. They all said how much they'd enjoyed it, what a good time they'd all had.

Folk said this to me I hadn't spoken a word to. Guys I know really well. I saw them leaving, headed them off at the door and gave my pathetic apologies for not spending any time with them. I said we shouldn't wait for an excuse before we all got together and did something like this again. Everybody was in agreement.

Everybody said it was a great night out, one of the best ever, if not the best.

Soon, all that remained was myself, the guys off the shift, and our respective partners. Myself and the guys off the shift at one end of the big, long banquet-style table, our partners at the other end.

All we wanted to do was talk about Kaye and Lairdy. Kaye, we all agreed, was one in a million, one in ten million, one in a billion even. And Lairdy? Well, Lairdy was alright, but, in the parlance of the day, the guy was simply not worthy, the guy should never've had a look in with the likes of Kaye.

D'you know not a word had passed between the pair of them all night? Not a single word. Fact: from the moment they arrived right up until the moment they left there was always one of us within earshot and we knew for certain that Kaye and Lairdy had not spoken so much as a single word to each other all night.

One of the guys suggested that maybe they weren't getting on, that maybe they weren't speaking. It didn't seem like that, though. Nah, it just seemed more like they were into going off and doing their own thing. Kaye ranting, Lairdy dancing.

After a while, our conversation dried up. This wasn't entirely surprising, mind you, seeing as how we had, after all, lost our muse. There was also the fact that we were all of us as sober as a pile of bricks. A work's night out and all.

We all just sat there, me and the guys off the shift, the nine of us, wondering about things, wondering about how things had turned out, wondering about what was happening.

I was just about getting ready to call it a night when I noticed as how the other end of the table had fallen silent as well. All our various wives and girlfriends, all of them that had not so long ago been out there acting it up like a bunch of teenyboppers, making right proper arses of themselves, they were like we were, not saying anything, not looking like they were going to say anything either. All of them just kind of looking at us, in the same daft way that all of us were kind of looking at them.

THE MAN WHO BELIEVED IN LOVE

Much as it all started off as a joke, with me gagging at the mention of his name, or making my excuses and leaving whenever he appeared, if truth be known, I never wished for Robbie anything but the worst.

The guy just really irritated me. Give you an example: I was trailing round Willie Lows one day, getting in the messages, when this announcement comes over the tannoy, 'Would Mr William Burnett please report to the cream of tartar section. Mr William Burnett. Thank you.'

That's right, cream of tartar. Ever tried to find cream of tartar down Willie Lows? Not an easy job. Anyway, eventually, I did find it. So there I was, straining my eyes, doing my Mr Magoo, as I browsed intensely through all these wee containers of cream of tartar, bicarbonate of soda, glacé cherries and the like when up hops Robbie.

'Boo!' he goes. 'Boo!'

'Cause Robbie always goes 'Boo!' when he hops up on you unexpected. 'Boo!' Like that. 'Boo!'

And whenever he appeared – at least whenever he sneaked up on me, at any rate – he would always be hopping. His leg would always be bothering him, and he'd've unstrapped it and be carting it about, hod-like, over his shoulder.

Robbie thought getting his auntie in the delicatessen to put a message over the tannoy requesting me to report to the cream of tartar section was funny, really funny. I didn't. I thought it was stupid, really stupid.

The next thing, of course, when Robbie was around, was the ritual sacrificing of the shoulder. 'Cause that's what you did;

when Robbie's leg was bothering him, and he had to carry it, you had to offer your shoulder for him to lean on.

So, picture it, there's me pushing a no-wheel drive trolley round a busy, first Thursday of the month, Willie Lows with this oversized parrot locking its claws into my shoulder.

Apparently, a few folk, when they got to hear of it – the cream of tartar business – did find it funny. Margaret thought it was funny. When I told her, she thought it was funny. When Robbie told her, she was in hysterics.

Anyway, that's just one example, one example of how I came to hate Robbie. Mostly, though, I hated Robbie 'cause of the grief he caused between me and Margaret.

See Robbie loved Margaret. It was no secret. Everybody knew about it. Went on about it all the time. Used to kiss her on the hand. Used to take off his leg, go down on his knee, kiss her on the hand, and go, 'Oh, Margaret, I love you.'

And I'd be thinking to myself; Aye, right, and I suppose muggins here's going to have to slip a disc getting you back up on all ones again, eh?

Of course, to be fair, it wasn't just Margaret he went on at. It was all the women. There he'd be, going round like something out of Mills and Boon, praising them all the time, going on about how 'young' they all looked, how 'beautiful' they all were, how he 'worshipped the very ground they walked upon'.

Robbie always said he had it the best way: he was in love with thirty women, none of whom had ever shown him the slightest grief. When they heard this, all the women would go, 'Ahhhh, that's nice.'

When I heard it, I would go, Ahhhh, that's pish.

But only under my breath. See, thing was, you couldn't really say a word against Robbie.

'But, Christ,' I would say, 'could he not even see about getting one that fit, getting a leg that fits?'

'In love with thirty women and never had any grief off any of them? Aye, that'll be right. Believe that and you'll believe anything.'

But in my attempt to share these notions, I was never

particularly aware of any kindred spirits piping up to voice their agreement. In fact, more often than not, my comments gave birth to a stony silence that only gave way when somebody said something like, 'Can't be easy for the poor laddie, right enough' or – the favourite – 'Terrible thing to have to happen to you, that'.

The question of whether or not folk actually liked Robbie had nothing to do with it. The fact was Robbie *had* to be liked, Robbie *had* to be put up with.

And I couldn't handle it. Couldn't handle it to the extent that where there should, on my desk, rest a beautifully framed, daily-dusted photograph of Margaret, there rests instead a beautifully framed, daily-dusted photostat of a *decree nisi*.

Believe me, I tried to get on with the guy. For the sake of Margaret, for the sake of our marriage and just out of common decency, I made every effort I could to sympathise, to make allowances, to understand how the guy must've been feeling, knowing that each and every day of his life he'd have to overcome difficulties the likes of which I'd a struggle to even contemplate.

I gave Robbie the benefit of the doubt. I tried to be mates. We went out for a few drinks, we went up the match, we went to the pictures, the arcades, we even went shopping. Always, though, it would be the same. Robbie would ask how Margaret was. 'She's fine,' I would say, 'she's fine.' Then Robbie would get all anxious, all worked up and worried about her. 'Listen,' he would say, 'just you stay and enjoy yourself. I'll away and keep Margaret company, alright.' 'Away you go,' I'd say. But, nah, with one mighty bound, Robbie was off. He'd always find some excuse relating to his leg – too hot, too cold, too damp, too much sitting, too much standing, too much moving about – that meant he was uncomfortable. And Robbie would never hear of me going home and all. Oh no, I was to stay out and enjoy myself. After all, he said, how often did I get time to myself. And you want to have heard the earful I got if I did go home. 'You keeping checks on me?' said Margaret. 'Away you out, out and enjoy yourself. Away you go. Out.'

I said to Robbie one time, 'Look, are you obsessed with Margaret or something?'

Robbie beamed. Of course he was. Margaret was wonderful. So beautiful. Such a warm, kind-hearted person.

Robbie told me about the happiest he'd ever been. It was a dream he'd had. In the dream he'd been working in Boots, on the ground floor, manning the perfume counter. Margaret had come into the shop. Margaret was so pleased to see Robbie she'd ran up and gave him a great, big cuddle. A cuddle that went on for ages. Hours.

Robbie was chuffed when he was telling me this. He wasn't smug. He wasn't confrontational. He wasn't ashamed or even embarrassed. If anything, he was euphoric. He said so himself, 'That was it,' he said, all dreamy-eyed with the memory, 'that was the ultimate.'

I'd never heard the like. Was this guy winding me up or what? A cuddle? In a dream? With my wife? And I was supposed to be pleased about this?

In no sense of the word could you've called Robbie a rival. He wasn't after Margaret for himself. Yes, he loved her. But he loved all these other women and all. He was always in love.

I queried whether this love – in a general sense – ever transgressed into lust.

Robbie was affronted.

He wasn't the only one.

The next time he seen Margaret I got every heartless, dirty-minded bastard under the sun.

'But,' I said, 'there's nothing wrong with him. Apart from missing a limb, there's nothing wrong with him. He's just the same as the rest of us. He's just the same as you or I would be if – God forbid – you or I ever had some kind of accident that meant losing a limb.'

'No,' Margaret said, 'there's nothing wrong with him, absolutely nothing wrong with him. But what you don't realise, sunshine, what you don't understand, is what's *right* with him, what's *good* about him.'

I told her about the cuddle, the dream cuddle. It wasn't news.

Robbie had told her ages ago. I hypothesised. 'But what if I'd told you I'd had that dream, and it'd been, I don't know, say, wee Jean Foster, what would you've said then?'

'But you,' said Margaret, 'are not Robbie . . . And, anyway, what's wee Jean Foster got to do with all this?'

First name that came to my head. Didn't save me from wearing my dinner, mind you.

Getting Margaret to turn against Robbie wasn't going to work – so I tried my hand at getting Robbie to turn against Margaret.

I made out how Margaret was awfy concerned about everybody, how it wasn't just Robbie. I even implied that there was another other man. Somebody Margaret was awfy pally with, somebody Margaret was spending an awfy lot of time with. Not somebody she was involved with, like, just somebody she was concerned about, awfy worried about. Mean really worried about. Of course, when I told him, Robbie just hopped off, grassed us off and I had some rather complicated explaining to do.

Nevertheless, I persevered.

I tried to exert my influence.

I tried irritating Robbie. 'One leg, eh? Must be a few funny stories happened to you over the years, Robbie. Tell us your funny stories then. You not got any funny stories? Surely you must have funny stories, Robbie? Come on, Robbie! Think!'

I tried to be paternal, tried to induce some kind of guilt. 'Now look, Robbie, listen, take it from me, right, this is for your own good, but teasing and making trouble for folk isn't big, it isn't clever and you know, nine times out of ten its practitioners are found to be wanting, mean seriously wanting. Get a life, pal.'

I tried to get Robbie fixed up. 'How 'bout those two over there, eh? Let's go for it, my man.'

And that was the beginning of the end.

'What?' said Margaret. 'You were out chasing women?'

I explained my intentions. If Robbie had a woman of his own, then maybe he wouldn't be hanging round everyone else's.

'If Robbie wants a woman, he's big enough and daft enough to go out and get one. What I want to know is what *you* were up to?'

I explained my methodology. Robbie was a bit on the shy side. Working as a team we'd be more likely to succeed. That was how you did these things.

'You seem to know an awfy lot about all this, all this chasing women business. And what was she like, this woman you were after?'

I made myself clear. I wasn't after a woman for me, I was after a woman for Robbie. The woman in question – the woman for Robbie – was a nice wee lassie, a nice ordinary wee lassie, just a lassie.

It was then I worked out a new plan. Male-bonding.

'Look,' I said, 'you maybe think you know Robbie, but deep down inside, Robbie's still a man, he thinks male thoughts, deep down inside, he thinks the same as me, and, deep down inside, I think the same as him. I know what he's thinking.'

It was one of those historic moments when I thought what I was saying was the smartest thing ever said by anybody.

So you can appreciate my wee bit surprise when Margaret went up the stairs, packed a couple of bags, took the car round to her mother's and, a week later, citing mental cruelty and philandering, phoned to say she'd initiated divorce proceedings.

It went to court. I had to stand up in court and talk about all this.

And for ten days I did stand up in court and talk about all this. Giving it the truth, the whole truth and nothing but the truth.

I expected a degree of recognition. I expected folk to say, or at least think, 'Aye, I see what you mean, right enough. I can understand what you're saying.'

But when I looked up at the increasingly packed galleries, all I ever saw were all these shaking heads that didn't have a clue what I was on about.

Don't ask me how, but the story made the papers. The tabloids wanted blood. *Mine*. The *Sun* ran a feature – 'The Jealousy Junkies' – wherein my photo appeared alongside those of Adolf Hitler, Saddam Hussein and Jeffrey Dahmer. The *Record* ran a feature – 'The Jaundiced Junta' – wherein my caricature appeared alongside those of Napoleon, Freddy Krueger and the Devil.

Meanwhile, to add insult to ignominy, Robbie was getting groomed for nothing less than sainthood. The *Sun* did a 'Robbie's Guide – Twenty Top Tips On Griefless Love'. The *Record* did a 'Robbie's Guide – Twenty Top Tips On How To Love Your *Women*'. Robbie became the first person to appear with both Richard and Judy and Anne and Nick in the same morning. He made a programme with Esther Rantzen and some handicapped kids. Robbie was a hero to the kids. A national celebrity, full of goodness, full of love, who'd triumphed in the face of adversity, who'd overcome terrible odds, who'd suffered both physical torment and mental anguish, yet had come through it all unscathed, unrepentant and undaunted.

A lot of folk were surprised I didn't get put away. It was, after all, only a divorce. Even so, I got hate mail. Sackloads of the stuff. I got my windows put in. I had to give up my job, due to 'ill-health'. Then one day I seen kids spraying 'Jealous Bastard' on the side of my car. I chased them down the street. Later that night, two guys with baseball bats reminded me of this as they kicked down my door and proceeded to smash my legs to bits.

I ended up in hospital. Robbie came to visit me, accompanied, as ever, by reporters and photographers from the *Sun* and the *Record*.

The photographers wanted what they called 'natural light'. This meant closing every curtain within a three-mile radius then setting up a lamp the likes of which could easily have sufficed as the gravitational centre to a small planetry system.

I was needing my bed-pan changed. My lawyer, though, who'd got word of the visit, was getting me to wheesht. Not that anybody would've bothered, mind you. Robbie was around. Orderly queues were forming to get his autograph. Relatives were saying, 'You couldn't possibly come over and have a wee word with my Auntie Bessie, could you?'

Eventually, it came time to do the photos. The guy from the *Sun* said, 'Right, Robbie, catalogue shots. Okay?'

Robbie sat on the edge of my bed.

I wondered what the hell was going on. *Catalogue shots?*

The photographer guy clicked his fingers. 'Three two one . . . Go.'

'Hey,' said Robbie, 'look over there.' I looked over there.

'Hey,' said Robbie, 'what's that?' I looked down in my lap.

'Hey,' said Robbie, 'look at this.' I looked at his palm.

And that was that. Catalogue shots.

'Thanks, Robbie.' The guy from the *Sun* started packing up. 'See you around sometime.'

The journalists came forward. 'Anything to say, Robbie?'

Robbie nodded. 'I just want to say that I think violence is a terrible thing. I think that things like this are terrible. Thank you.'

The journalists turned to me.

'Well . . .'

But before I could snarl out another syllable my lawyer was manhandling everybody away out the road. 'Come on now,' he said, 'let the lad have his rest.'

Robbie got up to go.

'So,' I said, 'how's Margaret these days?'

Robbie nodded. 'Fine. Doing away. She sends her regards.'

'Good,' I said. 'I'm pleased to hear that – that she's doing fine.'

'Well,' said Robbie, 'you look after yourself, okay. I hope everything turns out alright for you.'

Robbie offered his hand.

I tellt him what he could do with it.

'No, Robbie, I'm not one for forgiving and forgetting. You've caused me a lot of grief, pal, grief I've as yet to see the back of, grief that'll probably be with me till my dying day. No, Robbie, take your hand. There's plenty round here would be glad of it.' I fixed him in the eye before I added, 'But always mind, I'm not one of them.'

Robbie shook his head.

'You just don't understand, do you?' he said. 'After all you've ever been through, after all you've ever said – to me, to Margaret, to everybody else – all your lecturing, all your snidey wee comments, all your stirring, all of that stuff in the court, all your theories, all your daft wee ideas, you just haven't understood that you're the only person who thought any of this mattered, that it made the slightest bit of difference to anybody.'

I pointed towards the door.

'I'm going,' said Robbie. 'I'm going. Like the man says, see you around sometime.'

And with that, Robbie walked away: only faltering to exaggerate his limp when a pretty nurse came round the corner.

CHOOSING

The whole town was on about it. I'm not saying that they were all on about it all the time, like, but guaranteed, they were all, each and every one of them, at least going out of their way to mention it.

That is, to mention the subject of Troy's new woman.

To be precise: Troy's new woman with them seriously pingable wing-nut lugs; Troy's new woman with that right tight, right severe, jet-black straight as a die ponytail; Troy's new woman that's never as yet been seen to surrender so much as a slip of a smile; Troy's new woman that's got all the meat of a dosser's last roll-up; and Troy's new woman that's always in skin-tight Levi jeans, big, baggy Levi jackets and plain black T-shirts.

In other words, Troy's new woman that's the living and breathing double of none other than the town's number one weirdo; the one and only Danny Lamb.

Danny Lamb, man.

Talk about a total bugsy.

'Cause like everybody round here knows Danny Lamb. Noh, well, hold on, that's not what I mean, what I mean is everybody round here knows *of* Danny Lamb. In the same way as we all know all the prozzies, all the druggies and all the nutters, we all of us know the Danny Lambs of this world. Like I say, just a total bugsy, man, just a file-under-avoid-like-the-plague. Take Our Denise, she even stays up the same stair as the freak. Not have nothing to do with him but. As she says: it's them wing-nut lugs of his; that right tight, right severe, jet-black ponytail; that face that never smiles; and that denim-clad, see-thru skinny, emaci-ated excuse for a body.

And as for Troy, man; well, mean what can you say? Mean Troy always does alright with the lassies. Christ, I could rhyme off a whole stream of his exes without even having to bother myself with stopping and thinking about it. Always been like that and all. Troy was into women when nine out of ten of the rest of us still had dicks called Willie. Inasmuch as there was a town stud then Troy was that very man.

And, while I mind, another thing; not only that but Troy's not one of them that goes out and makes his porridge out of paracetamol when he has to go without his ride. Mind one night when he was over talking to us, when we were on about that very subject, when what Troy had to say on the matter was how he couldn't stand the likes of that, guys who when they got dumped by a woman, or finished with a woman, whatever, just went out and flung themselves and all their fivers at the feet of the nearest available bit of skirt. Panicking, Troy called it, the sign of a weak man; the sign of a weak, desperate and pathetic man. Christ, he said, that was no way to treat a woman, you had to treat a woman with a wee bit respect, had to treat a woman like she was something special, somebody special, like, 'cause, hey, come on, to you, she had to be special or else you wouldn't've blasted well chose her in the first place, now would you? 'Cause see that's what it was all about, according to Troy, like, *choosing*. That was the word, that was the very word, the exact word. If I mind right, what Troy's actual words were, what Troy actually said was, 'If you've got a choice, then you choose, you take your time and you choose.' There you go. Quoted.

And what Troy had went and chosen was as near as damn the living and breathing double of the one and only Danny Lamb?

Talk about your thought-provoking.

Aye, tell me about it.

You had to wonder what Troy was playing at. Mean surely to God he must've realised, must've noticed, must've been aware. Come on. We're not talking passing resemblance here, by the way, we're talking Harmony Hairspray stuff, we're talking *is that or isn't it?* When I say Danny Lamb's double, I mean Danny Lamb's double. Same hair, same lugs, same height, same size, same shape, same clothes, same look, same flaming bloody everything.

In addition to all this – what for want of a better word you'd call the evidence – there were a couple of fairly substantial rumours doing the rounds: one had it that the lassie's name was actually – wait till you get a load of this – Danielle; it was also being uttered in certain quarters that before she teamed up with Troy that this Danielle character had a wee bit weight about her, that her hair was all different and that to all intents and purposes she was quite a cheery kind of soul who favoured flowery frocks and sported a pair of lugs that had never been known to merit so much as the merest of mentions.

Either way, whether all that was all right or whether all that was all wrong, that didn't alter the facts of the matter, and the facts of the matter were as plain as the lugs on their skulls – the lassie was Danny Lamb in all but gender.

Not that I was saying that, of course. Not that any of us were saying that. Word gets round when you start saying things like that. Like I say, anything likely to earn you a burst mouth and there'll always be plenty queueing up to point the finger in your direction, point the finger at you for being the one that actually went ahead and said it. And, believe me, Troy's not the type you want to give an excuse to. Mean he's a mate, like, and he's alright, like, but see for all that he's calmed down over the years; well, let's just say there's not too many of us as would bet against him dishing out a few skelps if the mood so took him.

Especially when you consider the subject at hand. Talk about delicate.

It ended up with the situation where, say, you'd maybe bump into one of your mates, walking down the road or whatever, and after a wee while your mate would maybe cagily say something along the lines of, 'You've no seen the new bit of stuff Troy's kicking about with, have you?'

Then you'd go, 'Aye, think I seen them over the town the other day there . . . Kind of minds me of somebody, though.'

'Aye?' your mate would say. 'Well, it's funny you should be saying that cause I just heard somebody outside, eh, ih, eh – now where was it again? Argees? Aye, Argees, Argees it was – and what they were saying was how the lassie in question bore more than a slight resemblance to that bloke – now what is it that you call him again, him that stays up over Richie's Court, up the top?'

'What, Danny? Danny Lamb?'

'Aye, aye, that's the fellow.'

'Aye, suppose so. Aye, suppose when you come to think about it. Aye, I can see what they mean, right enough.'

'. . .'

'. . .'

And that's about as much as you'd get. From that moment on panic would ensue, thoughts would turn to burst mouths and the conversation would tan a hairpin that would see you talking about something that was about as undeniably bland as the affairs of Troy, Danny Lamb and Danielle were undeniably interesting.

And that was about the size of it – the classic case of something going on being something you weren't able to go on about.

Talk about doing your head in.

Talk about doing *my* head in.

'Cause I'll warn you here and now; see me, I am the world's worst when it comes to minding my own business. I've got to know everything. I've got to tell everybody. I tell wives what their husbands've been up to. I tell husbands what their wives've been up to. See them chat-lines things? Telling you, I ran up a bloody fortune on them. Used to put the light out, put a hankie over the mouthpiece and spend my nights going on about all what was going on round about here. Another thing – see I love talking to the police. I see one of them walking down the road, right, I'll cross the road to talk to them. It's no something I'm proud of, like, but there you go, that's yours truly for you, that's what I'm like. As my mother always says, 'See you,' she says, 'you're nothing but a clipe.'

If there's one thing, though, that's guaranteed to keep my trap shut, it's the potential for physical violence. Know it sounds like an awfy obvious thing to say and all that but I am terrified of violence. Petrified. I mean real violence, like: real pain; real blood; real broken bones. Know this, I'll not even sit down to watch the wrestling without quaking in my boots.

And that's why I was never saying a thing. That's why none of us were ever saying a thing. When we were mentioning it to each other, that's all we ever did, we *mentioned* it. Them rumours I was telling you about, that was all early stuff, that was all ages ago, that was all nipped in the bud as soon as the fear factor became the first and foremost factor.

Mean I've plenty of mates, like, plenty of folk I stop and have a blether with, but there's none of them, not one of them, I would trust about as far as a broken-legged bairn could overhead kick them. For all I knew, I'd be telling them, they'd be off telling Troy, and I'd end up with a gig in accident and emergency.

Aye, right.

No chance.

My lips were so tight you couldn't see the join.

Then one night – when I was just sitting here watching the telly, like, just watching a wee bit of the old bit snooker, you know – it dawned on me, there was one guy I could trust to go round and see and talk about all this, one guy I knew for certain who wouldn't be rushing off round to Troy and grassing us off.

Obvious when you come to think about it, eh; who else other than the man himself, the one and only Danny Lamb.

Talk about your flashes of inspiration.

I turned down the snooker and worked out all the possibilities, all the potential pitfalls. I'd get to say all what I was wanting to say, but I'd get to say all what I was wanting to say in the form of questions. It would be Danny Lamb as would be making all the directly quotable comments, and in the cold light of day, when any burst mouths were getting dished out, it would be Danny Lamb as would be 'the attributable one'.

As to when I should go round; well, I decided it would have to be after one of my back-shifts. That way I'd be under cover of darkness for when I was heading out and also, obviously, I'd be under cover of darkness for when I was heading home. Mean it's not as if I'd be wanting to be seen up at Danny Lamb's now, would I? Christ, no. Christ, under normal circumstances you wouldn't want to be seen anywhere near the likes of Danny Lamb's even if it said in the papers that the freak was standing there dishing out free tenners. And, hey, this was anything but your normal circumstances.

Anyway, that was me made my mind up. I was going round to Danny Lamb's.

The day of reckoning duly arrived – my next again back-shift, like. I set about getting myself ready: first, I put on an old army surplus coat of mine the mother gave us for my Xmas years ago but which I'd never once got round to actually wearing; next, I turned the team's tammy outside in, then put it on back to front; finally, I put on five pair of socks before I put my shoes on. You get given a lot of shite up the TA but one thing I always mind them telling us was how you could always recognise one of your own from the way they walked. It's true and all. Telling you, see if I see someone, no matter how far away they are, as long as I can see them, and as long as they're moving, I can tell you all you'd ever need to know about them.

It was round about the back of midnight when I eventually headed off. Everything was going just as I'd planned it. By the time I was halfway, I was limping so bad you'd have thought my pins were made of molten rubber. Perfect. To've recognised me you'd've needed to've been a regular with at least twelve years' service.

Round about half an hour after I'd left the house I was finally standing outside the entrance to Danny Lamb's close. But, before I headed up the stair, I was wanting to carry out just one last precaution.

I was wanting the close lights out.

I went along the line of lock-ups. The last of the doors had a sign on the front: 'DANGER!' it said. 'Electricity,' it said. 'Improper use carries a maximum penalty of £1000 fine or six months' imprisonment.'

I got out my screwdriver.

Talk about a piece of piss. The lock was that jiggered, if I'd wanted to I could've tanned it with a toothbrush.

Behind the door, mounted on the wall, was a nest of wires

leading to a rusty old panel. On the panel were two switches. One of the switches was green, the other switch was red. One had to be for the close power, one had to be for the close lights.

A stereo was going on on the bottom landing. If I hit the wrong switch, the music would cut and me and my five pair of socks would have to high-tail it faster than the proverbial rodent tanning the proverbial aqueduct.

I minded my training.

Combinations.

Greenhouse? Greenclose? Redhouse? Redclose?

Nah.

Initials.

GH? GC? RH? RC?

Nah.

Associations.

Red for stop? Green for go? Red for danger? Green for go!

Aye, aye. Hold on. That was it.

Green for go. Go outside.

I hit the switch, the green one.

The lights went out.

I listened.

The stereo stayed on – just like I knew fine it would.

I hitched up my socks and tanned the steps three at a time. Eighteen mighty bounds later I was gasping for breath outside Danny Lamb's door.

I opened up the letterbox. Just to have a wee listen, like. Just to see if I could hear the freak stoating about.

Aye, and I could hear him alright, oh aye I could hear him, could hear his telly blaring away. That's exactly the type of weirdo we're dealing with here, by the way. Christ, imagine it, imagine watching telly at this time of night.

I chaps the door.

Next thing I hears is a wee confab going on out in the hall, going on out in Danny Lamb's hall.

Talk about surprise.

Talk about me shitting it.

What if it was Troy that was in there? What if I'd disturbed them? What if they were up to . . .

I thought about tanning a runner.

It was too late.

The door was opening.

And there he was.

The wing-nut lugs. The right tight, right severe, jet-black ponytail. The face that's never been seen to smile. The jeans. The black T-shirt. And that body – you want to see the thing. Talk about the gable-end of a five-pound note.

'Alright, Danny,' I says.

Danny gives us a nod. 'Brizo, innit?'

I nods. 'Was just passing round, like. Thought I'd maybe pop up and see how you were doing. Long time no see and that, you know.'

Danny nods. He steps aside to let us in.

As I walks up the lobby, the smell of spleg hits us like a kick in the ribs.

But that's nothing compared to the surprise I gets when I gets through the living-room and sees, sitting on the settee – sitting on Danny Lamb's settee, like – none other than my mate Rusty with Rusty's mate Jed. Not only that but lying on the floor is Tango from the TA and Smudge from my work.

Not that you'd've recognised any of them, mind you. Not from what they were wearing at any rate. Talk about disguises. Aye, I'll give you disguises alright. I thought I was bad with the five pair of socks, but Tango, Christ, he must've had on about ten. And as for Rusty, Jed and Smudge, well they'd all had a serious attack of the retros, and were all done up in first-generation rave gear with all the hooded tops, baggy jeans and boots the size of wheely-buckets.

Just as I was beginning to think I'd stepped into the house of Mr and Mrs Twilight Zone, this squeaky wee voice pipes up, coming out of the living-room cupboard, going, 'Is it alright, Danny. Can I come out now?'

I looks over at Danny. Danny looks over at me.

I goes over and opens up the cupboard door.

'Alright, Denise,' I says.

Our Denise, mind, that says she'd never in a month of Sundays be having anything to do with the likes of Danny Lamb; and here she was hiding in one of his cupboards with one of our mother's best wigs half on all because somebody had dared to chap his flaming door.

Talk about dee-dee dah-dah dee-dee dah-dah.

Aye, right.

'Eh, be back in a minute,' says Danny. 'I'll just away down and shove the close lights back on.'

Danny left us. I took the opportunity to stare Our Denise out and think about things; pretty soon reaching the less than startling conclusion that all of us less than great minds had kind of all went and all thought alike.

Not that I was wanting to say that, of course, so I just said the first thing that came to mind: 'What the hell are you doing here?'

To which the reply was – nothing. Not even a loud blink. So I just thought, right, fuck it, just go for it, my man, just ruffle a few feathers, on you go, sunshine, you can do it, just ask the biggie. 'Okay,' I says, 'tell us then, eh, what is it that's going down between Troy and Danny Lamb?'

But still, no response. Just a case of everybody shaking their heads, shrugging their shoulders and displaying their nonplussed ten to two palms.

Danny returned. Something flickered between the eyes of him and the eyes of Our Denise. Next thing anybody knew Denise was saying, 'See yous all later then,' and her and Danny were heading back out into the hall.

Danny made a point of shutting the living-room door behind him.

I made a point of going over and pressing my ear right up against it.

Whereupon I heard the distinctive sound of smoochy giggles.

Talk about love's young dream.

I was just about to pass some crappy comment when I couldn't help but notice as how the others were all somewhat otherwise engrossed.

Smudge was skinning up. Rusty, Jed and Tango, meanwhile, were all sitting there busy watching the telly.

And, in keeping with everything else that was going on, what was going on on the telly was downright weird and all, 'cause what was going on on the telly was the new Big Arnie, the new Big Arnie that wasn't even on up at the pictures yet.

Danny came back in.

'Hey, my man,' I says, pointing to what was on the telly, 'where d'you get this from?'

'The brother,' says Danny. 'Works as a projectionist down in London. Sends us up these copies of all the new releases.'

'Nice one,' I says and gets the jacket off just as Big Arnie flings this bloke off the roof of this multi-storey office building.

'Oh, ya fucker,' I says and tans a hit of Rusty's spliff as the guy lands smack right back on the roof of this big olive-green stretch limo.

'Jees-oh,' I says and helps myself to a decent slug out this big bottle of juice that's lying in the middle of the floor as the car explodes with more flames than your Mr and Mrs Pyromaniac could ever hope to dream of.

Then we're all dead quiet, all dead silent, so's not to miss the comment, so's not to miss Big Arnie's punchline.

Big Arnie, he just looks down, just looks down on all the carnage and goes, 'Many times do I have to tell you? No fucking sugar.'

What a line. What a fucking line. 'Many times do I have to tell you? No fucking sugar.'

And then, would you believe it, the bastarn fucking credits go and roll. What a bummer. I'm sitting there, all disappointed and everything. 'Hey,' I says, 'any chance of a second show, my man?'

But Rusty and Jed, like, they're getting up, saying as how they've got their work in the morning. Tango, though, he's on days off. He says he's into it. It's all up to the Smudge-ster; oh, fuck it, he says, he's due one of his annual sickies, anyway.

We all look pleadingly at Danny.

'All the same to me, boys,' he says. 'Tell you what, though, could do with stocking up on the old bit munchies routine.'

So we all dips into our pockets and I increases my popularity by bringing out my emergency fiver – which, incidentally, I always store in my wallet in the compartment next to my library ticket.

Then we do one-potato two-potato to see who's going to have to trail all the way over to the all-night garage. Smudge and Tango lose out. I has a wee laugh to myself trying to imagine Tango and his ten pair of socks traversing the good old rickety-rackety railway bridge.

Now with Rusty and Jed off for the night, and with Smudge and Tango away for the munchies, you'll have worked out that that just left myself – myself alone with Danny.

Danny Lamb.

And his wing-nut lugs.

And his right tight, right severe, jet-black ponytail.

And his unsmiling face.

And his jeans.

And his black T-shirt.

And his see-thru skinny, emaciated body.

I was watching him.

Danny put on some cool sounds – right mellow stuff, kind of jazzy, like, kind of trip-hop stuff, you know, but not too wanky, know what I mean – and started dancing about, all that chill-out leading with the jaw kind of vibe.

Me and my five pair of socks started dancing and all, getting into the grooves, man, just trying to relax, just going with the old bit grooves, you know.

Anyway, fuck it, it was time to do or it was time to die, it was time to go for it or it was time to go home, it was time to put up or it was time to shut up, it was time to broach my subject: the subject of Troy, Danny Lamb and the mysterious – nay, extraordinary – duplicature that went by the name of Danielle.

But before I moved on to that, though, there was one other wee small matter I was wanting cleared up.

'Eh, Danny,' I says, 'you shafting Our Denise?'

Danny just kept going with the grooves, passed us over the spliff, fixed us in the eye and gave us a big, slow nod.

Fair enough, I thinks to myself, and 'Fair enough,' I says. Not that myself, you understand, personally speaking, that I was bothering my arse one way or the other, like, just kind of curious that was all.

Anyway, that was the wee small matter out the way, it was time to move on to the great big matter.

'Eh, Danny,' I says, vibing away, 'you seen the new bit of stuff that Troy's kicking about with these days?'

Aye, said Danny, he'd had seen her alright. Aye, said Danny, he'd noticed the slight resemblance. But, no, said Danny, other than that there wasn't what you'd call a whole heap more to say on the matter. Mean, don't get me wrong, we talked about it, like, me and Danny, talked long and hard about it, in fact. I asked all sorts of questions, Danny came away with all sorts of answers, but there was nothing coming forth that could in any way, shape or form be called intriguing let alone illuminating. There was no goings-on between Danny and Troy – never had been – and there was no bit of history that even remotely connected the pair of them.

'But, Christ, Danny,' I says, 'the lassie's your double.'

Danny just laughed.

It wasn't long till the Smudge-ster and the limping, lop-sided, agonised Tango returned and we all settled down to feed our faces and watch Big Arnie's latest. What a classic it was and all. Telling you, it never even spoiled it knowing the ending. 'Many times do I have to tell you? No fucking sugar.'

It was round about the back of four when we eventually called it a night. I pulled down my tammy, Tango and Smudge pulled up their hoods, and the three of us bid our farewells to Danny and headed off into the cool of the early morning.

You'll not be surprised to hear we had a bit to talk about as we made our way down the road. Tango and Smudge explained as how they'd gone round to Danny's for pretty much the same reason I had – their noses had been bothering them. But as to any kind of further information, any sort of enlightenment; well, like Danny, they were about as much use as a black bulb.

The one thing that did stir my sense of curiosity, mind you, was when they let on just how long they'd been going round, been going round to Danny's. This was them on their eighth visit. They'd been going round there for over a month now. And they weren't the only ones: Jessica was a regular, and Stevo, and Frog, and Butlins, and Daegsy. All sorts of folk. Apparently, according to Smudge and Tango, like, when Robin Forsyth went round he had on his sister's clothes.

That, I just didn't believe. That, I just had to see.

And that I have seen.

Yeah, that's right, I've been back, back round to Danny's, back round to Danny Lamb's. Been about three months since my first visit now. Usually go round a couple of times a week – when I'm on my back-shifts, like – take in a flick, smoke some blow, see my mates and feed my face. No bad, eh? Nah, but it's good round at Danny's. Kind of strange, like, but good, a good night out.

The latest regarding Troy and Danielle, by the way, is that they're shacked up the gether. The latest regarding Danny and Our Denise is that they're heading that same way and all. Fine by me. I like Danny. Grown to be quite fond of the fellow actually. Quite often go away with him at the weekends, when he's away flogging them dodgy videos of his round the markets and car-boot sales. You've maybe seen us sometime. To be honest, these days, Danny's just about near enough my best mate. Funny, when you come to think about it, though, eh. Mean funny how sometimes you choose your mates.

LIFE ON A SCOTTISH COUNCIL ESTATE VOL. 3 CHAP. 3

Okay, it's the middle of February, it's one o'clock in the morning, so where do you reckon me and my visitors decided to go once we'd prepared and necked the mushies? Why, up the woods, of course – where, given the month, the day and the hour, it is pitch black and seriously fucking freezing. The Big Man is well freaked out: he's got a slight problem with disappearing digits. 'Anybody seen my fingers. I've lost three fingers.' He keeps counting them. 'One, two, three, four, five, six . . . Oh, no. God, help me! Help me, God!' God, meanwhile, would maybe be better advised to protect poor Stuart. 'Cause poor Stuart is in real danger of dying up here. As in, death by murder. He's going round asking everybody all the time what their hit's like. Regardless of answers, Stuart's all pompous and going, 'No, no, no. It's no like that, it's like this. It's supposed to be like this.' On and on he goes. 'No, no, no. You shouldn't be feeling like that, you should be feeling like this . . .' Talking of all things termination, by the way, Wee Harry and Wendy aren't far from Murder One either. Wee Harry has decided to go green. 'Look,' he says, pointing to the trees, 'it's all artificial. It's all the same fucking tree, man. To think, some cunt took all this down, and then some other cunt went and put it all back. But it's all the same fucking tree. It might as well be fucking concrete. Look!' Then he goes and points to a tree. 'Look!' Then another. 'Look! All the same!' As ever, Wendy manages to take extreme issue with the importance and accuracy of everything Wee Harry says. In the midst of all this, The Tank is telling everybody he's off home. He's been saying this since we arrived. Aye, he says, he's having a good time and everything, but he's heading off home.

At least seventy-six times he's told me this. He's looking me in the eye when he's talking to me. He never looks me in the eye when he's talking to me! He asks what we're doing in the morning. 'Eh,' I says, 'maybe you'll come round, maybe play some records, maybe we'll head down the town. Maybe go down the library, eh?' 'Wow,' says The Tank, 'the fucking library, eh. Brilliant.' The Tank starts giggling. Then he goes away to tell somebody else he's off home. Next thing I know, the E boys – Edwin and English Edgar – are clambering all over me. Completely out their nuts, they're going, 'Come on, let's go for it!' They're wanting to play The Snake. Now The Snake's when you run through the woods, as fast as you can for as far as you can, bawling, screaming, and giggling your tits off. 'Yeah,' says Hamish, who hitherto has been dancing away with Carmel and the exes, 'The Snake, man. Let's fucking Snake the bastard.' He starts The Snake chant. 'Sna-ake! Sna-ake! Sna-ake! Sna-ake!' This causes The Big Man to be convinced that there is now some lethal reptile on the loose. I'm watching the exes, the ex-girlfriend and the ex-psychotic big brother. My sneaky plan lies in tatters. They're helping each other through this. I'd half-thought that getting my ex-psychotic big brother back on the mushies would bring out the bastard in him. I'd half-thought that my ex-girlfriend would, as a consequence, freak out, then fling herself back at me. Carmel comes over. 'She's not your type,' she says. The Big Man's curled up on the undergrowth and crying. He's shivering with the cold and panic. Carmel says, 'It's for the best. Can't you see how happy they are?' Hamish and the E boys are going, 'Sna-ake! Sna-ake! Sna-ake! Sna-ake!' Carmel's going, 'She-e's! No-ot! You-ur! Ty-ype!' Wendy and Wee Harry are arguing. It seems like they're arguing about me. The exes are laughing. It seems like they're laughing at me. The Big Man's crying. All these straight, identical trees have become his lost fingers. 'Look,' he says, 'look. My fucking fingers.' We all look. We all see what he means. Every cunt's pissing themselves apart from me and The Big Man. Carmel says, 'She-e's! No-ot! You-ur! Ty-ype!' The E boys and Hamish are going, 'Sna-ake! Sna-ake! Sna-ake! Sna-ake!' I'm freaking out. Stuart comes over. He asks me how I'm doing. He wants to know what my hit's like, if it's helping me out. There's only one thing for it. I just scream in his face, 'SNAAAA-AAAAAKE!'

I'm off. Racing through the trees like something's after me. The Predator. The Viet Cong. The trees are as brittle as breadsticks. It's like I'm running through a maze of paper streamers. I'm running through the carnival in Brazil. I'm stumbling. I'm slipping. I'm sliding. I'm Dr Richard Kimble. I'm the Rogue Male. I can hear them shouting, I can hear my name, but it's faint. They've given up. I'm bashing myself off the trees. It's like running through a maze of lampposts. My arms, my knees, are getting battered to fuck. I slow down. I try and identify some sort of path. It seems like ages, but before long, I'm walking hand in hand with the crapness of reality. I'm okay. I just want to say sorry to a lot of folk. I'm tired. I'm sore. I've no idea where I am. The woods *do* all look the same. I could be anywhere.

Eventually I come across what looks like a well-used path. It goes up, it goes down. I choose down. After a while, I come across some houses. A row of old houses. They're vaguely familiar. I think I know where I am.

And then I sees this amazing sight. This lassie out walking her dog. She's gorgeous. She looks like, she looks like . . . well, that's the thing, she doesn't really look like anybody. I'm sure she's aware of me. I don't want to scare her. 'Excuse me,' I says, getting her attention. 'Excuse me, I was wondering if you could help. I was with some friends, but I've kind of got lost from them. I was wondering about getting back to town.' The lassie smiles. Who does she look like? She looks like, she looks like . . . No, she doesn't look like anybody. She points over to her right. There's a road. 'That'll take you into town,' she says. I think I recognise the road. Yeah, I know where I am. 'Thanks,' I say. I look at the lassie and her dog. I starts laughing. 'What's up?' she says. She's laughing and all. 'This is just crazy,' I says. 'I've never told anybody this before but I've always wanted a dog.' The lassie laughs. I go on. 'See whenever my old boy's having a go at us, or anybody's having a go at us, I'm always thinking how he never got us a dog. I blame everything on that. Never told him that.

Never told anybody. Stupid, eh?' The lassie laughs. 'No,' she says, 'I can understand.' This is doing my head in. What's going on here? What's she doing out at this time of night? Who is she, anyway? She says, 'You look like you've had a rough night.' I laughs. 'Yeah, I've just lost my girlfriend to my brother. My mates are all completely out their faces somewhere back up there, and I'm fucking knackered.' She laughs. 'What do you do?' she says. 'Eh,' I says, 'I stay in the house all the time, play records. Sometimes I go over the library.' 'Sounds alright to me,' she says. I asks what she does. 'Oh,' she says, 'I stay in as much as I can. Play records. Sometimes go to the library.' This is intense. I'm totally straight. I'm hungry, tired, embarrassed. Straight. 'I take it you don't work,' she says. I laugh. She laughs and all. 'Do you?' I says. 'Oh, aye,' she says. 'Just part-time, though. In fact, I'm just in, just in off the late shift.' Then she smiles. Christ, I've waited all my life for a smile like this. I asks her, 'What do you do then?' 'Oh,' she says, as if by way of some long-winded explanation, 'I'm the one that mans the reception up at Megabowl.'

THE END

FAMILY CARES

Frank parked next the taxi rank. He checked his watch as he made for the phone.

'Hi,' he said, 'just me. Now you're sure you're not needing anything, eh?'

There was one of her silences, one of her panic-stricken silences.

Then, a sigh.

Then . . .

'Well, I don't know, mean there's bound to be something, there's always something; yet I've raked and I've raked and I can't see a thing. Are the trains running okay, a-ha?'

'Yeah,' said Frank, 'the trains are running fine. No need to worry yourself about the trains. Now, last time, you're sure, you're absolutely positive, you don't need anything?'

Another silence.

Another sigh.

Then . . .

'I don't know. Sure as I can be, I suppose. But mean you don't really know what they're eating these days, what they're no eating these days, what they're into these days, what they're no into these days. Mind last time, I'm sure Vicki said she was stopping eating eggs. You no mind of her saying that, no? I'm sure she said that, positive she said that. I should've asked when she phoned, I should've. Stupid, bloody typical. Oh, see me. But see, they're spending all that money when they phone, you just never stop to think, you just never stop to think about it. Costs them a bloody fortune and all, phoning all that way. Costs them an arm and a leg. Costs them damn near . . .'

Frank butted in. 'Okay. Okay. Calm down. I think she'd've told us if she'd stopped eating eggs. Anyway, it's not as if you're boiling an egg for their tea, is it?'

'No, smartie. But, listen, I got this really lovely cheesecake out of Mathieson's. Tell me, is there eggs in that, eh? How am I supposed to know if there's eggs in that? For all I know, there could be eggs in flaming Rice Crispies.'

She was starting to panic again.

'Come on,' said Frank. 'Come on now, hen. That's enough. Everything'll be fine.'

Another silence.

Another sigh.

Then . . .

'Well: I can't help it if I get myself all het up and flustered. Only happens once a year. It's supposed to be special. It's supposed to be flaming special.'

The pips sounded.

'Look,' she said, 'are you warm enough? You've only got that wee, thin jacket on, mind. Don't you go catching a cold now, you hear me? That's all we bloody need. You sniffling about with the house full of visitors.'

'I'm fine, I'm fine. It's a bit fresh, that's all.'

But before Frank could say any more the line went dead. Just as well really, all said and done.

Frank wandered over to the seat nearest the footbridge. It would've been warmer to've stayed in the car, of course, where he could easily've amused himself with the radio and doing some tidying, but Frank felt he was as well to stretch out and savour these last few minutes, these last few minutes of peace.

The kids were due off the trains, due up for Christmas. For the past six years they'd been based in London: where the laddie worked in insurance; where the lassie was a journalist with some local radio station.

Like last year, this would be the only time the family would all be together. It seemed like a long time to say it, a year, but, in truth, it didn't seem anything like twelve months since Frank had last drove up and waited at the station. Not like twelve months was supposed to feel, anyway. Not like it used to feel.

Frank yawned. He stretched himself out, let his arms run the length of the bench and crossed his legs at the ankle.

In all, they'd be up for the best part of five days. They'd appear for their meals, and they'd arrange to get ferried round the relatives – with Frank as chauffeur-cum-chum – but most of the time they'd just be hanging out with their pals. Truly, honestly, they'd've been as well to stay with their pals.

Thing was, there was never that much to say to them, for Frank to say to them. When you thought about it, really, all you ever ended up talking about with the laddie was football and politics. You ended up talking about football as if you were halfway interested in it. Same with politics; mean you cared alright, cared about how folk were treated and all of that, but you were never really what you'd call bothered.

In a way, it was like talking to a stranger, talking to the laddie. Polite conversation. Small talk. They shared next to nothing. They knew next to nothing about each other. Sure, they looked the same, they were obviously, genetically, father and son, but they could hardly talk. The funny thing with the laddie, of course, was that he would, at some point or other, come away with some problem that was troubling his mind – some friend or that, some bit of skirt. It was like he was trying to convince you of something, that he was interesting or whatever, by going on about it. Trouble was, it never was interesting. It ended up you just wanted to find an excuse to get away and leave him to wallow in it. It was a bit sad really, the laddie going on like that. It was a bit worrying and all, worrying that Frank was still the only person he had to confide in. Mind you, when you came to think about it, for the sake of the laddie, the really worrying thing was that he went on at everybody like this.

The lassie was about as opposite as you could get. She would never tell you anything, anything that was bothering her. True, she would near enough fling herself at Frank when she seen him, all hugs and kisses in the middle of the bloody platform, and from the moment she arrived till the moment she was gone she would never let up. She noticed the stupidest things. Soon as she got in the door it would be, 'Oh, that's new; oh, that's lovely. You know I seen one like that in blah–di–blah, where was it again?' She was always saying that. Blah–di–blah. Bloody blah–di–blah.

The strange thing with the lassie was this thing about never going on about herself. Whereas the laddie didn't communicate by being, alternatively, mute or depressingly intense, the lassie didn't communicate by just boring the effing pants off you. If you asked, 'How you getting on?' she'd rally forth for what seemed like ages with some God-almighty, stultifyingly dull trivial little mishap that had befallen her on her travels. Whereas if you asked her something interesting, something like, 'How's your love life?' she would a) feign indignance and go, 'I beg your pardon?' or b) feign sleeze and go, 'Fine, fine' or c) feign frustrated failure and go, 'Don't talk to me about men!' You'd've got more sense out of Harpo flaming Marx. You could never work out really whether she actually was interesting, and she just didn't want to tell you, or whether she actually was boring, and she didn't want to tell you that either.

And, who knows, maybe she was, maybe she was boring. Maybe she was like that all the time and all. Blah–di–blah. Blah–di–blah. Blah–di–blah. Could well be. Truth be known, Frank didn't know. Truth be told, Frank wasn't bothering his arse one way or t'other. 'Cause when you got to this stage in the proceedings there was near enough bugger all you could do for them anyway. They were okay for money. They were big enough and daft enough to make decisions for themselves. All you had to do was phone every so often, see they were okay, and try and make some kind of conversation.

'Malt loaf!'

Frank turned round.

It was the boy that manned the station, the ticket boy. 'You Frank with the wee, thin jacket on, aye?'

Frank nodded. He supposed so.

'The wife – Faye, is it, her name is? – says you've to stop off and get a malt loaf.'

Frank shook his head. 'She's daft,' he said. 'We'll be eating all this stuff for weeks. Half of it'll just end up getting horsed. Oh, and next thing she'll be complaining about being fat. Guaranteed, that one.'

The ticket boy sat himself down. 'Family coming up, is it?'

'Aye,' said Frank, 'laddie and the lassie. Up from London.'

'Glasgow?'

'Eh, the laddie's Glasgow. The lassie's Edinburgh. Different sides of the town they stay on. Different trains and all of that.'

The boy checked his watch. 'Due any minute. No problems.' The ticket boy lit up a fag then said, 'Tell you a story, wife of mine, right, had her sister and the family up from Stafford for a weekend there, September weekend. Ended up we'd to go back down the town and return stuff. Wife'd got that much she couldn't fit it all in the freezer. What a brasser to give somebody, though, eh? Going back into Farmfoods with all these carrier bags. "Eh, excuse me, doll. Any chance of a refund? Wife got a wee bit carried away, like, you know." '

Frank laughed. 'Know the feeling, pal. Been there, seen it, got the T-shirt. We've got this old biddy stays next door takes in stuff. Just in case, you know. Just on the off-chance you get a bus-load of great aunts dropping in from Echelfechen or something.'

A couple appeared. They looked like they were wanting tickets. The boy acknowledged them.

'Ach well, no rest for the wicked, I suppose. See and try and have yourself a good one, though, eh.'

'Aye,' said Frank, 'yourself and all. Doubt it, mind.'

Frank yawned again. He checked his watch and stretched himself out.

In a way, all this Christmas, all this festive season carry-on, it was a bit too much like being on your holidays. Looking back, looking back at your photos and all of that, thinking about it, it always seemed like you'd did loads of things, but at the time all you ever seemed to be doing was waiting. Queuing up for this, hanging round for that. For all that you were supposedly getting away from it all, enjoying that much-deserved break, you were never really that in charge of what you were up to; in many ways you were even more blasted dependent than ever you were.

That's what the next few days would be like. Frank would be doing hundreds of things; true, things he never normally did, but most of the time he'd just be waiting.

The phone would be non-stop. Every time you settled down; calls for the laddie and lassie, calls from the laddie and lassie. Funny but nowadays they always wanted you to know what they were up to. Never used to be like that. No, used to be you never had a scoobie as to what they were up to. Once they were out the door, they could've been anybody.

The boy that manned the station came over again. He sat himself down and re-lit his fag.

'See,' said Frank, leaning forward, 'the thing about all this, all this Christmas carry-on, right, you're either sitting about doing bugger all or there's two or three things you could be doing. It's like the telly; only time of the year they put decent stuff on, and what do they go and do? They put it all on at the same time. And the wife, of course, she wants you to go and wash and get changed 'cause somebody might, maybe just might, be coming round, you know. Or the lassie, she wants you to give her a run up to see her Auntie Greta, and just now is the only time she can go, like. And she's at you, she's on at you, she's going, "Are you sure it's alright? Are you sure it's okay?" And it's not okay at all, 'cause you just can't be bothered, can't be arsed, but you never say anything, do you? Just bugs my flaming happiness, so it does. See, the thing with the laddie and the lassie, right, mean ken they're flesh and blood and all of that, but I've nothing to say to them. I've nothing in common with them. Mean, I mind them when they were wee. I liked them when they were wee. I'd a wee bit of a say then. But see nowadays, nowadays if you mention anything about when they were wee, they go spare. "Oh no, dad, you've got it all wrong. Oh, you're making all that up." Oh no, they deny everything. Look at you like you're half-daft. That's the only thing we've got in common too, when they were bairns. Nah, these days, all I'm really bothered about is that they're alright, that they're doing alright for themselves, and you don't really need to go through all this palaver to ken they're doing alright. Mean a bloody phone lets you ken they're doing alright. Mean . . .'

'Uh-oh,' said the ticket boy, 'talking of bloody phones, I think I hear the dreaded single-tone. Buggers must be checking up on us. Only so many times I can be seen out watering my plants, especially this time of year, though, eh?'

'Eh, aye,' said Frank. 'Aye. Suppose so.'

The boy went away. Frank checked his watch, folded his arms and crossed his legs at the knee.

Folk were waiting on the opposite platform now. Folk not so much waiting for the train as for what the train was bringing. Oh aye, you could tell these things. No bags. No big jackets. The way they checked their watches all the time. That was always a giveaway: regular commuters only ever checked their watches when their train was late, or when they were late. There was this one particular woman, with just a loose-knit cardie to brave the cold. She kept leaning out as far as she could, seeing if she could see the train coming. Then she would look at her watch. Then she would look out again, looking the other way. Then she would look at her watch again.

As if it would matter, as if it would make the slightest bit of difference.

Frank got up. He walked out as far as the yellow line, the yellow line you weren't supposed to cross when the trains weren't stopping, lest you got sucked in and Moulinexed by the undercarriage. Frank put his hands in his pockets, his trouser pockets, and walked along the yellow line as far as the ticket office. The boy in the ticket office acknowledged him, then quickly turned away and picked up his phone.

Frank returned to his seat. In the interim, a woman, a woman that about aged with Frank, with a case and a shoulder-bag, had parked herself down on his bench.

Frank sat down beside her.

'This you escaping all the hullaballoo, is it?'

The woman nodded shyly. 'Darlington,' she said, 'down to see my sister.'

'Darlington?' said Frank. 'Think the wife's got a second cousin stays down there. Now, what one is it again? Iris? Jean? Think it's Iris. Can't say as I've ever been there, mind. Nice, is it?'

'Sorry?'

'Darlington? Nice?'

'Oh, you know. Just a normal town. Wee bit of everything.'

'Been to Middlesborough. That near there, aye? Not to stay, like, just to pass through. Maybe stopped for petrol or something, you know.'

The woman nodded.

'Darlington, is that no where they've got the famous spire?'

'You not thinking of Durham, the cathedral?'

'No, no, no. The spire. The twisted one. The crooked one.'

'What, Chesterfield?'

'Chesterfield, that's right. That's the one . . . That near Durham, aye?'

'No,' said the woman, 'not really. It's not near Darlington either.'

'Oh . . . Where is it again?'

'Sheffield.'

'What, in Sheffield? Chesterfield's in Sheffield?'

'No, near Sheffield. About twelve miles from Sheffield.'

'Oh, right,' said Frank, 'gotcha.'

The woman looked at her watch. She leaned and looked the one way, then she leaned and looked the other way.

See, she was doing it and all. She was looking both ways.

Now, they couldn't all be like him, they couldn't all be like Frank, they couldn't all be waiting on both trains. And the woman sitting next to him, she was definitely only waiting on the one, cause she was going somewhere. She was waiting for the train that would take her east. So what was she doing looking east for? That's why she was on this platform, she was on this platform 'cause she was waiting for the train that would take her east, the one that was coming from the west. Now, if she was wanting to go west, she'd've been on the other platform. If either platform was an option, then surely she'd've positioned herself halfway across the footbridge or something, something sensible like that.

Frank looked the one way. Then Frank looked the other way. *He* was entitled to look both ways.

Nothing was coming.

To pass the time, Frank started counting things. Those on this side of the platform versus those on that side of the platform. The number of women versus the number of men. The number of seats. Flowers. Buckets. The number of rivets per panel on the footbridge.

'That's amazing!'

'Sorry?' said the woman.

'Look,' said Frank, 'the footbridge, the last panel, see it? Notice how the pattern of the rivets is the exact same as on all the other panels but if you count them you see how there's one less on the last panel than there is on all the others, on all the other panels. See what I mean? See? That is amazing. Like an optical illusion or something, eh?'

The woman looked at Frank, then at the footbridge, then at Frank again.

'Wonder if it's safe,' said Frank. He thought for a second then added, 'Well, obviously, of course it's safe, it's not as if it's going to fall down or anything like that, what I mean is is it sound, is it structurally sound.'

The woman started to gather up her stuff.

Frank looked. Her train was coming.

Frank looked the other way. The other train was coming and all.

Frank checked his watch.

The 0800 hrs from London King's Cross via Waverley was bang on time. But the 0830 hrs from London Euston via Queen Street was three minutes early.

Frank shivered with the cold.

The laddie's train was early. Paul's train was early.

As he made his way to the yellow line, Frank wondered what was wrong. He wondered if everything was alright.

QUESTION NUMBER TEN

So I goes for this job interview and the boy says, 'Right, name fifty singles by The Fall.'

I goes, '*What?*'

The boy goes, 'You heard me. Come on. Two minutes. Two minutes and counting.'

And I needed it . . . but I did it.

The boy puts a wee tick in this ledger-type book that's lying in front of him.

'Right,' he says, 'next: you know how some folk screw their faces up when they smoke, and how some folk straighten their faces out when they smoke?'

I goes, 'Aye.'

The boy puts a wee tick in his book.

Then he stares us right in the eye. 'Reincarnation,' he says, 'what d'you reckon?'

I shrugs. 'Kind of looks like it to me,' I says.

The boy puts down another tick. Tick number three. Nice wee column of ticks developing.

'Question Number Four,' he says, 'Question Number Four, what d'you do when the adverts are on?'

'Play back the week's goals,' I says.

The boy looks chuffed. Another tick goes in the book.

'Four out of four,' he says. 'Not bad.'

The boy has a wee laugh to himself.

I has a wee laugh and all. Give him his due, this guy's alright.

'And in summer?' he says.

He's caught me off guard. Then it dawns on me – *he's trying to be fly.*

215

'In summer,' I says, 'when the adverts are on I try and get the zero on the video counter using only the rewind and fast forward buttons.'

The boy's into it. He puts down a tick then goes into this wee drawer of his, pulls out a sheet of tracing paper, peels off a wee gold star and sticks it down beside tick number five.

'Incidentally,' he says, 'much money you got on you?'

'Eh,' I says, digging into my pocket.

'No,' he says, 'hold on, I want you to tell me, son. You mean you don't know?'

'Aye,' I says, 'course I do. There's two pound coins, a pound note, a fifty, three twentys, a five and four ones.'

'Well,' he says, 'that's what I was wanting to know, son. Mind: when folk ask you questions, you tell them answers, you don't waste their time.'

I nods to the boy. He's got a point. He puts a tick in his book and I breathes a sigh of relief. It was touch and go for a minute there.

'Right,' he says, 'two quickies – when was the last time you told a lie?'

''Bout five year ago,' I says.

The boy puts down a tick.

'And,' he says, 'long does half a pound of cheese last?'

'Twice,' I says.

The boy puts down a tick.

'You're doing well,' he says, 'doing well. Keep it up. Only two to go.'

I nods to the boy.

'Now tell me,' he says, 'have you worked how you would cheat on *Gladiators*?'

'Aye,' I says . . . but I holds back from telling him. See I'm no wanting to waste his time. I'm only telling him what he's wanting to know.

The boy stares us out. I stares him out.

The boy's got a big grin on his face. 'Well done,' he says, 'you're learning.'

The boy puts down a tick and makes a wee note beside it.

'Right,' he says, 'so far, so good. All I'm prepared to say, son, is that the ball's at your feet. Get my drift?'

I nods to the boy.

'Right,' he says, 'last question. Question Number Ten.'

'I'm listening,' I says.

The boy takes a deep breath. 'Question Number Ten,' he says, 'Question Number Ten – and, by the way, good luck, son.'

I nods to the boy.

'Okay,' he says, 'here we go. Question Number Ten – would you rather a) be good-looking or b) have a decent-sized knob?'

I thinks about it. It's a toughie. I says, 'Could you repeat the question, please?'

'Certainly,' he says. 'Question Number Ten – would you rather a) be good-looking or b) have a decent-sized knob?'

I'm all agitated. Jesus, you'd think I'd never thought about it before.

The boy puts a cross next to Question Number Ten.

He closes his book, puts his pencil down and leans back with his hands behind his head.

'Sorry, son,' he says, 'time's up.'

He puts the book back in the drawer he got the gold star out of.

'Now, sir,' he says, 'if you wouldn't mind just leaving your details with the girl at reception then we'll put you on file and let you know if any vacancies crop up in the near future. Thank you, that'll be all for now.'

The boy takes a report from the other side of his desk and starts skimming through it.

I sits there. I'm no moving.

The boy looks up. He's looking at us like I'm a dafty.

'That'll be all,' he says, 'thank you.'

The boy nods towards the door.

I says, 'It's the knob, eh? Eh, it's the knob.'

He says, 'I'm sorry, sir. You must understand I can't possibly go into your answers. Now, like I say, if you'd like to just . . .'

I leans over the table. 'No,' I says, 'it's no the knob, though, is it? No, it's no, is it?'

'Good day to you, sir,' he says. 'Now if you would be so kind as to . . .'

I makes a lunge at the boy. I grabs a hold of his lapels and starts shaking him.

'Come on, you,' I says, 'tell me, I want to know, I need to know this.'

As I goes for his throat I notice the boy's looking over to his left.

I looks over to his left and all.

There's a green light flashing above his door.

Two seconds later, two guys with short-sleeved blue shirts come bombing in.

And that's the last I mind of it.